Praise for Amy Yurk's
The Kind of Love That Saves You

"A startling and powerful novel, filled with love and an almost miraculous friendship."

> —Luanne Rice, *New York Times* bestselling
> author of *Summer Light*

"Endearing and often hilarious." —*Booklist*

"Heart-wrenching and life-affirming and hard to put down."
> —Jean Hegland, author of *Into the Forest*

"A heartbreaker . . . a great read and a great first effort."
> —*Greensboro News & Record*

Written by today's freshest new talents and selected by New American Library, NAL Accent novels touch on subjects close to a woman's heart, from friendship to family to finding our place in the world. The Conversation Guides included in each book are intended to enrich the individual reading experience, as well as encourage us to explore these topics together—because books, and life, are meant for sharing.

Visit us on-line at www.penguinputnam.com.

The Language of Sisters

Amy Yurk

NAL Accent
Published by New American Library, a division of
Penguin Putnam Inc., 375 Hudson Street,
New York, New York 10014, U.S.A.
Penguin Books Ltd, 80 Strand,
London WC2R 0RL, England
Penguin Books Australia Ltd, Ringwood,
Victoria, Australia
Penguin Books Canada Ltd, 10 Alcorn Avenue,
Toronto, Ontario, Canada M4V 3B2
Penguin Books (N.Z.) Ltd, 182–190 Wairau Road,
Auckland 10, New Zealand

Penguin Books Ltd, Registered Offices:
Harmondsworth, Middlesex, England

Published by New American Library, a division of Penguin Putnam Inc.

First Printing, September 2002
10 9 8 7 6 5 4 3 2 1

FICTION FOR THE WAY WE LIVE

REGISTERED TRADEMARK—MARCA REGISTRADA

LIBRARY OF CONGRESS CATALOGING IN PUBLICATION DATA:

Yurk, Amy.
    The language of sisters / by Amy Yurk.
        p. cm.
    ISBN 0-451-20700-9 (trade)
    1. Sisters—Fiction. 2. Young women—Fiction. 3. Rape victims—Fiction. 4. Pregnant women—Fiction. 5. People with mental disabilities—Fiction. I. Title.

PS3575.U75 L36 2002
813'.6—dc21   2002025518

Set in Cochin
Designed by Ginger Legato

Printed in the United States of America

PUBLISHER'S NOTE
This is a work of fiction. Names, characters, places, and incidents either are the product of the author's imagination or are used fictitiously, and any resemblance to actual persons, living or dead, business establishments, events, or locales is entirely coincidental.

For Angie

Acknowledgments

Thanks to Victoria Sanders; I could not conjure a better agent to have in my corner. To Dr. Julie Iverson, for creative brainstorming and technical information along the way. To my mother, Claudia Weisz, for emotional truth. To Kristin Cleary, for unabashed enthusiasm and racous laughter; you are truly the sister of my heart. To my husband, Eric, for never failing to believe in me. And to my children, Scarlett and Miles, for letting me love you both beyond anything I could ever capture on the page.

Prologue

I was at work when it happened. I had just finished folding pungent wild blueberries into the creamy muffin batter, thinking how the brilliant purple streaks that trailed each berry stood out like a bruise against white skin. I was about to fill the greased-and-readied pan when something stopped me. Something tangible, like the thump of a fist against my chest—I felt it. I felt my sister's voice for the first time in years, the way I used to feel it when we were children, coursing through me like my own blood, hearing her thoughts the way no one else could. Can you hear a whisper in your heart? Across the miles, the years, through callused layers of resentment and anger and pain, can a voice as familiar to you as your own slice through it all and find you? *Help*, she said softly, and the muffin tin fell from my grasp and landed with a clatter on the concrete floor.

Barry's head poked out from the dish room that punctuated the long, narrow kitchen in the back of the bakery. A heavy electronic drumbeat thumped in the air behind him, the radio tuned to the dance music station where his current boyfriend was an early-morning disc jockey. "Everything okay in there, champ?" Barry inquired, the familiar sight of his blond poodle-fluff explosion of hair and long, wiry limbs bringing me back from wherever I had been.

"Yeah, fine," I said, grinning at him shakily, my heart still resonating from the impact of Jenny's voice, my mind racing to think what trouble she might possibly be in, why she could need my help badly enough for me to feel it a thousand miles away.

Rubbing his large hands in the folds of a linen towel, Barry tilted the fuzzy tip of his goatee into his chest. "You sure, now? Not wishing you'd kept that fancy therapist's gig?"

I shook my head and reached for a clean tin from under my workstation. "Nah. Just checking to see if you were awake," I said, gesturing for him to go back to work with a wave of my hand. He acknowledged me with a tiny dishtowel salute, then disappeared into his cave.

Grateful for the brief distraction from the worry that had risen within me, I refastened my defiant red mop into a ponytail at the base of my neck and got back to work, preparing the clean tin and filling it with batter. As I slid it into the shiny convection oven behind me, I thought how lucky I was to work with Barry. We'd met six months before when I'd closed my budding therapy practice to become a baker. The decision to switch careers hadn't been a terribly complicated one: I'd simply realized that someone as screwed up as I was had no business telling other people how to remedy what was wrong with their lives. Barry didn't expect me to tell him anything; in fact, most mornings we barely spoke. We met at the front door of the bakery at three a.m., nodding our greeting. We understood that at this hour words were beside the point.

I had fallen easily into this routine of silent communication with Barry; it was a language already tightly woven into my subconscious, taught to me long ago by a sister whose profound disabilities had robbed her of words. The thought of Jenny's angelic, heart-shaped face stopped me in my tracks. Crossing my bare arms over my chest and leaning against the smooth edge of the counter, I stared blindly at the aged brick wall in front of me, surrendering to the insistent pull of the past.

It had been a decade since I'd seen my sister, since the day I walked out of the Wellman Institute, leaving her in the care of people she did not know, did not love or trust. I considered the ugly mixture of cowardice and passivity that had plagued me for the last ten years, and had kept me wrapped in the safe cocoon of a life I had created in San Francisco. I had no excuses. It was simply too hard. I could not stand the thought of seeing her in that place, soaked in the rancid odor of excrement and neglect.

Nor could I forgive what my father had done to our family by convincing my mother to place Jenny there, a decision that had given me the final push I needed to remove him from my life permanently. The little I knew about my sister's life I learned secondhand through infrequent calls from my mother. Those conversations were brief and awkward, smoldering with tension. I avoided them at any cost.

Help.

The word interrupted my thoughts and bounced through my body like an echo, the sound of Jenny's voice lingering in my heart like the shiver from a nightmare, the kind of shiver that clings to your skin even though you know whatever is haunting you was only a dream. That was it. I had to know if I was imagining things or if something had actually happened to her. Maybe my mother had called me at home and gotten the machine.

Shane never answered anything but his cell phone. I glanced at my watch and saw that it was just past six o'clock. After a year of living together, I knew he'd be awake, sitting at the small wrought-iron table in our Tuscany-style kitchen, his meticulously pressed navy blue suit setting off his eyes like an alarm. His blond head would be bent over the files of the cases he would prosecute that day, a forgotten cup of black coffee cooling on the counter. I didn't know why he bothered brewing anything; he was always too focused on work to remember to drink it.

A call from me would probably only annoy him, so I decided to swallow my apprehension and take the chance my mother would be awake, getting ready for the bank teller's job she had worked at since my father divorced her eight years ago. I picked up the cordless phone, slowly and deliberately punching in the number to my childhood home. It rang four times before she answered.

"Hello?" she said, the sound of her conjuring up a usually well-repressed pile of feelings into a small storm inside me.

"Hi," I exhaled. "It's Nicole."

"Nicky," she said, surprise wrapped around her voice.

I gritted my teeth at the childish shortening of my name. "Nicole," I corrected her as I glanced at the cloudy illuminated window of the oven to check the level of browning on the muffins. They needed just a minute more.

"Right. I know. I named you." She paused. "Did somebody at Wellman call you?"

Anticipation sent cold fingers dancing up my spine. "No. Is Jenny all right?" The pounding of Barry's radio matched the sprinting beat of my heart.

I heard her inhale several times, perhaps trying to keep back tears. It had been so long since I'd been around her, I couldn't be sure. Tucking the phone between my ear and shoulder, I grabbed the thick silver oven mitts and lifted the pan out of the oven, carrying it over to the cooling rack while I waited for her to respond. "Mom?" I prompted as the toasted butter scent of finished muffins filled the air around me with their sweet perfume.

She cleared her throat. "Sorry. It's just so strange that you'd call today. I only found out last night."

"Jesus," I said, exasperated. I felt like I was trying to coerce information from a reluctant suspect. I walked back over to my worktable and set my hands flat against its cool metal surface, pressing the phone into my shoulder with the side of my head. "Found out what?"

She paused again, then finally spoke, her voice quiet, barely above a whisper. "Jenny was raped."

The weight of those three small words traveled through the phone line and landed like a boulder in my belly. "Oh, no," I breathed. My heart shook in my chest. I had been expecting something, anything: a sickness, an accident, but not *this*. Hot, thick tears flooded my throat and I swallowed hard to keep my composure. *"By who?"*

"A nurse's aide, they think. They're pretty sure it was him." Her voice trembled.

"God∂ammit." I kicked an enormous bucket full of brown sugar. The lid popped off and jumped to the floor. I kicked it, too.

"God had nothing to do with this."

I let go of a disgusted sigh. I didn't give a rat's ass what she thought about God. I was surprised she still had anything to do with Him.

She digested the bitter silence that followed. "There's more," she finally said. "Your sister . . ." She trailed off, then quickly began again. "She's pregnant."

The storm inside me quickly progressed into a tornado, drowning out my senses. The bakery seemed to disappear; the world around me was suddenly reduced to a two-inch shell of insufficient oxygen. As things slowly began to fade back into focus, I realized my mother was still speaking. ". . . And so maybe it would be good if you could come. Will you come home, Nicky?"

The first words that came to me spilled from my lips before I could rein them in. "I'll be there as soon as I can," I said numbly. I hung up and dropped the phone to the floor, then sank there after it. I felt detached from my body; the too-short legs and slightly fleshy belly belonged to someone else. Someone who didn't have a sister who was pregnant by a monster. Someone who didn't have to face a past she thought she had left behind.

A moment later Barry strode out of the dish room, a stack of yellow dessert plates balanced in each of his wide palms. Seeing my sagging figure on the floor, he rushed to set his load on the counter. When he folded his body down next to me, I gratefully leaned into his strong embrace, my cheek pressed against the xylophone of his rib cage. "What's wrong, champ?" he whispered against my hair. His T-shirt was damp and smelled of detergent and healthy male sweat. "Muffins giving you a hard time?"

I made a noise that was half sob, half laugh, then whispered into his chest, "My sister's been raped." The words felt like a cat's claws against my skin. Knowing he'd understand my need for silence, I simply closed my eyes and let him hold me. I pressed my hand firmly over my aching heart, hopeful that Jenny might feel my touch and know her sister had heard her call.

I was finally going home.

At first, we had not known anything was wrong with Jenny. She had been such a stunning baby—much prettier than I ever was. When I was three and Jenny was a newborn, my mother took us to a small park in our neighborhood, where I could climb on the jungle gym while she held court and allowed other mothers to croon over her perfect second daughter.

Jenny came out of the womb with dark brown hair and skin creamy as milk splashed with brushstrokes of rosy peach. Her eyes were a deep, viscous indigo, huge and round in her tiny baby head, framed by rows of lashes so lush you longed to touch them to see if they were real. She was the human embodiment of a porcelain doll.

"She's just perfect!" the women would exclaim as my mother sat straight and proud on the park bench, cradling Jenny as though she might shatter if she were jiggled the wrong way.

Mom would smile the small secret smile of a mother who knew the exceptional beauty of her child. She'd gently brush a curl from Jenny's forehead. "Isn't she? She's an angel, too. Slept through the night the first week she was home."

There would be a collective gasp from the women, followed by several comments about their own children's nightmarish first-year sleeping habits.

"Oh, don't feel bad," my mother would assure them. "That's my first girl, Nicky," and she would gesture toward me as I proceeded to do something the exact opposite of perfect, like pour sand down the front of my dress or stick a lollipop into my matted red curls. "She didn't sleep more than two hours straight until she was fifteen months. I figure I was due for an angel baby."

An angel baby. I wondered later what that made me: Jenny's demon counterpart? I was definitely strong-willed where my sister was complacent. Our mother could leave her in her crib for hours at a time and Jenny would sleep, wake up and bat playfully at her mobile, then sleep again until someone came to get her. She rarely cried. I, however, ran like holy hell through our house until I finally collapsed on the floor and someone dragged me, usually kicking and screaming, to bed.

When Jenny was still an infant, I used to poke at her as she lay quietly on the floor to see if I could get her to cry. She might whimper at too tight a pinch, but mostly she just stared at me with her enormous dark eyes, cooing softly. We spent hours on the floor together. I became fascinated with her eyes, and through them, I heard her voice long before she ever spoke.

At thirteen months, Jenny was still not sitting up all the way; instead, she slumped forward at almost a forty-five-degree angle, using the muscles in her neck to lift her head to look at you. She couldn't walk yet, either, but managed a sort of combat crawl, her arms pulling her thin body across the floor. While our father insisted on believing that Jenny was simply a slow starter, our mother had begun to worry.

It was around this time that Jenny said her first word, and my mother's fears were temporarily quelled. It was a dark and blustery Northwest winter afternoon, unfit for outside play, so Jenny and I were lying on our bellies in the living room looking at our family photo album. Heavy gusts of wind propelled drops of rain against our house like bullets from a gun. There was a thick white towel beneath the upper part of Jenny's body to protect the gray shag carpet from the saliva that ran at a constant drip from her mouth. Mom was in the kitchen trying to get dinner ready before Dad got home from work; the rich aroma of roasted chicken and freshly baked yeast rolls laced the air around us. I explained the pictures to Jenny as she batted at the pages, trying to turn them herself.

"This is a cow, Jenny," I said, my four-year-old ego bursting at the seams as I showed her the shots my father had taken during our family's recent trip to the Evergreen State Fair. "A cow says, 'Moo-o-o-o.' "

Jenny stared hard at the page, her eyes seeming to suck up the image into her brain.

"This is me standing next to the cow," I continued. "Do you see me? I'm almost touching her leg."

Jenny swung her gaze sideways to look at me, then back to the page. "Nic," she said suddenly, the one syllable sounding more like a cough in the back of her throat than my name.

I stared dumbly at her for a moment, not believing what I'd heard. She had been making nonsensical noise for months, but never had her intent been so clear. The sound came again, more pronounced this time. "Nic." Her entire face blossomed with pride. She blinked several times, rapidly, her thick lashes brushing the apples of her cheeks like a butterfly's wings.

"Mom!" I yelled, jumping up from the floor and leaping excitedly onto the couch by the front window. "Come here! Jenny just said my name!"

Our mother walked in from the kitchen, wiping her hands with a white dishtowel, looking harried. Her willowy frame was clad in blue jeans and a red sweater, both dusted generously with flour. Her pale angled cheeks were flushed from the heat of the kitchen and the muscles of her slender heart-shaped face drooped with fatigue. Her dark brown waves hung loose around slightly sloping shoulders. With a bent wrist, she brushed a thin strand back from her face, frowning at me. "Please don't jump on the couch, Nicky."

"Nic!" Jenny exclaimed again, twisting her head to look at our mother.

Mom's pale green eyes, slanted like a cat's, glowed electric with surprise. I jumped gleefully on the cushions. "See? I told you! Yah, Jenny!" I yelled.

Mom went to Jenny, helping her to sit up. She held her younger daughter tightly, rocking her, not saying a word. I caught my sister's gaze with my own, and though neither of us made a sound, I remember hearing my name over and over again in the endless blue of her eyes.

Jenny quickly acquired a few more words: "Mama" being the next, then "kitty." But after our initial excitement it didn't take long for her to stop speaking entirely. She lost interest in most everything, often gazing off into space with a vacant stare.

What most disturbed my parents, though, was that Jenny stopped looking them in the eye. If they tried catching her glance, even using their hands to direct her gaze back at them, Jenny would twist her head and avert her eyes, as though the visual contact caused her some great internal pain. "Come on, sweetie," my mother would plead with her, trying over and over to get her attention. "You can do it. I know you can." The heavy ache in my mother's voice stung my heart and I, too, did everything my child mind could come up with to make Jenny respond. Nothing worked.

Profoundly retarded. Two words that loom in the back of every parent's mind like the threat of a diabolical storm. My father exploded at the news. "Not my child," he thundered at my mother, his sapphire eyes flashing. His freckled face burned scarlet and his carrot-colored curls stood out from his head in wild disarray. He looked like a lit match.

"My child is not retarded," he insisted. "The doctor is wrong." Then he pressed both his rough carpenter's hands flat over his face as though they could restrain his grief. It was the only time I ever remember seeing him cry. From the very beginning, Daddy took Jenny's disabilities as a personal affront, as though she were somehow offending him for being an imperfect child. He stood his long, thin body up straight and defied her disease, daring it to change his life in any way.

My mother took on the diagnosis as a challenge, a problem to be solved. It immediately became her mission to find a name for the monster that was robbing her beautiful child of a normal life.

For me, Jenny simply remained my sister. At five, all I knew was my instinct to protect her, to get her to laugh, and to love her. It took longer for me to realize her differences and then, later, to finally try to escape them.

In less than twenty-four hours my life in San Francisco was pretty well wrapped up, which made me ponder for a moment just how much of a life it actually was. I wasn't a terribly social person, so there were few friends to call. The weekend baker was more than happy to pick up my shifts while I was away. Barry had promised to take over my daily food deliveries to the park near the bakery, where I had recently befriended a homeless family; I simply could not stand the idea of their little girl going hungry. Shane would take care of my three-legged dog, Moochie, whom I had adopted from the shelter where I sporadically volunteered. I left a detailed feeding-and-walk schedule taped to the refrigerator, still a little fearful that the poor pup would starve to death while I was away. I left a message on my mother's answering machine, telling her I'd be arriving late that night. I was unsure whether she wasn't home because she'd gone to work or to Wellman to be with Jenny, but I hoped for the latter.

My biggest challenge had been in deciding what size suitcase to fill: a small one would say my visit would be short; a larger one might say I was planning to stick around. I finally settled on a medium-sized black duffel bag that I'd found stuffed into the back of the closet; I hoped it would simply keep its mouth shut.

As I packed, I tried not to give in to the sense of trepidation I felt swelling within me. Everything in my mind screamed for me not to go, to stay in San Francisco where it was safe, where I knew the boundaries of my life. Grabbing a handful of underwear from my dresser and shoving it into my bag, I tried to keep my thoughts focused on Jenny, what she must be feeling, how traumatized she must be.

I pushed away thoughts of seeing my mother again, facing the house where I grew up, having to deal with everything that happened within its walls. *Jenny*, I thought as I added two pairs of jeans to the messy pile in my bag. *Jenny*, I thought again, creating a chant out of her name. I counted the letters in her name, over and over again, keeping the image of my mother's face out of my mind. It was Jenny who needed me, Jenny I was going home to see. No matter the depth of my fear, nothing else mattered. I wouldn't let it.

By nine p.m. I was at the airport, alone. Shane had been appropriately horrified at the news of Jenny's rape, but was waiting on a verdict for the case he had just wrapped up that morning. He didn't think he could make it out of the courthouse in time to see me off. I was pleasantly surprised, then, to see his tall, athletic figure striding toward me at the gate, his black trench coat flapping furiously around his long legs as he waved his briefcase in the air to catch my eye. I noticed the airline attendant stand up straighter behind her desk when she saw him heading in our direction. Then she was smoothing her platinum-blond pageboy and smiling wide with bloodred lips. Shane had this effect on most women. Even in his sharp Armani suit, he had the look of that boy in junior high whose simple touch made you swear to your friends that you'd never again wash whatever body part had come in contact with him. So when he rushed up to me and dropped his briefcase to the ground for an enthusiastic embrace, the attendant lost her smile and looked away, probably amazed that a man as handsome as Shane was attracted to a short, slightly plump redhead like me. Most days it amazed me, as well.

Returning his hug, I smashed my face into the middle of his broad chest. "I thought you couldn't make it," I said accusingly, looking up to him and digging the sharp point of my chin into his breastbone.

He leaned down and kissed me soundly on the lips, then on the nose and both cheeks. "Mmm. Your freckles taste like cinnamon."

"Uh-huh," I said. "What about the jury?"

He grinned. "They came back sooner than I thought they would."

"And?" I prodded a bit impatiently, jiggling my arms around his waist, knowing he'd need to tell me his news before we could move on to the subject of my leaving.

"And you're looking at the only assistant D.A. to win five consecutive murder cases. I thought the boss would piss his pants, he was so happy with me."

I smiled wryly. "Wow."

"How are *you* doing?" he finally asked, tilting his chin down and looking up at me from under his eyebrows with concern.

"I don't really know." I shrugged, my ambivalence punishing him a little for not asking me right away. "I'm more worried about how Jenny is doing." I was terrified, in fact, to think what she must have gone through, how she must have felt when that bastard climbed on top of her. . . . I shook my head, trying to erase the horrifying image from my mind.

"Let me know if there's anything I can do." He hugged me again and I basked in the security I felt in his arms, not knowing when I might feel it again.

"I'll miss you," he said, smothering his face into my neck, the roughness of his slight five o'clock shadow sending electric shivers zipping through my body.

"Me, too," I said, swallowing a sharp lump in my throat. I waited for him to say he'd go with me, caseload be damned. He'd pack up himself and Moochie and come to Seattle with me. I waited for him to ask me to stay, to let my mother deal with the situation. But our good-bye was cut short by the final call for my flight. After promising to call him the next day from my mother's house, I boarded the plane. My stomach lurched as we ascended into the black night sky and I gripped the plastic armrests with cold fingers.

"Not a good flier, I take it?" the man in the seat next to me asked good-naturedly.

I shook my head. "Something like that." I wasn't about to explain to a complete stranger the real reason I was so shaky.

He lifted a substantial flask from his inside jacket pocket and wiggled it at me. "Me, neither."

I smiled politely, but turned my head away and continued my

attempt to hold myself steady. *Jenny,* I said to myself, making a little rhyme: *One-two-three-four*-five, *J-e-n-n*-y. A moment later, a flight attendant strolled by my seat, interrupting my internal chant.

"Ma'am?" she inquired. "You're more than welcome to take your seat belt off."

I nodded sharply to acknowledge that I'd heard her, but did not release my grasp. After she went down the aisle, I kept my seat belt on, wearing it tightly, checking its security again and again for the entire flight home.

*T*he midnight air in Seattle was sweet and cool, filling my lungs with much-needed relief from the packaged oxygen I had breathed on the plane. It was the middle of May, but a slight winter chill still tickled my skin as I stepped outside the terminal, the thin cotton sweater and worn Levi's I had chosen as traveling clothes doing little to protect me from the elements. Sea Tac airport was quiet at this hour; only a few scattered taxis lined the pickup lane and it wasn't long before I was sitting in the back of one headed north on I-5 toward the West Seattle exit. I shivered violently as I shifted against the cold leather of the seat. "Could you turn the heat on, please?" I asked my driver.

Reaching for the knobs on the dash, he cocked his head around to look at me. "Must've picked myself up a California girl."

I smiled halfheartedly, vigorously rubbing my biceps with both hands. "I've lived most of my life here, actually."

He nodded sharply. "You going home, then?"

"Looks like it," I said, the apprehension I felt taking up too much space in my chest, leaving little room for air. I certainly didn't feel like chatting, so I turned to look out the window, hopeful the driver would take the hint and leave me alone for the rest of the ride. The lights of downtown twinkled before me like the sun reflected on dark water, the Columbia Tower looming over the rest of the buildings as a father does over his children. The outline of the city looked odd to me, but it took a moment or two for me to realize what was missing.

Though I had watched the news footage of the Kingdome being demolished, the gray hatboxlike structure had remained in my memories: the time I had spent there at Mariners games with my dad, sitting on the hard metal bleachers of the one-hundred level, eating Red Vines and popcorn as he sipped a Big Gulp–sized beer and hollered at the players. I smiled a bit, remembering how much I enjoyed that time with my father each season, just the two of us heading out for a Saturday afternoon game.

Those outings stopped when Jenny began regressing again, her spine curving into a deeper S than was safe for the survival of her organs, the doctors telling us she might need major back surgery to correct the problem. My father began folding in on himself, spending more time at the homes he built for other people and less time at his own. Gradually, he became less like a person, less like a member of our family, and more like a shadow moving along the walls, jumping out to frighten us at unexpected moments.

I closed my eyes and a vision filled my mind: my father's broad-shouldered back moving into the darkness of Jenny's room in the middle of the night; the door closing softly, no lights turning on; the murmur of his voice behind those walls; the soft, insistent squeak of the bedsprings. My stomach swirled in acid at what I rarely allowed myself to think about. I willed the memory away.

My thoughts were interrupted by the driver prompting me to get out of the car. The trip from the airport had gone by in a blink and suddenly I was in front of my childhood home. I sat immobile, stuck to the seat. "Help you with your bag?" the driver offered.

"No. Thanks, though," I said, pushing the fare through the slot. I added a hefty tip for his silence during the ride.

He saw the size of the tip and gave me a happy yellow-toothed grin. "Peace, sister."

"Peace," I said as I opened the door and went to grab my bag from the trunk. The driver tooted the horn lightly as he pulled away and I had to quell the urge to hail him back. I longed to be anywhere but where I was; I wanted someone to save me from what I was about to do. I stood on the sidewalk and shivered again in the night air, my breath a silver cloud escaping me. How small the one-story Craftsman-style house looked. A child's playhouse in a backyard, not the seemingly rambling home I had lived in for eighteen years. The A-line white trim seemed closer to the ground; the four square windows on the front of the mustard yellow house looked about the size of dinner plates. Even the fragrant red cedar in the front yard looked shorter to me as I moved toward the crumbling brick porch.

A shaft of light flooded the steps as the door opened; my mother stood in the entryway. She hugged herself against the night's chill. The first thing I noticed was her hair. Once long past her shoulders, it had been cut into a sleek bob that followed the edge of her jaw, accenting the sharp point of her chin. Like the rest of her body, the line of her neck was still elegant and long, her heart-shaped head balanced perfectly at its top. Her clothes were plain: a navy blue sweat suit and white socks. I froze at the bottom of the steps, anxiety bubbling within me like a kettle about to boil. We stared at each other a moment longer.

Mom was the first to speak. "Come in," she said. Her voice was flat, careful.

I nodded, dipped my head down and ascended into the house, its familiar scent assaulting me like a slap in the face. The whisper of my father's pack-a-day habit still clung to the yellowed walls. I was surprised that our mother hadn't painted to erase any hint of him. The ceiling seemed too close to my head. Had the house always been this small? Did I make it larger in my memory? I hadn't grown any since leaving, yet I felt like a giant stumbling through a dollhouse. I dropped my bag to the worn gray carpet.

My mother stepped toward me and we hugged awkwardly, our bodies barely touching. She was warm and smelled of sleep. She patted my back in a stiff gesture, then pulled back to look at me. "You've gotten so pretty," she said, reaching to touch my hair, then pulling her hand back quickly as though she had thought better of it. "Your hair turned out so much darker than your father's."

I nodded again, not trusting my voice. While I had inherited my father's bold hair color and my mother's slanted mossy green eyes, my shorter, more voluptuous build was a gift of heredity from a grandmother I had never met. Jenny had been the lucky recipient of both our parents' slender tendencies. I fingered my copper curls self-consciously, keeping my eyes to the ground. Overcome by mixed emotions, I wrestled with the simultaneous urge to either slap this woman or throw myself into her arms, weeping. I kept every muscle, every nerve in my body rigid and tense, fighting for control. As we stood in the light of the hallway, I took in the details of how the last ten years had changed her. Her once-smooth pearlescent skin was now crinkled around her regal English features like fine white tissue paper. The lines around her mouth sliced her cheeks in deep parentheses and the gray in her chestnut hair grew in thick stripes on each side of her face. Her eyes were the same, in perfect echo of my own. Our eyes were the only indication we were related. Without them, we might simply be strangers passing each other on the street.

"I'm exhausted," I finally said, tearing my gaze away from her to the watch on my wrist. It seemed forever since that morning in the bakery when I first heard Jenny's call. It seemed a lifetime ago.

"Of course," she agreed, and gestured for me to move past her and into the living room. I noticed a few tan age spots on the back of her hand and it suddenly struck me that my mother was growing old and that I was no longer the child who had lived within these walls. I had grown, gotten stronger. I could get through this. I *would* get through it.

I picked up my bag and my body moved by remembered feel through the house; Mom followed close behind, watching me as-

sess the living room. The furniture was the same: dark wood tables and blue floral couches surrounding a brick fireplace. I
glanced down the dimly lit hallway that led from the living room
to my parents' bedroom and saw that family pictures still covered
that particular wall: bright false images of a happy existence. I
wondered whom my mother thought she was fooling.

I moved through the living room and into the small, square
kitchen, noting the chipped yellow paint on the chairs and the severely dated rust-colored appliances. I stepped carefully down
the short hallway from the kitchen, past the bathroom door, then
paused outside my old room. My mother stood right behind me.
"Am I staying in here?" I asked her.

"If that's all right with you."

I turned the doorknob. "Why wouldn't it be?"

She didn't answer me, but reached to one side of the door and
flipped on the light switch. The room hadn't changed much:
faded red-rose-flowered paper still dressed the walls; matching
bedspread and curtains completed the look. I set my duffel bag
down on the hardwood floor and went to sit on the bed.

"I put on fresh sheets," Mom said, gesturing to where I sat. "I
don't use this room much anymore. You might want to open the
window."

"Okay." I patted the bedspread nervously, then opened and
shut the nightstand drawer. Unspoken words traveled between
us like electricity in the air. "When can I see Jenny?"

"I took the day off, so we've got an appointment at Wellman
at nine." She started to leave, then turned back to look at me. "Is
that too early?"

"No, it's fine."

She paused again before shutting the door behind her. "I'm
glad you came, honey." The look she gave me was an open, fragile thing, full of hope; I was not expecting it.

I nodded, though unwilling to say I agreed.

"Welcome home," she said and a shiver ran through me at the
same words Jenny sent to my heart the moment the plane had
touched down.

❖   ❖   ❖

My call to Shane first thing in the morning caught him in his car on the way to the office. "Let me get my headset on," he said when he heard my voice. He talked on his cell phone so much while he was driving, I had insisted he start using one. After a moment of freeway noise and plastic rustling in my ear, he came back. "Okay, all set. So you got there okay?" he asked.

"All in one piece." I ran my finger down a long crack in the textured plaster wall. I stood in the hall across from my old bedroom door. As a teenager, since the phone was so close to the kitchen, I used to drag it inside my room for the illusion of privacy. I quashed the urge to do the same now. I was an adult; I didn't have anything to hide. "I'll see Jenny in an hour or so," I told Shane.

"Did you talk to your mom yet?" he asked loudly, his words broken up by static in the connection. "Is Jenny going to have the baby?"

"I pretty much went straight to bed when I got here. I doubt she'll have it, though. An abortion seems like it'd be the smartest thing to do."

"Um-hmm," Shane agreed. "Tricky legal issue, though. Who's her guardian?"

"My mom." I sighed, frustrated that he seemed more concerned about the legal aspect of the situation than the turbulent feelings that went along with it.

"What about your dad?"

Acid emotion rose up and burned the tender flesh of my throat. "He's not involved. He gave up his rights years ago." I stared at the door to Jenny's room, only a few feet from my own, feeling my father's presence in the house wrapped around me like cotton gauze. I hadn't shared the details of my childhood with Shane; in fact, I hadn't shared them with anyone.

"Didn't you tell me he pays for your sister's care?"

"Yes, but it was part of the divorce agreement that he'd get to sign away any responsibility for Jenny if he took care of her expenses. Nice, huh?" My voice rattled as I spoke and I pressed my forehead against the rough wall. "God. What am I doing here? I don't know if I can do this."

"You'll be fine," he casually assured me. He didn't know, didn't understand what I had come back to. He didn't know how I had left things. "Is there anything I can do?" he asked. "Do you want me to call the D.A.'s office in Seattle and see what I can find out about the rape case?"

"I'm not even sure if there *is* a case." I pulled away from the wall and stood up straight, rubbing my forehead with my free hand.

"Couldn't hurt to call." Static interrupted us again and we were suddenly cut off.

"Shane?" I said loudly. "Shane?" I hung up, then tried to reach him again but couldn't get through. "Dammit!" I swore softly under my breath as I slammed down the receiver.

Mom chose this moment to emerge from the kitchen, her coat and hat already on. "Who was that?" she asked as she pulled on a pair of brown leather gloves.

"Shane. I just wanted to let him know I got here safely. Don't worry. I used my phone card."

She stared at me blankly for a moment. "I wasn't worried. You can call whomever you like." She blinked, then shook her head. "Anyway. We should get going if we want to beat the traffic over the bridge." She looked at me expectantly; her eyes businesslike and efficient, the hint of openness I had seen the night before had vanished. "Is that what you're wearing?"

I had pulled on my traveling jeans and a slightly wrinkled embroidered peasant blouse. I glanced down at them. "Yeah," I said, the heat rising to my skin. I couldn't believe she was starting to criticize me already. "Is that okay with you?"

She shrugged. "Of course it is. I only meant you wouldn't have time to change. We need to go." She tugged at her gloves. "Your hair looks nice up like that."

I touched my upswept ponytail. "Thank you," I said, with an unsuccessful attempt to keep the surprise from my voice. I never knew what to expect from my mother. I could never read her intentions the way I could with other people. The way I could with Jenny. I took a deep breath and followed my mother out the door, hoping the sister I had neglected for so long wouldn't turn me away.

❋   ❋   ❋

The Wellman Institute perched like a boulder at the top of Capitol Hill, looking down over the downtown corridor of I-5. It was an imposing structure, square and sturdy, its faded brick facade strewn with ivy, its windows barred and closed. Spotty gray clouds moved over the morning sun, creating black ghosts that waltzed across the perfectly manicured lawn.

We pulled into the visitors' parking lot a few minutes before nine. A pointed crown of Douglas firs guarded the property like frozen soldiers; beneath them, thick rows of what must have been an abundant crop of daffodils hung their heads low, their petals pale and bruised. They looked how I felt.

When my mother got out of the car, I sat in the front seat, hands gripping my knees, trying to control my breathing. *It will be fine,* I told myself. *I can handle this. I am a grown woman. Jenny needs me.* I had repeated this mantra all night long. Unable to sleep, I had lain stiff in my childhood bed, overwhelmed by the enormity of my decision to come. Why hadn't I waited a day? Given it more thought? My therapist's training told me the answer to this: thinking is what had allowed me to stay away all these years. Reasoning and remembering, analyzing and rationalizing; these were the mental weapons I had brandished in defense of my behavior. Not thinking, allowing my instincts to finally take over, was what finally brought me home.

"Nicole?" My mother rapped at the window, startling me out of my thoughts. "Are you coming?"

I nodded. "Yes." I followed her into the building using the same heavily swinging metal doors I had escaped through a decade before. The stinging scent of ammonia did little to mask the cloud of stale human waste in the air. My eyes watered.

"You'd think they'd open a window or something," I commented after we signed in at the front desk and stepped into an elevator.

"They couldn't use the air-conditioning then," my mother said, reaching into her purse and handing me a couple of Altoids. "Here. These help a little."

I popped them into my mouth. "Thanks." The elevator's joints creaked with age. "What floor is she on?"

"Four. Dr. Leland told me he'd meet us in her room."

"And he's her gynecologist?"

My mother whipped her head around to look at me. "Jenny doesn't have a gynecologist. Dr. Leland is her case supervisor. He's been here almost as long as she has, overseeing all her meds and physical therapy, things like that."

"Do you like him?"

She shrugged. "I've never really thought about it. Jenny smiles at him, though, so he can't be too bad."

I smiled myself. Jenny's smile was like a blessing. The greatest gift because you knew she could not fake it.

When the elevator doors opened, the moaning hit me like a punch in the stomach—the aching sounds of communication for those who had no words. We walked slowly down the hall where the beige walls were lined with women and girls in various stages of undress, sitting in their wheelchairs or on the floor, their limbs twisted in odd angles away from their bodies. Many stared ahead, unblinking, unseeing, but an older woman in a wheelchair slammed her open palm against her forehead again and again, muttering and spitting as her other hand waved haphazardly in the air beside her. A nurse stepped over to her, reaching for the woman's arms. "Hush now, Connie," the nurse soothed. "You're all right. Everything's okay." It was gratifying to see such a prompt response to a patient's needs. I wondered briefly where this nurse had been while Jenny was being raped.

The smell was worse here than downstairs; I sucked hard on the mints in my mouth. Despite the foul odor, the surroundings at least seemed clean: the confetti-speckled linoleum was polished to a glossy shine, and if not completely dressed, the patients themselves weren't covered in vomit or their own waste the way I'd always feared. Still, I was uncomfortable, even if these walls didn't appear as sinister as I'd made them out to be.

My mother moved forward purposefully down the hallway, opening a pale green door marked HUNTER, JENNIFER. I steeled myself and followed her, eyes to the floor, ashamed, afraid that my sister would not know me, that the years I had been gone might have changed everything between us.

"Mrs. Hunter, hello," a deep voice said, and I looked up to see a black man with short graying hair. His stocky build suggested that at one time he might have been a wrestler. "This is your other daughter, I presume?" he inquired, sticking out his hand.

"Nicole Hunter," I said as I stepped forward to shake his hand. I glanced around the small, square room that was painted the same beige as the hallway. Across from the bed and dresser there was a TV/VCR combo and a small stereo; otherwise, the only other furniture was a chair by the window. Jenny stood next to it, her back to me. She could walk, but just barely. Her gait was unsteady, a jerky, uneven movement that threatened her balance with each step she attempted. Since she was eight years old we had had a wheelchair for her, but I knew it was important that she get a chance to stand on her own whenever she could. Perhaps in the same way it is important for us all.

"Jenny, look who's here," Dr. Leland said as he stepped around the bed and over to my sister. He gently rotated her to face me. I barely recognized her. Her glorious chestnut hair, once long and shiny, had been shorn just above her shoulders, its waves choppy and dull. She seemed huge, at least fifty pounds heavier than when I had seen her last, a substantial gain on her petite four-and-a-half-foot frame. In a shapeless purple house-dress, she was a swollen version of the angel I remembered. Her face, once heart-shaped like our mother's, was doughy and round. Her chin had virtually disappeared beneath soft flesh. I searched her blue eyes for a hint of the sparkle I remembered so well from our childhood, but found only the distorted reflection of my own face. Still, she looked at me intently, recognition rising slowly in her expression. Her twisted, callused hands patted together in a silent rhythm. My bottom lip quivered and my heart shook inside my chest as I hugged her to me. My chin still rested perfectly on top of her head; my body remembered holding her this way. She smelled of sweat and talcum powder.

"Jenny," I whispered. "Hi, sweetie." I pulled back but kept my hands on her shoulders. She stared at me, her eyes blinking rapidly, as though she could not believe whom she was seeing. "I'm so happy to see you!" I said, reaching out to tuck her hair behind her ears. It felt greasy to the touch. I used the corner of my shirt to wipe away the drool that ran a small river down her chin. "There, that's better."

Jenny's face froze suddenly and her indigo eyes flashed in anger. She slammed her fists together once, twice, then let out an aggravated yell. "Ahhh!" she exclaimed, driving her gaze into me like a knife. Her entire body shook with effort.

"I know," I soothed. "I know you're mad. You should be. But I'm here now." I leaned in and held her again. She was rigid against me, a low groan resonating from somewhere deep within her. "I heard you," I whispered into her ear so Dr. Leland and our mother wouldn't hear me. "I came because you said you needed help."

Her body relaxed at these words, and in a gesture of long-forgotten affection, Jenny rubbed her face against my sweater. When she pushed herself away, she looked up at me with a gooey grin, her eyes glowing. *Sister.* The word warmed my heart like the sun on my face. I could not believe I had stayed away from her for so long. Every minute of my life in San Francisco seemed a waste in comparison to the feelings that filled me in that moment of reunion.

My mother stood by the door watching our encounter, her expression soft around the edges. "I've told Nicole about Jenny's condition," she said to Dr. Leland, who had lowered himself into the chair by Jenny's bed.

I kept my arm around my sister, glancing down at her belly. "How far along is she?"

"We think twenty weeks," Dr. Leland said.

"Twenty?" I gasped. "How could that have happened?" I had thought she'd be a month, maybe two. Not five, not more than halfway through the pregnancy. Jenny swayed next to me from side to side, her hands patting together gently again. She stared intently at Dr. Leland.

The doctor looked over to my mother, who gestured with a flutter of her hand that he should go ahead and explain. Dr. Leland turned to me, leaned forward with his pointed elbows on his knees, fingers tented against each other. "Jenny has been on Depo Provera for several years. You know what that is?"

I nodded impatiently. "Yes. The birth control shot that keeps you from getting your period at all."

"Right. Pretty much. Most girls here who haven't had hysterectomies are on it, mostly for the sake of the staff."

"How nice for them," I commented snidely.

"Well, Miss Hunter, it's certainly less messy." Annoyance flashed briefly across his face. "Anyway, about six months ago, your mother expressed concern about all the weight Jenny had put on since being on the shot, so we took her off it. And since a normal side effect of Depo is missed periods even for a few months after it's been discontinued, Jenny's condition went unnoticed."

"Until now," I said pointedly.

"Yes, until now. When she missed her fourth period, one of the nurses felt her belly and suspected the pregnancy. We did the blood test yesterday."

I wondered if Jenny already knew she was pregnant or if the nurses told her yesterday and this was what prompted her to call me for help. I looked at my mother. "How often do you visit her? Couldn't you tell?"

"How?" she said defensively. "She'd put on all that weight . . ."

Dr. Leland stood up and pressed down the air in front of him with his hands. "There's no one to blame here. It went unnoticed. Now we need to figure out what to do with her."

"No one to blame?" I was incensed. "What about the bastard who did it to her? What about this institute, for hiring him? Haven't you heard of a little thing called background checks?"

"Of course, Miss Hunter." Dr. Leland's voice was low and smooth. "Jacob Zimmerman checked out perfectly. He'd worked in several institutions similar to this one and came with high recommendations. There was nothing we could have done."

"Nothing you could have *done*?" I repeated, my tone rising angrily.

"Nicole," my mother said, moving over to stand next to Jenny on her other side. "Please."

I shot her an angry look, trying to slow the quick beat of my heart. *Nothing we could have done.* Watching my father walk into

Jenny's room. There was something I could have done then. I could have screamed. I could have told. Told someone, anyone who might listen. But instead, I was silent. A child terrified. Not anymore.

I straightened my spine, pulled my shoulders back. "Someone is responsible for this, Dr. Leland. I assume you've contacted the police?"

"Of course. They're looking for Mr. Zimmerman as we speak." He walked over to help my mother, who was maneuvering Jenny into the chair he had just vacated. Her small body shuddered as they lowered her into the seat, uncertain where she might land. Dr. Leland gently laid his hand on my sister's head and spoke again. "What concerns us now is what to do about Jenny's condition. Your mother wants her to have the baby."

"What?" I exclaimed. My jaw dropped. "Isn't abortion legal until twenty-two weeks?"

"Twenty-four weeks here in Seattle," Dr. Leland corrected me. "One of our doctors could perform the procedure. Today, even, if your mother will sign the paperwork." His tone was suggestive, and his brown eyes gazed at her expectantly. Obviously, they'd already had this conversation.

My mother folded and unfolded her hands, chin down to her chest. "I won't," she said softly.

"What?" I exploded. "Are you crazy? She can't have this baby, Mother."

She raised her eyes to me defiantly. "And why not? She's carried it this long. Maybe she wants the baby. Did you ever think of that?" She held her head high on her graceful neck, though the pale skin on her chest flushed red, as it always had, with the stress of confrontation.

"That's ridiculous and you know it."

Dr. Leland strode to the door. "I'll leave you two alone to discuss this. Tell the charge nurse to page me if you arrive at a decision."

"Thank you, Dr. Leland," my mother said, kneeling down next to Jenny. My sister had been watching our exchange with hawklike intent, the same way she used to watch our parents fight: eyes wide, not blinking, drinking their words like a man taking in water at the end of a desert journey. My mother rested a light hand on Jenny's belly. "Everything's fine," she said, and I could not tell whom she was assuring, the baby or her own daughter.

I dropped on the bed next to them, leaned back on my hands. The patchwork quilt beneath me was soft, comforting against my skin. My mother must have brought it from home. I quickly scanned the room and noticed several other personal touches: a small pile of stuffed animals, two bright Monet prints, and a substantial library of *Sesame Street* videos. At least Jenny was surrounded by her favorite things. I redirected my attention to our mother. "What are you going to do, Mom, raise the baby yourself?"

"No," she faltered, then looked at me with sad eyes. "I don't know what I'm going to do. But it's just not right. This baby is alive. I can't be responsible for killing it."

"You wouldn't be."

"Yes, I would. I'm Jenny's guardian, so it's my decision whether this baby lives or dies. If it dies, I'm the one who made it happen." She shook her head. "I won't do it." She stood up, giving emphasis to her words.

I threw my hands up in the air. "Then what the hell did you want me here for, if you've already made up your mind?"

Her eyes lit up with tears, looking to Jenny and then back to me. "You're her sister, Nicole. I thought she might need you."

Jenny let out a tiny happy squeak, smiling at me again. I sighed, realizing I wouldn't convince Mom to change her mind so quickly. But then, the seed of an idea began to take root in my mind: a solution, a redemption. Something I could finally do to make up for what I hadn't done all those years before. "All right," I said. "Fine. But then we're going to get her out of here."

My mother's thin dark eyebrows lifted into small tents toward her hairline. "And take her where?"

"Home, Mom. I want to take her home."

After a long day of fruitless discussion at Wellman, I consented to leave Jenny at the institute one more night. Whispering in my sister's ear before my mother and I left, I promised her I'd do everything I could to be back the next day and take her home.

As we sat down to eat at the small, round kitchen table, my mother and I continued to argue. "You've never taken care of someone like that," she said. "You don't know how much it takes out of you."

I set my fork down next to my bowl, its contents cold and untouched. My stomach was whirling with emotion; the idea of adding soggy spaghetti to it was enough to cause a small gag in the back of my throat. "I watched it drain the life right out of you," I said spitefully.

Her eyes closed and her chin shot upward at this remark, as though someone had caught her with a sharp right hook. She lowered her jaw and looked at me with watery pale green eyes. "When did you get to be so cruel?"

My chest tightened with guilt. Strange how I could be so angry with her and yet feel such remorse when I hurt her. "Sorry," I said, pushing my bowl to the center of the table. "It's just . . . I guess I don't understand why you want her to have this baby, Mom. It seems like you'd be putting Jenny through an awful lot—"

"She's already been through an awful lot!" Mom snapped, interrupting me, slamming her fork to the table. I jumped at the noise, taken aback by her forcefulness.

"Having an abortion is not as simple as it sounds," she continued in a quieter tone.

"I know," I consented. "It just seems that it would provide a quicker solution than letting her go through with the pregnancy."

Mom stared at me, her expression deep and thoughtful. "Just because a solution is quick doesn't mean the consequences don't stick with you."

Her point hit home. I thought of my hurried departure ten years before, how the consequences of choosing to build a life without my family had left me feeling empty, uncertain about my career and living with a man I wasn't sure was right for me. Contentment seemed to elude me like a fugitive; just when I thought

I might turn a corner and catch it, it vanished. I readied for confrontation on this subject with my mother. "I left because I couldn't stand to see her in that place," I said defensively. "And yes, the consequences stuck with me. They're still sticking with me." My tone stepped up an octave. "I'm positively *sticky* with guilt, okay?" I made my voice hard, demanding.

She looked bewildered, then a little annoyed. "I wasn't talking about you, Nicole, however much that may surprise you."

I felt appropriately chastised, realizing that in the short time I'd been home, I'd made more than one false assumption regarding her intentions. But I was a little annoyed myself, feeling once again that I had to drag what my mother was thinking from her.

When she didn't go on, I asked, "Then who *were* you talking about?"

Placing her elbows on the table, she let her forehead fall against folded hands. "Me," she said. The sound was more a breath than a word.

It was my turn to look bewildered. "What about you?"

She didn't look up, but instead spoke to the surface of the table as though it were a priest to whom she was making confession. "My abortion." If her voice had been any quieter I wouldn't have heard her at all.

My jaw dropped. "What? When?"

"You were six months old. I didn't think I could have another child so soon. . . ." She trailed off, then took another deep breath before continuing, still not looking at me. "You think *you're* sticky with guilt." With this, she lifted her gaze to me, her thin lips pressed into a grim line.

I couldn't believe what I was hearing. "So you don't want Jenny to have an abortion because you feel guilty about yours?" Her reluctance made a little more sense now, though I wasn't sure if it justified putting my sister through the strain of pregnancy and childbirth.

She shook her head. "No. But what if she feels the same connection to her baby that I felt to mine when it was still inside me?" She swallowed. "Before I killed it."

"You didn't kill it, Mom." I recognized my own melodramatic

nature in her words and had the sudden urge to shower in order to wash off the similarity.

Her dark head bobbed insistently. "Yes, I did. I felt that baby's life inside me the same way I felt *your* life inside me, and I made the decision to end it." Her green eyes were pleading. "If Jenny has any sense of that baby's life, I will not be the one to take it from her."

We were quiet for a moment, both absorbed in our separate thoughts. I considered the significance of what she had revealed. "Okay," I said. "But why didn't you just tell me this at the hospital?"

"We've barely spoken for ten years," she said flatly, her eyes dark with restrained emotion. "Telling someone you had an abortion isn't exactly something you share with a casual acquaintance. Even if she is your daughter."

It seemed I wasn't the only person at the table capable of cruelty. My bottom lip quivered unexpectedly at the severity of her words, and as I averted my eyes from her gaze, I found myself having to blink back an onslaught of tears. I stared hard at the yellow birdhouse-patterned wallpaper that had hung in this kitchen for as long as I could remember.

She was right, of course. We were hardly more than strangers. And suddenly I realized how terrible that was, how much I had missed having her in my life. I felt her eyes still on me, expectant, but I still couldn't look at her. I certainly wasn't prepared to share what I was feeling, so I decided instead to try to set aside the issues we had with each other in order to figure out what was best for Jenny. "So, okay," I said, finally, consenting to her wishes. "Jenny is going to have this baby." I paused, turning my head to look at her. "Then she should come home."

She leaned back against her chair. Sighing, she tucked her hair behind both ears and held her hands there as though she didn't want to hear anymore. "I have to work, Nicole. I couldn't do it."

"But you wouldn't be doing it," I said stubbornly, crossing my arms over my chest. "I would." I swung one arm around the room in a wide circle. "She knows this house. It's still set up for her: the bathroom, her bedroom, the ramp on the back porch. You wouldn't have to do anything. I'd do it all." My voice shook under the weight of this promise, unsure whether I actually had what it took to follow through. I spoke purely on instinct, allowing my feelings, not my intellect, to guide my words.

She looked at me skeptically, her chin to her chest. "You have no idea what you'd be taking on."

"Maybe not, but you asked me to come because Jenny might need me." I held my hands out to her, open-palmed. "So let me at least *do* something." I had a difficult time understanding how she could be so adamant about Jenny having the child and hedge so much about bringing her home. It seemed I was offering her the perfect solution.

"What about *your* job?" she countered. "Can you afford to take so much time off?"

"Another baker is picking up my shifts. It's no big deal." This was true, I realized, and a little bit sad to think I was so easily replaced. I suddenly felt insignificant.

She sighed. "I still can't believe you left your practice. Your grandmother didn't leave you an education fund to have you throw it away like that."

I felt compelled to defend myself. "I'm not throwing anything away. I'm trying out a different career." I didn't mention that I had been extremely thrifty with my education fund; I was still living off its remains. It was the financial cushion that made my coming home possible. I stood up from the table, fingers splayed across its surface. "You're trying to change the subject. We need to make a decision here. I want to bring Jenny home."

She still looked hesitant, so I tried another tack. "Do me a favor, okay? Just think about it. Don't decide tonight. Sleep on it and see how you feel in the morning."

"Okay," she agreed, her green eyes tired. She stood as well, and we both retreated to our respective rooms, waiting silently for morning to come.

When I woke, the house was still quiet. I ventured into the dark hallway to call Shane before I talked to my mother. This time I caught him at home.

"Hey, babe," he said. "How'd it go with your sister?"

I fingered the springy telephone cord, smiling. "Pretty well, all things considered." I gave him a brief synopsis of the visit, then told him of my plan to stay and take care of Jenny until the baby was born.

He was quiet for a moment, then spoke. "You're staying four more months?"

I held my breath tightly in my chest. "I can't just leave her, Shane."

"What about your mom? She's the one who wants Jenny to have the baby, right? *She* should be the one to take care of her."

"I know. And I'm sure once Jenny is home the maternal instinct thing will kick back into full force and we'll take care of Jenny together." As I said this, I realized my insistence on bringing Jenny home was hinged on this belief: that once I got my sister here, Mom would spring back into the caretaker I remembered and help me. All she needed was a little prodding.

Shane was quiet until I spoke again. "Shane?"

"Yeah."

"Are you *mad*?" I asked, incredulous.

He sighed. "No."

"You sound mad."

"I'm not mad, Nicole. But you're always saying how screwed up your family is and suddenly you're back living with them instead of me." He sounded like a child who wasn't getting his way.

"It's not like I'm leaving forever." I made sure my tone reflected the annoyance I felt.

"Four months is a long time."

I sank to the floor, my back against the wall, the textured plaster scratching me through my thin cotton nightshirt. "So you're saying our relationship is over if I stay?"

"Of course not. Look, I have to get to work, okay? You do whatever you feel is right, I guess, and keep me posted." I felt dismissed.

"Okay, I will." I paused. "How's Mooch doing? Does he miss his mama?"

Shane snorted. "He's fine. Shedding all over everything, as usual." Moochie was a Husky/German shepherd mix; his thick coat made up almost half his body weight.

"If you brush him it's not so bad," I counseled. Shane had a difficult time with anything disordered or messy; he was the type of person who washed, dried, and put away all his laundry in one afternoon. I, on the other hand, tended to wash the pile of clothes on the floor only when it looked like it might stand up and walk to the laundry room of its own volition.

"I'll keep that in mind," Shane said, sounding as though he had no intention to do so. "Bye, babe."

"Bye." I softly hung up the phone and looked up to see my mother standing there. Her smooth dark bob was tousled from sleep. "How long have you been listening?" I asked, a little peeved she was sneaking around like I was a teenager again.

"I wasn't listening. Who's Mooch?" She smiled guiltily and I decided to forgive her eavesdropping.

"He's my dog. Shane's not nuts about animals, so it's a bit of a drama for him while I'm gone."

"Oh." She stuck her hands into the side pockets of her sweatpants and leaned back against the wall.

"So," I said, pulling my knees up to my chest and hugging them with both arms. The worn carpet tickled the soles of my feet. "Did sleeping on it help at all?"

She let her head fall toward one shoulder and then shrugged. "I'm not sure. I didn't sleep much."

"I'm sorry," I said.

"Me, too." She sighed. "I still don't think it's a good idea, Nicole. But if you're determined . . . I did ask you to come."

"So . . . ?" I prodded, rocking a bit on my tailbone.

She crossed one ankle over the other, managing to look both defeated and frightened at once. "So . . . okay. Bring your sister home."

The first few years after Jenny's disabilities made themselves apparent in our lives I don't remember very much of my everyday existence changing. I was a child, of course, self-absorbed in the innocent way children are, so I'm sure as I floated obliviously along, my parents were dealing with mind-bending emotional hurdles. But for the most part, Jenny's disease didn't make an enormous impact upon me until her screaming fits began. She was six when the first one hit, and these episodes quickly became the ticking bomb in our lives. From one moment to the next, we never knew when one might come, what invisible trigger would send my sister into agony so great we often thought she was dying right in front of us.

The fits struck in varying degrees of intensity, but for some reason a particular evening the summer I turned eleven sticks out in my mind as being one of the worst. It was after dinner and I was in our front yard jumping rope in the warm dusk air when an astonishing screech erupted from our house. Then came another, and another. It was a shrill of the deepest distress, an anguished peal for help. I ran up the porch stairs and into the living room, where both my mother and father were kneeling in front of Jenny, who sat on the couch red-faced and crying. Her bottom lip sagged; her blue eyes were wild with fear. The muscles of her small body were tense and rigid, like a volcano leaking lava, about to erupt.

"What's wrong with her?" my father demanded. He asked this every time Jenny began screaming as if it were possible for my mother or me to know.

Mom smoothed Jenny's messy dark hair, searching her child's body for evidence of trauma. "I don't know, Mark," she said loudly as her daughter continued screaming. She cupped Jenny's hot, wet face in her hands. "What's wrong, honey? Are you hurt? Are you sick? Please, tell me." Mom knew from experience that these questions were futile, but still she asked them, perhaps believing in some place in her heart that if asked enough times, her daughter just might answer.

Instead, Jenny screeched again, raising her clenched fists and slamming them into her open, drooling mouth. Blood oozed from the marks her teeth had made. I stood frozen; my sister's screams reached deep inside me, scratching at my soft, pulsing flesh. I wiggled in discomfort. "Mom, *do* something!"

My father stooped down and grabbed Jenny by the top of her thin arms. "Stop it!" He shook her. Hard. Her head snapped forward and back on the top of her neck. "Stop it right now!" I turned my eyes away and began counting the bricks of the fireplace. I made a deal with myself: if I could count all of them without taking a breath, Dad wouldn't hurt Jenny anymore. I had to exhale before I even got to twenty.

"Mark, don't," Mom pleaded, pushing him away, still trying to soothe Jenny with her touch.

"There's nothing wrong with her, Joyce!" Dad bellowed, throwing his arms up in the air, disgusted. "She's like a baby, wanting attention. You need to stop coddling her, dammit! This is why she should be in a home. They know how to handle these things. You don't."

My mother's eyes shot daggers at him, but she didn't respond. It was an old argument, one neither of them planned to lose. My father stormed out the back door with his car keys and cigarettes in hand. Jenny's screaming continued.

We tried everything, my mother and I. We had to. Even though nothing had helped before, we couldn't just listen to her scream. We sang to her, we tried food and water, we checked her diapers, laid her down, walked her around, and still she screamed. Mom held her arms down so Jenny wouldn't slice her fingers to ribbons against her teeth. Being restrained only seemed to incense my sister more. The banging of her fists to her mouth seemed to give her relief, the same way punching a pillow or slamming a door made me feel better when I was angry.

After three hours, my insides felt twisty and disoriented from the sound of my sister's cries. As usual, she slowly petered out, resting her head on my mother's belly as they swayed together in the living room. My mother's exhaustion was written across her face in tear streaks and dark shadows. "Help me get her to bed, Nicole," she whispered and the two of us walked Jenny through the kitchen and down the hall to her bedroom where finally, mercifully, she quieted and fell asleep.

Images of this night tumbled through my mind as I packed up my sister's belongings at Wellman. I considered whether I was insane for wanting to take her to my mother's house, to be utterly responsible for her needs over the next four months. And her needs were immense. Dr. Leland had fought me tooth and nail to keep Jenny at the institute, citing my sister's medication schedule and extensive physical therapy needs. "Do you really think you can handle this?" he asked me as we stood on opposite sides of Jenny's bed. "Do you think you're qualified?"

"I'm her sister," I snapped. "I helped take care of her for fifteen years before she came here. I think that qualifies me." I didn't want to think about this. I only knew I had to do it. I looked over to Jenny, who sat quietly in her wheelchair by the door, watching me pack her things. I tried to send out only positive thoughts so she wouldn't sense any of the hesitation I felt, any of the fear that I was making an enormous mistake.

"Have you ever given her an enema, Nicole?" Dr. Leland inquired pointedly. I stopped packing for a moment and looked startled. He continued. "She needs one almost every day—did you know that? And what about the baby? Other than here, where are you going to find a doctor willing to take on a severely disabled mother?"

"I'll find one." I hardened my gaze along with my determination. "If I were you, I wouldn't be worrying about my sister's enemas. I'd be worrying about what this institution's lawyers are going to do when the media gets wind of what happened here."

"Miss Hunter, there's no need—"

"No need for what? To let the public know what really goes on in these places every day? What gets brushed under the rug because the victims don't have voices?" My words shook with emotion. "Well, Dr. Leland, Jenny has a voice. She has my voice and I intend to use it."

I sounded more confident than I felt. I didn't actually have a plan to approach the media; I wanted to talk to Shane first and get an idea of how stable our legal position was before I did anything.

For the moment, all I knew for sure was that I was going to care for Jenny the way I should have when I was eighteen. How unfathomable it had been to me then—fresh out of high school, thrilled to escape the suffocating confines of my family—to drop the potential of my life and take care of my sister so my parents wouldn't place her at Wellman. How much I tormented myself over leaving her there when I could have stood up to my father's ultimatum: "Either commit her or I will leave you, Joyce." How deeply I hated my mother for choosing a man over her own daughter, a man who ended up leaving her anyway. The life I'd created in San Francisco didn't seem worth it now, after all the time I'd lost with Jenny, after what had ended up happening to her. Her pregnancy gave me the chance to finally redeem myself, to be the sister I wished I had been.

When Dr. Leland realized I would not be swayed, he grudgingly handed over the names of a couple of obstetricians who had had some experience with special-needs patients. He also gave me a list and schedule of Jenny's medications and informed me that any that might be harmful during pregnancy had already been discontinued.

"Could the damage have already been done?" I asked fearfully.

Dr. Leland gave a short nod. "Possibly. She wasn't taking anything considered especially harmful to a fetus, but you'll just have to wait and see."

I looked the list over. Zantac, for severe acid reflux, twice a day. Milk of magnesia, for constipation, as needed. Klonopin, for muscle spasms, once daily, with food. Dantrium, a muscle relaxant, as needed, with food. Instructions for giving an enema. I leaned over the back of Jenny's wheelchair to kiss her cheek. "Quite the pharmacy, sis. Don't worry. We'll figure it out."

I thanked Dr. Leland and wheeled my sister down the hall to the elevator and then to the car. My mother was waiting for us at the house, her disapproval of Jenny's homecoming clear. As I loaded her few things into the trunk, Jenny closed her eyes and lifted her round chin, the soft spring sun on her pale face and dark hair like a graceful caress. She smiled, her closed hands patting their gentle dance. Her gaze caught mine and I smiled back into her deep blue eyes. *Home,* I said without a sound and she laughed, a sound so pure and clear it smoothed the edges of my ragged soul.

*F*or six years after Jenny first began to show signs of her disabilities, our mother took her to an unending line of specialists, neurologists, and pediatricians who had nothing to give us but more forecasts of my sister's impending death. "If I were you," one had actually said, "I'd want to get some tests done to find out if she's playing with all her marbles." But despite the negativity she encountered, my mother led a determined search for the name of the monster who had invaded our lives. More than once, we had been told Jenny could die any day.

"She's regressing," several specialists concluded. "More likely than not, she'll continue to regress until her brain simply stops functioning. You should prepare yourself for losing her." Not one of them could tell us why this was happening. Not one of them could give it a name.

My mother came home from these appointments tearful and depressed, often locking herself away in my parents' bedroom for hours, leaving me to care for Jenny. I did my best to entertain my sister; she loved to watch me make silly faces and sometimes even attempted to mimic my expressions. At three, she had begun to look us in the eye again, an occurrence my mother took as a sign of her ability to be healed. Anything could be a sign: a smile, a laugh, a particular movement of Jenny's hand. My mother interpreted them all as proof that her daughter was simply ill, not permanently damaged. Back then her hope was a bright thing, sometimes dulled, but always burning.

But the professionals she consulted provided little encouragement. So when Jenny was nine, Mom decided to look away from medicine and into the spiritual world for answers. There was a healer, a supposed miracle-creating interpreter of languages unheard by the rest of us. Mom found out about her from a friend who swore the woman was God's unnamed daughter. "She knew things about my life I've only prayed about," the friend said. "You have to take Jenny to see her."

My mother made the appointment. She didn't tell my father, sure he would only scoff at the waste of time. She did, however, insist that I come with them; if the healer said or did something worthwhile, I could back her up when she told Dad about it.

"But I don't *want* to go," I had whined when she told me of the appointment. It was the summer I turned twelve and the days were hot. My best friend, Nova, and I were spending as much time as possible at Coleman Pool in Lincoln Park, practicing our high dives and giggling over the boys in their wet swim trunks.

Helping my mother take care of Jenny at home was one thing, but going out in public with them had become another. I was easily embarrassed, painfully vulnerable to every sidelong glance sent our way, every whisper of a child who asked his mother, "What's *wrong* with that girl?" I had learned that the safest response to these situations was to ignore them. Too many times I had watched as my mother attempted to introduce Jenny to an inquisitive child only to have that child's mother yank him out of Jenny's reach, as though her disabilities were a virus that might be caught.

This was not the only lesson I learned about life as the sister of a retarded child. Unwilling student that I was, I learned that no matter how many times my parents tried to convince me differently, I always came second. By simple necessity, Jenny's needs were foremost, pushing me into the role of less important child even when I had accomplished the most. My straight As won a quick smile; Jenny's managing to get a spoon to her mouth won her an hour of cooing and congratulations. This realization forced me into a subconscious hyperachievement drive, compelled to be more, do more, as though it were my task in life to make up for Jenny's disabilities.

Not wanting to give my mother more than she already had to handle, I rarely misbehaved. I struggled to match Jenny's angelic demeanor, though on some level I sensed I would always fall short; I would always be the imperfect daughter. And since Jenny didn't have the capacity to misbehave, the standard I set for myself was completely unreachable. Still, I reined in my rebellion as best I could, the ache I felt for normalcy binding me like a too-tight blanket.

But that morning, of all the lessons I had learned, duty to my sister spoke the loudest. As my mother got Jenny dressed, skillfully sliding her daughter's stiff limbs into a calico sunsuit, she looked at me, her eyes hard at my reluctance to accompany her. "I don't care if you don't want to go. Take that bathing suit off and get your clothes on."

"But Nova and Star are supposed to pick me up in fifteen minutes. . . ." Star was Nova's mother and her father was Orion; a couple of hippies who had met and married in a commune, they had stuck with the celestial theme in naming their only child.

"Nicole Hunter!" my mother snapped. "Get dressed. Now. Call Nova and tell her you have something else to do today and you'll go to the pool tomorrow."

I looked at the floor, scowling, scuffing my bare foot against the carpet.

"Did you hear me, young lady?"

Jenny was silent, her eyes large and liquid, looking at me, not blinking. *Please,* I heard her say, so I twirled around and stomped out of the room. I called Nova from the phone in the hallway.

She was disappointed. "But why can't you come? What am I going to do all day without you? Who's going to put baby oil on my back?" Both pale-skinned with a tendency toward wild freckling, Nova and I approached tanning with scientific vigor. I knew her shining sandy-blond waves would look better next to a Copper Tone tan than my red mess of corkscrew curls, but since she was my best friend I tried not to hold it against her.

"My mom is making me go with her to some stupid appointment for Jenny." Nova was the only friend I ever felt comfortable bringing around Jenny, the only friend who embraced my sister as special, hugging her, wiping away her drool, and singing her the "Alphabet Song" in a Cookie Monster voice. Jenny, in turn, adored Nova, lighting up whenever my friend appeared. I raised my voice so my mother would be sure to hear how angry I was with her. "She's so dumb."

My mother called out from Jenny's room. "Watch it, kiddo. Keep it up and the pool is off-limits for the rest of the week!"

I spit air out of my mouth like it had a bad taste. After telling Nova I'd talk to her later, I got dressed and we left. I kept silent for the entire drive, staring out the backseat window as we headed through our local shopping district, the West Seattle Junction, and up Thirty-fifth Avenue toward White Center. When we pulled up in front of a beaten-down brown house with a rotten-looking roof and sagging front porch, I finally spoke. "This place is a dump."

My mother whipped around to look at me, her hands still gripping the steering wheel, her knuckles white. "That is a terrible thing to say. Maybe it's all she can afford."

I crossed my arms over my budding chest. "Then she's probably not that good. If she was, she'd make more money and live in a mansion on Lake Washington."

"Get out of the car, Nicky."

With one of us on either side of Jenny, we gingerly led her up the front steps, careful to avoid the soft-looking spots of wood. A small handwritten sign hung in the window next to the door that read EDEN SMITH, PSYCHIC HEALER. I rolled my eyes.

Before we had a chance to knock, a woman came to the door. At a little over five feet tall, she was small-boned, petite enough as to appear childlike. Her dark black straight hair fell to the middle of her back. Her skin was pale, her eyes piercingly gray. She wore a purple robe with a hood, its hem edged in gold rope. "Welcome, you must be Jenny," she said to my sister, her voice low and melodic; then she paused. "Yes, I've been waiting to meet you, too," she continued as though my sister had spoken to her.

I snorted at this, but when she directed her eyes at me, I shivered. "Hello, Nicole. Your mother told me you'd be coming. I'm so happy to meet you all. Come in, please." She gestured with her winglike arm for us to enter the small living room.

The space was dimly lit; heavy velvet curtains hung over the windows, blocking out the bright morning sun. Sweetly scented candles burned in several corners of the room and dark tapestries depicting scenes from the Bible insufficiently covered cracked plaster walls. Eden motioned us to the large couch by the door while she sat opposite in a deep, comfortable reading chair. There was a short wood table between us, lined with a pretty piece of burgundy fabric, candles, and an ornate deck of cards. She folded her hands gracefully in her lap.

"What can I help you with, Joyce?" she addressed my mother.

"Well," my mother said nervously, her fingers busily fiddling with the straps of her purse, "like I said on the phone, we want to know what's wrong with Jenny. The doctors can't—" She swallowed; I watched her voice box bob up and down her slender neck. "They say she's as good as dead already . . . ," she whispered, her voice faltering as she lowered her chin to her chest. "I—"

Eden reached out for her hand and squeezed it. "I understand. You want to know if the disease that grips your child's mind is hopeless. If it can be named, it might be healed."

My mother nodded once and whispered, "Yes."

Then Eden looked at me. "And you, Nicole—what do you want to know?"

I froze, then shrugged my indifference.

"Nothing?" Eden smiled, her eyes twinkling. "Well, we'll see if there's anything your sister wants to tell you."

"She already tells me things," I shot back at her, my eyes narrowed. "We don't need you for that."

"Nicole!" my mother exclaimed.

Eden's arched eyebrows rose to the middle of her forehead, tiny black birds about to take flight. "It's all right, Joyce. We'll just see what happens, then, shall we?" She reached out to hold Jenny's hands in her own. Closing her eyes, her lips began to move silently, her head wobbling in short nods, forward and back on top of her neck.

Jenny was quiet, staring at this woman intently. When Eden opened her eyes, she bore her gaze into Jenny, completely focused on my sister's face. It seemed every muscle on Eden's face was still; she didn't blink, her nose didn't wiggle, and her mouth stayed slightly open. Jenny, in turn, was motionless as well, her blue eyes as open and accepting as I had ever seen them. The only sound was the breath moving in and out of their bodies in perfect synchronicity. A translucent energy flowed between them; I was sure that if I reached out my hand I could touch it.

My mother sat on the other side of Jenny, leaning forward. She looked anxious; I could not tell if she sensed the same connection between Eden and Jenny that I did.

Eden still did not speak, but continued to hold Jenny's hands, pulling them to her small chest and cradling them there like a child. This went on for several minutes; my muscles began to twitch from sitting so still. I felt invisible, as though I were intruding on some incredibly private moment. My eyes ached from focusing so intently on their interaction. Then, out of the silence, a giggle erupted from my sister, the sound of tinkling bells, happy and pure. Eden laughed, too, finally releasing Jenny's hands and leaning back into her chair.

My mother looked awkwardly around the room. "Umm . . . ?"

Eden smiled at us. "There is a name for your daughter's disease, Joyce, but she does not know it. She wants you to know she is happy."

"But can you heal her? Can you make her well?"

Eden shook her head. "She's not meant to get well. But she's not going to die soon, either. Jenny is who she is supposed to be. She's who God created her to be. She is His gift to you."

My mother was silent, her hands folded tightly together as

though in prayer. Disappointment radiated from her body like steam from wet pavement. "How much do we owe you?" she asked finally, her voice flat.

"I accept donations only. Whatever you feel is appropriate."

My mother reached into her purse and slid out a dollar bill, carefully laying it flat on the table. "Ten cents a minute," she whispered. "Better rates than the phone company. Pretty good racket you've got going here." She stood, pulling Jenny with her and looked above my head at some unseen point. "Let's go, Nicole."

Eden watched us move to the door from her chair. "I'm sorry you're disappointed, Joyce. I did tell you how unlikely it was that Jenny could be healed. She needs your acceptance, not a cure."

My mother shot her words at Eden like poisoned arrows. "Don't tell me what my daughter needs."

We left, and it was my mother's turn to be silent on the drive home. Tears escaped the corners of her slanted eyes and she angrily wiped them away as fast as they appeared. I sat with Jenny in the backseat, holding her hand. My sister smiled a secret smile, humming and moaning happily to herself. I felt my mother's pain like a vise around my chest, but could not help thinking that Eden had gotten it right. Jenny was exactly who she was supposed to be. It wasn't our job to fix her. But my mother's life was anchored around a cure. Eden, like all the doctors and specialists who had seen Jenny before her, took that anchor and dislodged it further, leaving my mother to sail aimlessly along, a waning flicker of hope her only guide.

The first morning at home with Jenny it took almost an hour simply to get her dressed. Wrangling her stiff limbs into clothing was a far more difficult prospect than I had remembered. Her twisted fingers caught in odd places, bending them back and rendering from her shrieks of pain that lit panic in my stomach like a fire.

"Shit!" I exclaimed as I once again failed to get her arm through the hole of a knit shirt. We were in her yellow-painted bedroom; the contents of the two boxes of clothes I had brought home from Wellman were scattered across the bed down onto the pale green carpet. Jenny sat precariously on the edge of her bed as I stood over her. She was naked from the waist up and looked a little frightened of me, her eyes wide and inquiring, as though she wondered if I knew what I was doing. *I* wondered if I knew what I was doing. "What am I doing wrong?" I asked her, exasperated by my own incompetence. I tried to figure out how the hell I was ever going to get her dressed.

Mom stuck her head into the room. "Everything okay in here?" When I had gone to pick up Jenny the previous afternoon, Mom had straightened up Jenny's old room, changing the sheets and vacuuming the rug. I had taken her industrious behavior as a sign that she was ready to help, but when Jenny and I got home, Mom disappeared into her bedroom, proclaiming she had a migraine. Jenny and I had spent the evening alone in her old room, watching *Elmo in Grouchland* until she finally fell asleep.

"Ehhh," Jenny cried when she saw our mother. A pitiful edge tinged her voice. Her small shoulders shook uneasily; her eyes were bright.

An all too familiar feeling of inadequacy raised its ugly head in my belly. Leaving the shirt hanging around her neck, I hugged Jenny to me and glared at our mother. "Everything's fine."

Mom glanced around the messy room thoughtfully. A small set of worried wrinkles swam briefly across her forehead. She adjusted the thick brown belt she wore around an emerald green cotton dress. "Okay," she said. "I've got to get to work, so I guess I'll see you girls later." She turned to leave.

"Mom?" I called out, stopping her.

"Yes?" she said. I could almost smell her trepidation.

"I'm taking Jenny to a salon this afternoon. I thought she could use some pampering."

Mom nodded slowly. "That sounds nice." Her tone was careful, entirely neutral.

I stepped toward her, gesturing to Jenny. "Should I make the appointment for the three of us?" I thought of the look she had given me the other night, the hope it had held. It had taken courage to open herself that way to me; I wanted to answer her with some of my own.

Mom gave me a half smile, but shook her head. "I really can't afford to take any more time off this week." She waved at Jenny. "Have a good day, you two." And then she was gone.

I turned to Jenny, stepping back to face her. "Well, so much for bonding with Mom, huh, Jen?" I kissed the top of my sister's hair, then wiped my lips, trying to ignore the sting of our mother's refusal. I felt like a child who had reached out for her mother's hand to hold only to have it slapped away. I picked up another shirt from the pile on the bed and held it up to examine. "Okay. Back to the task at hand. The problem is these are all just too small. We need to go shopping, sis."

Jenny smiled, a small, hesitant gesture.

I touched her soft pale cheek. Her skin had always been perfectly clear; I don't think she ever had a pimple. As a teenager plagued by monthly bouts of acne, I remember asking my mother why Jenny never had a problem with it.

"Angels don't get acne," Mom answered lightly, as she brushed Jenny's smooth skin with the tips of her fingers. At the time I figured the zits Jenny would have gotten if she hadn't been such an angel were simply passed on to her demon big sister.

I shook my head at the memory, attempting to clear it from my mind. "Hold on a second," I said to Jenny. "I'll be right back." I dashed down one door to my room and picked through my old dresser for a sweater. I finally found one I had worn in high school; it was too small for me now, but I hoped it would fit over Jenny's newly expanded shape.

When I stepped back into her room, I heard a muffled cry, then saw that Jenny had fallen sideways on the bed and had her face stuck in a pile of clothes. I had forgotten that, like an infant, she needed pillows around her at all times or she would tip right over. I rushed over, lifting her as gently as I could back into a sitting position. Her eyes were glossy with panic and tears, her round cheeks flushed. She was panting, her breath hot. I brushed her dark hair back from her face and held her again. Despite her weight gain, she still felt like a child in my arms. "I'm sorry, Jen. There's so much I've forgotten."

"Ehhh . . . ," she moaned lightly, rubbing her face into my

chest. Her bare back was cold to my touch so I quickly showed her the sweater.

"Let's try this one," I said as I carefully maneuvered her head into the new top, following with one arm at a time. The green sweater clashed a bit with the hot pink elastic-waist stretch pants I had already managed to get on over her diapers, but I wasn't about to be picky.

I spent the rest of the morning unpacking her few belongings while she sat in a nearby chair, watching me. Her ankles were crossed and she rocked in a small forward and back motion, her hands clenched. She seemed uncomfortable; again, I wondered if I had done the wrong thing in bringing her here. Wellman had been her home for ten years. Despite what had happened to her there, maybe she felt the same way I did: displaced, the way you feel when you drive down an unfamiliar street in a city you thought you already knew by heart. Maybe she missed her routine and the familiar faces that had surrounded her for the past ten years. I experienced a stab of guilt knowing my face was not among them.

"Do you want your things folded or hung in the closet, Jen?" I asked her, carrying on a one-sided conversation as I sorted through the few bits of clothing she had. I was definitely going to need to find her some maternity clothes.

"Uhhn . . . ," she groaned, a low, unhappy sound.

I squatted down in front of her, resting my rear on the back of my heels. I took her callused hands in mine. "What's wrong, hon? Are you tired?" I reached up with one hand to straighten her dark hair.

"Uhhnnn . . . ," she groaned again.

"Not tired, huh?" I surmised from her tone. "Are you hungry?"

She stopped moaning and stared at me, her blue eyes round and wide.

"What do you say, sis?" I prodded. "Do you want to eat?"

"Ahhh!" came her happy reply. We had figured this game out as children: I would ask her questions, and when I finally asked the right one, her low, negative moans would suddenly escalate into a lilting, positive exclamation.

"All right," I said, clapping my hands together. "Let's eat and then we'll head down to the salon. It's about time you and I had a sisters' day out."

The Filigree Day Spa was only a few blocks from the house, and since the cornflower sky held only the promise of a beautiful spring day, I decided to walk Jenny to her appointment. After a quick lunch, I transferred her into her wheelchair, then carefully maneuvered it out the back door and down the ramp that led into the yard.

As I pushed Jenny up the driveway to the sidewalk, I noted how the yard had been carefully tended in a way it never was when I was a child. Mom had always been too busy with Jenny to bother and Dad hadn't seemed to care if the lawn was overgrown or if dandelions were the main flowering plant under the trees. But now, the enormous lilac bushes that lined the entire property appeared ready to burst, bunches of tiny and sweet lavender knots swimming in the potential of their amazing perfume. A clematis vine wove wildly through a trellis along the south side of the house; its mauve buds were swollen with life, about to give birth. The rest of the yard overflowed with other plants and flowers, most of which I couldn't name but appreciated for their sheer abundance. As we headed down the street, I considered that perhaps with Jenny at Wellman, Mom had channeled her caretaking tendencies into the land. Or then again, maybe she had just hired a gardener.

I pushed Jenny along California Avenue, one of the main strips that ran through West Seattle. The faces of the buildings looked familiar to me; as a child I had walked this maple-tree-lined street countless times with Jenny, forever aware of the heads that turned in cars, trying to catch a glimpse of the drooling dark-haired girl in the wheelchair. I felt the curious eyes on us now, too. I sighed as we approached the front door of the spa, wondering what it was that drew people to stare. It drove me crazy when we were younger. "Take a picture—it lasts longer," I'd whisper under my breath. I quashed the urge to do the same now.

A light-tinkling bell announced our entrance into the spa. The night before, I had decided Jenny needed a trip to a professional, when getting a brush through her matted hair proved to be an impossible task. I had thumbed through the phone book until I found a few salons nearby and the Filigree had been the only one that could take us both on such short notice. I explained to the woman I spoke with on the phone that Jenny had special needs but was assured that it wouldn't be a problem. We were both getting our hair done, as well as pedicures.

The receptionist greeted us, then led us to the back of the salon, where two empty black barber chairs sat waiting. The walls were sponged in a feathery terra-cotta paint and the mirrors were all edged in scrolled black filigree, the fancy wrought-iron detail found on the buildings in New Orleans' French Quarter. We appeared to be the only customers. "Your stylists will be right with you," she said, then gestured toward Jenny without really looking at her. "Do you—I mean, does *she* need anything?" She was obviously uncomfortable.

"No, we're fine," I assured her and she went back up front. I slid Jenny's wheelchair in between the two barber seats and sat down next to her, smiling at her in the mirror. She appeared slightly dazed. Her eyes were glazed over and her bottom lip drooped; her hands were clenched together but motionless in her lap. "This will be fun, Jen," I told her. "I promise." She didn't respond. Then I looked at my own reflection in the mirror and cringed a little. My red corkscrew curls frizzed wildly about my makeup-bare, freckled face. I usually managed to at least swipe on some lipstick, but as I'd been so focused on getting Jenny home and busy with her since, I hadn't even showered since arriving in Seattle. I glanced around self-consciously, then gingerly lifted an arm to see if I was obviously ripe. *Not too bad*, I thought, lowering my arm and crossing my legs under the floral print skirt I'd chosen to wear. At least I remembered to put on deodorant.

In a few minutes two women appeared behind us. The stylist who was going to work on Jenny inquired if she needed to be careful of anything while doing my sister's hair. "Keep your hands away from her mouth," I joked, in an attempt to put her at ease. "She bites." A horrified look popped up on the woman's face. "I'm *kidding*," I relented, reaching out to wiggle my fingers in front of Jenny's wet lips. "See? Completely harmless."

She laughed a bit awkwardly, her palm to her chest. "Geez, you scared me," she said. "I'll just work on her in her own chair. Is that all right?"

"Sure." I settled back and let my stylist begin the unenviable task of untangling my hair. Jenny remained quiet while her hair was washed, deep-conditioned, and trimmed, her expression still fairly blank. I wondered if she was overstimulated, if bringing her to the spa had been a mistake. Maybe I should have just kept her at home to help her get readjusted to being there. When the stylists moved us to the pedicure station, I took Jenny's hand in mine. "You doing okay, sis?" I asked. "Your hair looks great." Though not as long as they used to be, her dark waves shined softly around her face again, the layered bob complementing the new round curve of her jawline. I glanced around until I found a handheld mirror and put it up in front of her. "Look at you! You're gorgeous!"

The fog over her eyes seemed to lift and a light began to fill her face as she stared at herself in the mirror. A small smile tickled the corners of her full, rose petal lips and she ducked her chin down to the left in the tiniest motion, flirting with the image she saw reflected back at her. *Pretty*, I heard her say and I smiled in relief.

The rest of our visit went by quickly. Jenny giggled the entire time her feet were in the bubbling footbath, and since she was extremely ticklish, the poor pedicurist had a heck of a time getting a pale pink polish on my sister's tiny round toenails. But all in all, the appointment seemed a success and I was glad I had brought her. I paid the bill and tipped well, promising to spread the word about the service we had received there.

As I pushed Jenny back to our childhood home, I thought more about what drove people to stare at her. It suddenly struck me that perhaps it was the same phenomenon that caused commuters to slow down as they passed a fiery crash on the freeway; the there-for-the-grace-of-God-go-I syndrome. They looked at

Jenny and counted their blessings. So did I, I realized, looking down at the dark cap of my sister's head as we turned the corner that led down our street. My heart ached with emotion I had forgotten I was capable of experiencing. I counted my blessings, too, but for entirely different reasons.

*T*hree o'clock in the morning and she was moaning again. Every two hours; I could almost set my clock by the noise. The thin wall between our rooms did little to mask the sound. It reached into my chest and twisted my heart, pulling me from a fitful rest. "Jenny, *please,*" I groaned into my pillow. "I need to sleep." God, I was tired.

The first two weeks of her waking in the night had not bothered me too much. My body was used to being active in the dark and I had immediately run to soothe her, to adjust her pillow, to turn her over so she wouldn't develop sores. But the long hours awake with her during the day—feeding her, walking her around, changing her diapers, giving her her medications—had drained me. I longed for a four-hour-straight block of sleep like a starving man longs for bread.

Jenny's needs were constant, their strength like the tide, coaxing me to her even as I tried to pull away, tried to take a shower or finish a cup of coffee. My lower back screamed from lifting her swollen pregnant body. A dull ache had settled in behind my eyes like an unwanted visitor. My sister woke several times a night and rose early; she needed to be fed, showered, diapered, and dressed. Then there was her medication schedule, which I had scrupulously charted out and stuck to the refrigerator, but often passed by without consulting. "Take her back to Wellman," a small voice within me cried. "You can't do this. It's too much." I felt inept, lost in the wilderness of what caring for her demanded of me, afraid I might never return to the freedom of the life I had known.

I wanted to leave, to go back to San Francisco. I missed Shane. I missed Barry. I missed the simple solitary pleasure of taking Moochie for his afternoon walk. I wanted to be able to go to the grocery store without having to think about the logistics of pushing a wheelchair *and* the shopping cart, or whether I had packed enough diapers for an hour away from the house. I wanted to be able to take more than a five-minute shower without worrying that Jenny had fallen out of her bed and cracked her skull. I wanted to take back all my lofty promises, to take back what had happened to Jenny and return to the life I'd lived for the past ten years.

My mother wasn't helping stem these feelings of regret. I watched her move around Jenny and me as though we were polite but uninvolved acquaintances. I did not understand her. Putting aside my own complicated issues with my mother, I had truly believed that having Jenny home would soften her, bring her back to the mother she had been to Jenny before Wellman. "Help!" I longed to plead. "Help me do this! She's your daughter. What's *wrong* with you?"

She seemed to float above us like a balloon attached to our wrists, tied to us forever but distant, inanimate. She slept at the other end of the house in the same room she shared with our father when we were children. She wore earplugs, something she said she had done since Jenny moved to Wellman. "After she left," my mother told me, "even the tiniest sound would wake me. I'd be sure it was Jenny crying, needing me." She shook her head. "A woman's hearing becomes supersonic when she becomes a mother. Intently tuned to the sound of her children's cries. Even the illusion of them. If I didn't wear these"—she held up the earplugs—"I'd never sleep again."

But despite her words, the first time Jenny had woken up in the middle of the night, I'd stepped back into the hallway after comforting my sister and sensed my mother's presence nearby. I also smelled something burning. I caught her sitting at the kitchen table in the dark, smoking. Her legs were crossed and her dangling foot wiggled furiously. "What are you doing?" I asked. I was sure she had come to check on Jenny, but I wanted her to be the one to say it. To admit she cared.

She looked at me, her pale, angled face suddenly illuminated pink by the glowing tip of her cigarette. Her expression resembled a rubber band that had been stretched to its limit. "I was hungry," she said. There was nothing to eat on the table in front of her, only a saucer filled with ash and two spent cigarette butts. She jutted her chin toward the hallway to Jenny's room and tapped her cigarette with her finger. "Everything okay?"

I wanted to say, "No, everything's not okay. Jenny's knocked up and I'm exhausted." But I bit my tongue, unwilling to share how I was really feeling. After her refusal to visit the salon with us, I hadn't reached out to her; I sheltered my emotions under deep cover, unwilling to let her hurt me again. "When did you start smoking?" I demanded, ignoring her question.

"I've always smoked." That explained the still-yellow walls in the living room.

"I thought you hated that Dad smoked."

"I hated that he smoked in *front* of you." She looked at the end of her cigarette as though it might have something to tell her, then squished it in the saucer. "It's not something I do every day," she said without looking at me, and I had left her there in the dark, wondering what else there was I didn't know about my mother.

But now, Jenny's cries worsened, tightening their hold in my chest. I trod out my door and into her room, the rancid stink of fresh excrement attacking my nose with its fist. I flipped on the light. She lay on her back, her hands clawed and in her mouth, fat tears rolling from the corners of her eyes to the pillow, mixing with the drool there. The long hairs around her round face were damp with sweat.

I covered my mouth with a hand and pulled back her covers. The dark stain spread out from her diaper to the edges of the twin bed. "Oh, Jen, what happened? Are you sick?" I felt her forehead; it was cool. Then I remembered. Last night's botched enema. I didn't know what I was doing and look what it had done to her.

She moaned again, her eyes pleading with me. She could not stand this, I knew—the horror of lying in her own waste, unable to move, unable to do anything but wait for someone to come. How could anyone stand it? I imagined her at Wellman, her cries muffled by thick walls and other patients, how long she must have lain there, helpless.

"Come on," I said, swallowing, as best I could, the rolling wave of nausea that traveled up my throat. I bent down and slid my arms under her back as levers, sitting her up and swinging her to the side of the bed so I could get her to the bathroom. She'd need a shower and I'd have to change the sheets—the white lace-trimmed sheets I'd picked out as a child for my baby sister's new big-girl bed. My mother had tried to get me to choose a darker color, perhaps foreseeing the impractical nature of my first choice, but had relented when she saw how excited I was to give them to Jenny. I wondered how many times Mom had been stuck doing laundry in the middle of the night, running these ridiculous sheets through the bleach cycle.

I pulled Jenny into an upright position and she stood, shaky, a pitiful cry hiccuping from inside her: "A-huh, huh, huh." The stench reached down my throat like a finger and I gagged, once, twice, but managed to keep from throwing up on the rug and making the situation worse.

Again, I had to stifle the urge to call my mother for help. *This is her job,* I thought petulantly. *I shouldn't have to do this alone.* I just didn't understand why she was holding herself away from Jenny when she obviously loved her. Maybe it was me she was keeping away from. Still, I didn't think that was enough to justify standing by and watching me do this alone.

But you said you wanted to, a voice reminded me. And I knew it was true: I did want to. But I honestly didn't know whether wanting to would be enough.

It took about an hour to get Jenny cleaned up and the bed changed. She stood patiently in the shower as I washed her, her fleshy belly slightly raised and hard beneath my touch. I wondered if the baby was moving yet, if Jenny felt it tumble inside her. If she knew what had happened to her. What was going to happen to her. We had an appointment in the morning with an obstetrician who had agreed to take Jenny as a patient—one of the doctors Dr. Leland had recommended to me. Dr. Ellen Fisher had worked with developmentally disabled patients before, though never one as severely handicapped as Jenny. She had been businesslike in our brief conversation, so professional in her tone that I almost felt chastised for not having dressed better for the call. I was a little apprehensive about meeting her.

It was after four when I tucked Jenny back into her bed, lying on her left side. I kissed her and smoothed back her hair, making sure she was adequately propped up by pillows so she wouldn't roll off the bed. Exhausted, I stumbled back under my own covers and slept, mercifully, until the moon faded away and the sun took its turn at lighting the world.

"Did she always wake up like this?" I asked my mother over a huge mug of industrial-strength coffee that morning. "I don't remember."

My mother smiled a little wistfully. "Yes. Not every night, but often enough." She sat down carefully at the table, wiping away invisible crumbs from the front of her dove gray, pin-striped suit. She glanced at the clock on the kitchen wall. The bank didn't open until nine, but since she walked the eight blocks to the Junction's Washington Mutual, she needed to be ready to leave by eight-thirty. Her dark hair was pulled into a tight French twist and she wore a pastel pink lipstick that did little to brighten her already pale face. She needed to find a new shade.

"How come I never used to hear her?" I asked, my eyes heavy with lack of rest. And the unasked question: *How did I hear Dad go into her room and not you?*

"I was quick. I could hear her before she even started." She patted my hand, then leaned forward to tighten the laces around her too-white tennis shoes. When she sat back up she looked at me, obviously considering something. "Nicole," she started, but didn't go on right away.

"Yes?"

"What does Shane think of your being here?"

I bristled at the inquiry. "He's fine with it. He supports me." At least, that was what he had said the last time we'd spoken. But then again, he hadn't called me since then; the few messages I'd left for him had gone unanswered. I felt hurt and a little angry at his lack of concern, but I wasn't about to tell my mother that.

"He doesn't have a problem with you being away so long?" she asked.

"No," I said, hopeful my face didn't give the truth away.

"Well, he must be an exceptional man." Then she stood, grabbed her purse, and moved toward the hallway that led to the front door. "I've got to get going."

"Are you sure you don't want to come with us to Jenny's appointment?" The question tumbled from my mouth before my defenses could stop it. Something deep within me wanted her to be involved in this process; she'd always been the one to deal with Jenny's doctors. And if I was honest with myself, she'd always been the one to deal with Jenny. The short time I'd spent caring for my sister had shown me that. Whatever assistance I thought I'd provided as a child was nothing compared to what my mother had done all day, every day, for Jenny for fifteen years. I felt a newly developed, grudging respect for my mother. Perhaps that was why I asked her to come to Jenny's appointment.

My sister moved her eyes from her toast to our mother, seemingly interested in her answer.

Mom hesitated, but then shook her head briskly. "I can't. I can't do it all again." It seemed she said this more to herself than to me. "But you can tell me about it tonight," she offered, then paused, considering something. "Wait. I've got dinner with my book group tonight. I won't be home until late."

My molars squeaked against each other inside my mouth as I stood and moved next to my sister's wheelchair. "You're going out again?" She had been home for dinner with Jenny and me only three times since we had been there.

She looked at the door and not me. "Yes."

"Fine." That settled it. I definitely would not reach out to her again.

"What's that supposed to mean?"

I stepped over to the sink and began washing the few dishes there. "It means nothing. It means, fine, go out to dinner. Have a wonderful time." I hated my voice. I hated this nagging-mother role that had overtaken me without my permission.

She sighed. "Nicky—"

"Nicole," I corrected her sharply.

Her green eyes hardened. "Okay, *Nicole*. Don't take your frustration out on me."

"I'm not frustrated."

She snorted softly, twisting the straps of her purse in her hands. "Oh. Okay. I take it you're just naturally this pleasant, then?" Sarcasm crackled in the air between us, dancing around all we did not say.

"Good-bye, Mom."

She shut the door firmly behind her. I felt my anger like the sharp sting of a canker sore. I was unable to keep from tonguing it, if only to make sure it was still there.

"It wasn't *me* who decided you should have this baby," I said to Jenny, who blinked her gaze away from the door, focusing on an unknown point on the refrigerator, ignoring me. Disappointment clouded her round face. I sighed, then stepped back next to her, running my fingers through her curls. "Sorry, sis. Mom's just pissing me off. It's not your fault."

She looked at me like, *Well, I already knew that.* I set a cup of chopped canned pears on her tray and watched her scoop them to her mouth with a grabbing motion of her right hand. Her left hand was tucked under the tray. She managed to hand-feed herself fairly well, though she had lacked a pincer grasp since she was three. Meals were a messy prospect; I had learned quickly to not dress her before she ate or I'd end up having to change her all over again.

I checked the time. Our appointment was at ten and I still needed to clean Jenny up and get her dressed. After last night's unfortunate incident, I figured I could skip her morning shower; her hair still felt clean. I grabbed the cordless phone and dialed Shane's work number.

"San Francisco District Attorney's office. How may I direct your call?" a nasally voiced operator inquired.

"Shane Wilder, please."

"One moment."

He came on the line. "Shane Wilder." His tone was intimidating, lawyerlike, daring anyone to contradict him.

"Hi. It's me." I sat down at the kitchen table, hooking my feet around the front legs of my chair.

He paused, his voice softened. "Hi, you."

"How are you?"

"Busy. As usual. And you?"

"Fine. A little overwhelmed, but fine. How's Mooch?"

A longer pause, full of a hesitancy I didn't understand. "Missing you, I'm sure."

"And how about you?" I prodded, reaching for the carafe on the counter to warm my forgotten coffee.

"What?"

"Do you miss me?" I hated having to push him to tell me how he was feeling. I longed for a man who was comfortable expressing himself. If one actually existed.

He sighed. "Of course I do. I miss you like crazy."

"Enough to come see me this weekend?" I ventured.

"Nicole . . ." He sounded tired.

"What?"

"I can't, honey. Things are way too busy here. I've got four briefs to write and a deposition to prepare for this weekend." He paused. "Plus, what would I do with your child?" Referring, of course, to Moochie.

"Bring him."

"Honey, I don't know what you want from me."

"Support, Shane. I need your support." If my mother was going to think he was supportive, he'd damn well better be supportive.

"I told you, you have it. I talked to the D.A. up there and he said the case is under investigation, but the police haven't found the guy yet. I also have calls into several lawyers who could represent you in a civil case against Wellman. I don't know what else I can do right now."

"You could come and be with me." I knew I was being unreasonable but I could not keep the petulance from my voice.

Jenny emitted a short, high-pitched shriek. "Ahh!" I looked over to her and saw that she had cleared all the food from her tray.

"What was that?" he asked.

"Jenny."

"What's wrong with her?"

"Nothing's wrong with her," I snapped, making a nasty face at him through the phone. "She's just done with breakfast and wants me to get off the phone and pay attention to her."

"You got all that from 'ahh!'?" He sounded amazed. Or maybe it was disgusted.

"Yes." I grabbed a washcloth and ran it under warm water before using it to clean Jenny's face and hand.

"I can't really talk right now, Nic. I'm due in court in five minutes." He was always due in court in five minutes.

"Okay. Call me later. You have the number here, right?" He didn't answer, just shuffled papers. He had already left the conversation. "Shane?"

"Hmm? Oh, sorry, hon. I'll call you later."

"You'd better," I warned. "Love you."

"Me, too. Bye, babe."

I hung up and looked at Jenny, whose eyes were sly with understanding. I felt the need to defend myself. "Yeah, he's being a jerk, but he's really okay, once you get to know him. I promise."

She slid her gaze into mine with a wisdom deeper than I was ready to see. I looked away. "I love him, Jenny," I said, unsure of whom I was trying to convince.

*F*or as long as I could remember, my mother had been a religious woman. She encouraged me to say my prayers each night and delivered me to Sunday school while she sat with Jenny in the sanctuary of our local Unitarian church, hopeful my sister would not start screaming in the middle of the sermon. At Mom's request, the congregation prayed every week for Jenny to be healed. But just as the medical establishment's failure to cure Jenny drove our mother to Eden the Psychic Healer, her church's inability to produce a miracle soon drove her to desperation.

A few months after our visit to Eden, Mom saw an ad for an evangelical service on late-night television and sunk her teeth into this final shred of hope for Jenny's cure. She told everyone she knew about the pastor who performed weekly miracles during his sermons. "People who've been in wheelchairs their entire lives just stand up and walk after he touches them," she said excitedly to anyone who'd listen. I stood by her at the front door as she told the postman how Jenny would be cured and watched his expression fade from one of interest to pity. When my mother took the mail and moved into the living room out of sight, he looked at me sadly. "You don't let her get to you, young lady," he said.

I was mortified by my mother's religious exuberance. Each time she spoke of visiting the new church with Jenny, recklessness danced in her eyes like a flame in the wind. It got so that I could barely stand to look at her. She held on to her hope like a man who was drowning in the middle of the ocean would cling to a sinking boulder.

Before we left to pick up Nova the morning we were to attend the service, my mother stuck her head into the living room, where my father lounged comfortably in his recliner at the beginning of his sports-viewing day. "Are you sure you won't come, honey?" she asked him, her tone bright. I was glad I had convinced Nova to come so I wouldn't be bored out of my skull.

"I'm not going to waste my time at some sideshow religious service. I'm not an idiot." He looked pointedly at her, then back to the television.

My mother held her head high on her neck, white skin flushing rosy pink. "You don't know what you might be missing. What if this man can heal your daughter? What will you say then?"

"I'll say it's a cold day in hell, because that's when it might happen." He reached for the newspaper that lay in his lap and snapped it open in front of him, signaling the end of the discussion.

Though I resented the meanness of his words, I agreed with my father. I agreed with him more when we walked into the metal-sided, barnlike structure where the services were held. With its cement floors and bare wooden rafters, it looked more like a discount furniture warehouse than a church. The place was packed with people, some of whom already stood facing the stage as though the service had started, their hands waving above their heads, their tongues wagging an indecipherable language, wearing their desperation like perfume. One woman rolled on the floor, twitching and moaning.

"That woman's having a fit, Mom," I whispered urgently as we pushed Jenny's wheelchair toward the stage.

"She's just full of the Spirit, Nicky. She's overcome." Mom seemed not to see the dime-store religious adornments that littered the place: a grinning, plastic Jesus hung every couple of feet on the walls, each illuminated by loudly colored blinking strings of Christmas lights. She focused her eyes on the stage, on the spot where she imagined her daughter would be healed.

"She's over *something*," Nova whispered and I giggled. "Smoke?" she murmured even more softly, and I nodded. We had found an unopened pack of Winston Lights in my father's truck a few weeks before and were not so successfully trying to start a habit.

"Mom? Nova and I are going to the bathroom, okay?"

"Okay. I'll save your seats. Hurry back." Her white skin was tight and shiny, her smile a painted red slash above the point of her chin.

Nova and I wove our way through the crowd of zealots, out the side door to what we hoped was the alley. We walked a few doors down from the church, where we found a woman already standing by some garbage cans, puffing away. She was thin, painfully so; her black hair was stringy and loose around her pale face. She wore jeans and a shabby silk blouse with a large bow tied at her neck. She nodded in greeting, sucking on her cigarette like a straw.

We nodded back, pulling out our half-full pack from Nova's purse. "Shit," Nova said, shaking her bag around as she fingered through it. "No matches."

The woman held out a lighter and flicked its tiny wheel with a dirty thumb until a flame appeared.

"Thanks," I said as both Nova and I used the flame to light our smokes, coughing lightly as we inhaled.

"Pastor Pete tell you to smoke down here, too?" the woman asked with a voice that sounded as though she had swallowed a handful of pebbles.

"No," I said, slightly confused. "My mom brought my sister for him to heal."

The woman looked uncomfortable, gazing at the ground as she snuffed out her cigarette with the heel of her worn black shoe. "Ummm," she mumbled incoherently, then walked around the corner of the building and out of our sight.

"That was weird," Nova said, tapping the tiny bit of ash from the end of her cigarette. She held it out from her body and then tapped it again without putting it to her mouth. Neither of us liked the smoking thing very much.

I looked at the cigarette in my hand, ugly and unnatural between my fingers. I dropped it to the ground and squished it out. "We should probably get back." Nova took a final puff, coughed violently, then squished hers out, too. I sprayed us both with a plentiful dose of White Shoulders and we headed down the alley to the church.

By the time we got to our seats, the service had already begun. Pastor Pete, a rotund, white-skinned strawberry-blond in a badly cut pea green suit, stood in front of a microphone, praying. "O dear heavenly God, our Father who looks down upon us with everlasting, ever wonderful love. We pray to You, O God, that today, through Your strength, Your will, that we will be filled with Your spirit. Amen."

The crowd murmured a collective amen, my mother's voice among them. Jenny watched the pastor with a skeptical eye, her twisted hands silent in the lap of her daisy-printed, short-sleeved dress, drool leaking a thin stream onto her chest. My mother had taken the time that morning to style Jenny's chestnut hair in a long French braid and had even allowed me to brush a little sheer blue eye shadow on my sister's lids. Among all these supposedly holy people, she was the only one who resembled an angel.

Nova elbowed me as the pastor continued. I elbowed her back. "Before us today, dear friends," Pastor Pete said, "is Jane Riley. A young woman stricken with a terrible disease. The horror of not being able to speak. Found on First Avenue, that horrifying den of iniquity in our fair Seattle, she has not spoken a word since the day she was born. When I found her, she was selling her body silently for the nickels it cost her to eat. Come before us, dear Jane, and let the spirit of our heavenly Father come down upon you and make you whole!"

My mouth dropped open as the woman we had met in the

alley shuffled onto the stage. I looked at Nova, who was shaking her blond head, disgusted. "What a crock," she whispered. "Tell your mom."

I moved my eyes to my mother, who was sitting enraptured, hands clasped together in perfect prayer as she looked longingly at the stage where the hoax was taking place. Jenny's eyes caught mine and the only word that filled my head was *please*. She knew what was happening. She knew my mother's hope had gone too far, crossed into dangerous territory. I swallowed hard and tugged at my mother's sleeve.

"What?" she hissed through her teeth, not taking her eyes from the stage. "I'm trying to listen."

"I know, Mom. It's just . . . Well, Nova and I talked to that lady outside. She *talked* to us, Mom. There was nothing wrong with her."

My mother turned her head slowly to look at me. Her green eyes blinked, unbelieving. "What were you doing outside? I thought you went to the bathroom."

"Uh, we needed some fresh air. It's so crowded in here." I paused. "She talked, Mom. This is a bunch of crap. Can we go?"

"No, we cannot go. You must be mistaken, Nicole. You must have seen someone else." My mother looked at the stage again, where Jane Riley was awkwardly stuttering her supposed first words. "P-p-praise J-Jesus!" she said, holding her hands to the sky. She looked down and saw Nova and me in the front row, then winked.

"Did you see that, Mrs. Hunter?" Nova exclaimed as she sat forward and pointed excitedly. "She winked at us! God!" She threw herself disgustedly against the back of her chair, blond waves bouncing like springs.

"Please don't take the Lord's name in vain, Nova," my mother said absentmindedly. She stroked Jenny's bare arm, staring ahead, not blinking, not seeing for several minutes. Her chin quivered and she gave her head a little shake, as though to clear it of unwanted thoughts. People shouted and cried around us, but it felt as though we were inside a bubble, separate from the entire room. When Mom finally swung her gaze to our surroundings, she carefully took in the garish and glittered decor, disdain shadowing the sharp angles of her face. She scowled at the writhing figures who clutched their Bibles and spoke in different tongues. Her veins pulsed like little blue rivers beneath the thin parchment of her skin, a new understanding flowing through her blood. Each breath she took was deliberate and deep, the pause between each long enough to make me worry she might not take another.

"Mom?" I urged, touching her thigh. "Are you okay?"

"Your father is going to love this." She looked at me, the obvious false brightness of her smile sending fear tap-dancing around in my stomach. Tears illuminated her eyes like pearls of dew on green grass. She let loose a shuddering sigh and lifted her eyes up to the ceiling. "Dear God, what was I thinking?" she whispered.

Nova took my cold hand in her warm grasp but did not look at me. Jenny sat quietly next to our mother, as though respecting the weight of the moment. I watched as Mom finally turned to her, Jenny's eyes holding a liquid blue mixture of compassion and sorrow. *Mama,* I heard her say, then once again, louder in my heart, *Mama!*

Mom smiled and hugged Jenny close, then pulled back to touch the end of Jenny's nose with her own. "I'm okay, sweetie. Mama's okay." Before that moment, I had never heard my mother refer to herself as Mama; she was always Mom or Mother. I wondered then if she had heard Jenny's cry. If they might share a language all their own.

"I guess it's over, then," Mom finally said. "Let's go." We walked down the middle aisle, wheeling Jenny's chair around prostrate worshipers. My mother held her shoulders high and back, the defeat she felt reflected only in the slowness of her pace and the dim light of her sad eyes.

Mom stopped going to church after that day. She still prayed; she still read her Bible every night before she went to bed. But her church became a private thing, something she held within herself. No one was invited in. We never mentioned Pastor Pete or the smoking lady again. The constant appointments with new specialists for Jenny became a thing of the past. My mother no longer seemed to have a mission. She moved through each day with Jenny with careful, deliberate routine, her determination to find a cure silenced by a God who finally gave her an answer to her prayers.

God told my mother no.

*D*r. Ellen Fisher practiced out of one of many nondescript stucco office buildings near Children's Orthopedic Hospital. I had a little trouble finding a parking spot nearby, but it was a gray and rainy Northwest spring morning and I circled the block again and again until one opened up. I was determined to not push Jenny's wheelchair any farther than I had to.

When we finally got to the office, I saw that the reception area was a small rectangle consisting of six plastic chairs and a carpeted play area for children. Happy spider ivy burst out of several pots on the windowsill and a dark-hued oil painting of a robust, heavy-with-child woman adorned the wall above the receptionist's desk. When I informed her of our arrival, she apologetically let us know the doctor had had a complicated delivery early that morning and was running about forty-five minutes late. I wheeled Jenny into the waiting area where two obviously pregnant women sat thumbing through magazines. One of the women, her round belly taking up most of her lap, set her reading down and smiled at me.

"How far along?" she asked.

Without thinking, I answered her. "Twenty-two weeks."

The woman's eyes shot open. "Really? You aren't even show-ing!"

Realizing her mistake, I backpedaled. "Uh, no. It's not me." I couldn't believe I hadn't thought of this. Of having to explain. My cheeks flamed crimson.

She looked confused, then rested her gaze on Jenny's stom-ach. "Oo-oh," she said, drawing the sound out in understanding. She glanced at me quickly, deliberately not looking at Jenny again. She picked up her magazine, suddenly deeply interested in whatever the ancient *Newsweek* had to say. The other woman stole short looks at Jenny and both women shook their heads in small motions of what I'm sure they thought was invisible disapproval. I briefly considered asking her if I actually looked fat enough to appear pregnant, but thought better of it. Instead, I sat erect, ir-reproachable with dignity. Of course, Jenny chose this moment to open her mouth and let loose a wet, gurgling burp. She giggled after the noise, pleased with herself. I busied myself wiping her mouth with the towel I had learned to keep with me at all times for just such a purpose.

The front door opened again and in ran three small children, all bouncing with honey blond curls and energy. A woman's voice called out behind them, "Rebecca! James! Isaac! Stop right there. Do you hear me?" Her body soon followed her voice through the door. A fake but full-leafed Ficus plant blocked most of my view; I could only see her from the back. She was about my height, five-three or so, with a plush and curvy figure swelling beneath her swishing Bohemian-style embroidered dress. Her hair was twisted into a messy blond bun on the top of her head, fastened with what looked like a couple of small cro-chet needles. When she turned to the side, I could see she wore a baby sling, bulging obviously with a little life.

The boys made an immediate beeline for the stack of colorful toys in the corner of the room, but the girl ran up to stand in front of Jenny, fingering the shiny metal wheel of her chair.

"Why does she have this?" the child asked me, her round face open and curious. Her eyes were like ripe blueberries. I figured her to be about four. I wasn't exactly sure how to answer her question. How much would a child understand? I settled on the simplest explanation I could imagine. "It helps her get around better. She has a hard time walking very fast."

The girl, whom I assumed was Rebecca, widened her eyes. "Oh." She paused. "I have a bicycle with wheels like these. I can ride it very fast." She glanced sidelong over to her brothers. "Faster than Isaac."

"Liar!" the older boy cried out when he heard this.

"Don't call your sister a liar, young man," the blond woman ordered as she stepped up to the front desk. I still hadn't seen her face, but her voice was warm, tinged with fatigue. It sounded oddly familiar.

"No sitter today?" Annoyance shadowed the receptionist's tone.

The blond woman ignored the stab. "God, I wish. Ryan left for Alaska yesterday and my mother's at a jewelry show in Vegas."

At the mention of her husband and mother, I suddenly realized why I recognized the woman's voice. I stood up quickly, almost tripping over Jenny's outstretched footrests. *"Nova?"*

The woman whipped her head around to face me. She was heavier than I remembered, but there was no mistaking those sandy blond waves, that glowing smile. "It's Nicole," I offered. We'd kept in contact after I moved to San Francisco, writing and calling each other on a pretty regular basis, but when she got married and had her first two children we had gradually drifted apart. As a full-time graduate student, I remembered feeling detached from the life Nova was living: marriage, children, being a stay-at-home mom. I simply couldn't relate. But now, as I stepped over to her and she pulled me into a deep hug, somehow managing to keep her sling-covered belly free from impact, her embrace felt like an old, familiar blanket wrapped around me.

"Nicole!" she exclaimed as she pulled back to look at me, strong hands still gripping my shoulders. "I don't believe it. What's it been? Four years?"

"Three, I think. The last time we talked you were pregnant for the second time."

She dropped her hands to her sides, remembering. "That's right. You moved and never let me know your new address or phone number."

I ducked my head sheepishly. "I'm sorry."

The nurse called the two other women in the waiting room back for their appointments and Nova waited until they were gone before continuing. "So, what are you doing *here*?"

I gestured toward Jenny. "It's a long story."

Nova moved over to kneel in front of my sister, carefully adjusting the sling against her substantial chest. She grabbed Jenny's hand. "Jenny! It's so good to see you." It was heartening to see that time had not changed her comfort level with Jenny.

My sister's eyes brightened at the sight of Nova's smiling face; she kicked a foot in excitement and let out a small, happy yelp. Rebecca, who had been standing quietly next to Nova during our conversation, clung to her mother's arm, unsure. "Mama, what's wrong with that lady? Why is her face all wet?"

"Because she's drooling a little, honey." Nova used the sleeve of her dress to wipe Jenny's chin. "See? All better."

I smiled at this, feeling a hint of the same easy connection we had always shared. The two boys, suddenly interested in their mother, stepped over to stand next to Jenny, who smiled broadly at them both, her round cheeks pushing her eyes into thin slits. She patted her hands together and cooed loudly, a lilting, happy sound.

"Why is she clapping like that?" the taller boy asked Nova.

"I think it's because she hears music no one else can," Nova answered, smiling at me. She squatted down to her children's level and spoke to them. "Jenny's brain has a hard time telling her body what to do. It makes her look a little different and do things differently than we do. That's why she drools a little and makes different sounds than us." I was impressed with this succinct but accurate explanation.

Satisfied with this response, the boys went back to their toys and Rebecca joined them. I tentatively touched the now-wiggling bulge in Nova's sling.

"*Four* kids? Wow."

Nova grinned. "Yeah, well, what can I say? I'm a breeder."

I laughed. "Nice!" She definitely seemed to be the friend I remembered.

She laughed, too, cradling her child as she adjusted the sling and a hidden slit in her dress to allow the baby discreet access to her breast. My gaze lingered on them for a moment, oddly touched by this tender, yet unfamiliar vision. "Layla is definitely the last," she said. "Four under five years old is about all I can handle, I think. If Bill Gates thinks running Microsoft is a challenge . . ." She paused, looked at Jenny's stomach, which, I supposed, if you knew what you were looking for, was beginning to announce her condition. "What *happened*?"

I sighed, rubbed Jenny's arm. "Like I said, it's a long story. But basically"—I lowered my voice so the children wouldn't hear—"she was raped by a nurse's aide at Wellman. We think she's about twenty-two weeks along."

Nova's pink mouth dropped open in horror but she kept her tone low, also. "My God. Is she going to have it?"

I nodded. "My mother's decision."

"And do you agree with her?" Nova asked.

"I don't know. At first I was sure it was a mistake. Now, not so much." Tears stung my throat, I was so happy to have someone to finally talk to about all this. Happy that someone was Nova, who already knew me so well. There are people in this world you can be apart from for years, and yet when you come back together, it's almost as though no time has passed at all. You find yourself falling right back into the same rhythm of friendship you shared before. I hoped with everything in me that Nova was one of those people. "This is our first appointment with Dr. Fisher," I told her, "so hopefully I'll get a better idea of what to expect."

Nova held my hand and squeezed it. "She's a great doctor. Very much the patient's advocate. She's delivered all my kids except Isaac."

I looked over to the kids, their blond heads bent collectively over a stack of blocks. "Now, Isaac was your first, right?"

Nova took her hand away from mine and pointed each child out. "Right. He's five. Then there's Rebecca, who just turned four last week and James, who's two. Layla here is six weeks." She leaned down to smell her baby's head.

I whistled, a low, amazed sound.

"Yeah, they're a handful. But, man, I love them." Her face glowed for a moment with a joy so obviously private I felt a momentary pang of embarrassment for having witnessed it.

"Well, I have a child, too," I said. "Moochie."

Nova looked confused.

"He's of the furry variety. No diapers, just kibble."

She laughed again in understanding. "And where is he?"

"Back in San Francisco. My boyfriend is taking care of him." San Francisco suddenly seemed so far away, a place where I had lived long, long ago.

"Is it serious?"

I shrugged. "We live together, if that's what you mean."

"For how long?" she prodded.

"A year or so."

"Sounds serious. Have you washed his underwear for him?"

"What?" I giggled, and Jenny laughed, too, watching our conversation with obvious pleasure.

"The underwear test. I told Ryan I knew I'd marry him the day I saw his dirty underwear on the floor and willingly picked it up to throw in the wash. Sure enough, two months later, he proposed."

"Well, Shane would rather die before letting me touch his laundry. He's afraid I'll destroy it, turn his whites pink or something."

"Ah," Nova said, nodding. "Trust issues."

The nurse appeared from the back again, calling out Jenny's name. "Well," I said, standing and turning Jenny's chair toward the door. "That's us."

Nova hurriedly jotted down something on a scrap of paper. "Here's my number. What's yours?" I told her and she wrote it down, too. Then she continued talking. "Call me, okay? Ryan works the fishing boats in Alaska and he's gone for at least a month. I'd love to see you again. Catch up on things."

I took the paper and smiled. "Me, too." I waved to her as I wheeled Jenny back to the doctor I hoped would convince me everything was going to be okay.

Dr. Fisher was a tall woman, elegant in a manner that suggested it wasn't something she had to work at very hard. She appeared to be in her late thirties or early forties and had a bit of the exotic about her: her eyes were large and brown, burning with intelligence you couldn't ignore. Her lips were full and slightly pink; her straight, shoulder-length black hair was the perfect frame for the smooth, olive-toned skin of her oblong face. She wore a simple black top and slacks under her white doctor's coat and no jewelry save a stethoscope slung casually around her neck. Jenny looked her over with skeptical eyes, turning her chin away from the doctor and toward me. I imagined that over the years of endless doctor's visits, white coats had become like red flags to my sister, warning her of impending disaster.

"It's okay, Jen. Dr. Fisher is going to help you get through all this." *Please,* I thought, *please help her. Help us both.*

Dr. Fisher glanced at me. "How much does she understand?"

"About what?" I replied, confused.

She gestured in a big circle. "Everything. The world. What you say to her. The disabled patients I've worked with before have all been able to communicate on some level. Should I be talking to her or you?"

I was a bit taken aback by what sounded like impatience in her words. "To her, please."

She redirected her attention toward my sister, her tone softening a bit. "All right, then. Now, Jenny, I'm going to have a look at your belly. I'm going to touch it a little, to see how that baby is doing in there." She held up a small black device for Jenny's viewing. "We're going to use this to listen to the baby's heartbeat." She pulled up Jenny's shirt and prodded her stomach with straight fingers.

"Aren't you going to do an exam?" I asked, uncomfortably motioning in the general direction of Jenny's legs.

"Not today." Dr. Fisher squirted a blob of a clear jellylike substance on Jenny's stomach. The lubricant must have been cold because Jenny jumped and shuddered a bit when it hit her skin. Then Dr. Fisher pressed the Doppler device against Jenny's abdomen, moving it around as she spoke again. "Her records state she's never had a pelvic and I don't want to scare her. In fact, in cases like these, I'd rather she be unconscious. But we can talk about that later." She inched the Doppler over a little and suddenly a loud, echoing rhythm filled the air. "There," she said, satisfied, tapping the fingers of her free hand against her thumb, counting.

I was stunned by the intensity of the noise. "Is that the heartbeat?" Overwhelmed by the rush of emotion that filled my blood, I found myself having to hold back what felt like a river of tears. My mother was right; Jenny had a *life* inside her.

Dr. Fisher nodded as she wiped Jenny's belly dry with a white towel. "A nice and steady one hundred fifty beats per minute." She smiled, the first since we entered the room. Its warmth surprised me. "Sounds like a girl."

I squeezed Jenny's hand, then swung my head over to look at the doctor. "Really? You can tell that from the heartbeat?"

Dr. Fisher shrugged. "It's an old wives' tale, mostly. Just kind of fun to think about."

The rest of the appointment was spent with her answering my many questions about Jenny's medications, her diet, what kind of exercise I should be helping her to get. Toward the end, Dr. Fisher turned the tables and asked me a question I had barely allowed myself to think about.

"Have you decided what will happen to the baby when it's born?" Her face was blank, not judging.

It was then I realized when the doctor spoke to Jenny she had been saying "*the* baby" and not "*your* baby." Subtle, but noticeable. I shook my head. "This is all relatively new to me. I'm still trying to get used to taking care of her. It hasn't been easy."

She nodded briskly. "I'm sure."

"I've also got to find a new placement for Jenny after she gives birth. There's no way I'm letting her go back to Wellman."

"That's understandable. But when you think about placement

for the baby, I want you to consider there's only limited testing we can do to see if it will be normal. Since we don't know what caused Jenny's disabilities, we can't be sure the baby won't be stricken by them as well."

"Okay," I whispered, overwhelmed by all I had to think about, and terrified I just didn't have it in me to do this.

Dr. Fisher saw the fear in my face and patted my hand quickly. "The baby sounded good. We'll schedule an ultrasound and get a better idea of what we're dealing with. Until then, make sure Jenny gets her vitamins and lots of water." She rose and stepped toward the door.

"Dr. Fisher?" I called out.

She stopped, her hand on the doorknob. "Yes?"

"I . . ." I faltered, wanting her to reassure me, to tell me I was doing the right thing, the admirable thing, in taking care of Jenny. I was looking for affirmation, but the hurried expression on her face told me I would not find it there. She was a doctor simply doing her job. I shook my head. "Nothing. Just thank you, I guess. For seeing Jenny."

She bobbed her head sharply and then left, softly closing the door behind her.

*I*t was a rainy Saturday afternoon during the fall of my freshman year and my mother was gone. Her best friend's husband had died suddenly and she had begged my mother to come to Portland to help her with the arrangements. As always, my father balked at her leaving.

"I won't change diapers, Joyce," he'd insisted when she told him about going. We were all sitting at the kitchen table over the remains of our meal. Mom had spent the afternoon in the kitchen, the smell of fried chicken tipping me off that a confrontation might occur. She always made his favorite meal when she had to tell him something she knew he wasn't going to like.

I was unsure whether my mother's expression was one of pity or disgust. "I know that," she said. "Nicole will be home. She'll take care of all that." She looked at me expectantly. "Right?"

"Can I still go bowling Friday night?"

"Of course you can," my mother said.

"All right, then," I consented. I was used to taking over my mother's role when she left. I didn't really have a choice.

My father shook his head slowly, considering all this. "I don't know." He looked at her sternly. "You'll only be gone one night?"

"One night. I'll leave early Saturday and be back Sunday."

Dad looked at Jenny, then at me, his eyes full of an emotion I couldn't name at the time. But his expression stuck with me over the years, hanging in my mind like a dark painting. Looking back, I believe it was dread.

After my mother left, Dad spent most of Saturday reclined in the family room, beer in hand, eyes glued to the roaring action of a football game. I was in the kitchen, dying to finish feeding Jenny so I could call Nova and talk about Jason DeLong, the dark-haired sophomore with smoky eyes who had bought me a Coke at the bowling alley the night before. He had brushed my hand with his fingers when we parted; the touch sent shivers to places I never knew existed within me. I couldn't wait to tell Nova all about it.

After rushing her through lunch, I set Jenny up on the couch, her headphones playing Chicago's latest album. I figured she was probably tired of all the uppity classical stuff my mother made her listen to; I thought she might like to be more like other girls her age. Jenny loved any kind of music, patting her hands softly against each other and swaying, squealing in loud, happy approval when a particular tune struck her fancy. Her small body would rock back and forth, her eyes dancing in time with the song. In those moments she seemed free, unfettered by the twisted muscles and stunted bones of her disease.

She smiled at me that afternoon as I made sure she had enough pillows around her, ocean eyes sparkling, lit from within. I often wondered where her joy came from, what gave her such peace and happiness inside a body that caused her so much pain. When she slept, I imagined she was free, dancing and climbing trees, twirling and singing and calling my name. Perhaps she visited her dreams while she was awake, the relief she felt in that world shining through her eyes like the sun.

"Dad?" I said softly, looking over to his recliner in the corner of the room.

"Mmph?" he mumbled, not bothering to look at me. His eyes were heavy, half-lidded shades.

"I'm going to my room for a bit, okay? Jenny's hanging out on the couch. Just call me if she needs anything."

He waved me away, his eyes snapping open at a particularly vigorous roar from the television crowd. "Offsides, goddammit!" he yelled. "What are you, blind?"

I went into my room, pulling the hallway phone with me. Expecting my call, Nova picked up on the first ring and we immediately fell into the excited linguistic squeals comprehended only by teenage girls. We were debating whether Jason would ever get the nerve to call me when suddenly the siren of my sister's scream wrapped around my body and pulled me to my bedroom door.

"I have to go," I told Nova urgently. I felt the pounding of my father's feet across the floor; the walls vibrated with his movement.

"Is everything okay?" she asked, concern filling her voice.

"Jenny's yelling. I have to go." I started counting the pink stripes on the lampshade by my bed; if I could count them twice before I hung up, Jenny would stop screaming.

"Okay. Call me later."

I dropped the phone to the floor and raced into the living room. My father was standing over Jenny, his arm raised above his head. Jenny's body was rigid, her face twisted into a wretched expression, her skin flushed and her mouth open wide, releasing another heart-wrenching shriek. Her fingers were clawed together, poised to ram into her mouth. She stared at my father's arm as though it were an item detached from his body, watching it slice through the air like a knife.

"Dad, no!" I pleaded, running over to the couch. I felt the sting of his fist as though it had hit my own face.

In the stunned silence that followed, he knelt down in front of Jenny, gripping her shoulders, shaking her. "Quit it!" he bellowed. "Stop this right now. I will not allow it to go on. Do you hear me, young lady? I have had *enough!*"

Jenny trembled violently, her full bottom lip rolled out in a deep pout; tears ran like large, silent raindrops down her China doll face. She began to weep in earnest, misery racking her twisted body. A swollen crimson mark rose on her cheek, just below her right eye: the shadow of my father's fury.

Her eyes searched his intently, unbelieving. *Why, Daddy?* The words found my heart and I wept as well, sitting next to her and pulling her tiny body to me, sheltering it under my more substantial frame. She screamed again, though softer than before. "Shh," I whispered. "It's okay. Everything will be okay." I looked at my father as though he were a stranger. Jenny's muscles were solid stone beneath my touch.

My father stood, blue eyes wide, backing away from us with his callused hands up in front of his body defensively, as though we oozed some life-threatening disease. His orange curls twisted out from his scalp like tiny flames; they wanted to get away from him, too. Shock tensed his long limbs and he stepped woodenly toward the back door. "Shit," I heard him whisper. Then he was gone.

The television droned on in the background as I sat holding my sister. I could not believe what had just occurred. Usually my father left the house as soon as a fit began, but lately he had stuck around, using his voice as a weapon against each attack. And now my father's violent words had progressed to action, as though he somehow believed normality could be beaten into his already broken child.

My mother had tried everything: dietary changes, hot baths, cool showers, herbal teas, but nothing seemed to help. And sadly, no one seemed to care. The doctors could tell us nothing; they'd offer tranquilizers and institutional recommendations. I found my mother in Jenny's room one afternoon, watching my sister sleep, whispering to her.

"Come out where I can see you," my mother had said, her voice shaking and tearful. "I can't fight what I can't see, dammit. How am I going to fix this if I don't know what's broken? How am I going to save my baby? God help me, I can't *do* this anymore!" The tremendous force of desperation behind her words had rattled me to the core. I did not know how I was going to explain the now-purpling mark on Jenny's face to her; I was sure my father would not admit what he had done.

Late that night, after I had settled Jenny to bed, I heard him return. He crept through the house, the stink of cigarettes announcing his presence outside my door. He kept moving, and as the door to Jenny's room creaked open, I jumped out of bed and stuck my head out of my own door, watching in disbelief as my father's tall shadow stepped softly into my sister's room.

I quietly closed my door and held my breath as I stood with my ear against the wall that separated our rooms. I heard the squeak of Jenny's bed, the sound of added weight. "I love you, Jenny girl." I could barely make out my father's murmur. "I'd never hurt you, never. You know that, right?"

The bed squeaked again as more inaudible notes of my father's voice played through the air. I slid back into bed, lying tense and ready to hear him leave her room, but for too long a time he stayed, the only noise the creaking of her bed, its high-pitched moans sounding eerily like a child's cry for help.

During the week that followed our first appointment with Dr. Fisher, Jenny, Mom, and I were sitting in the kitchen together eating the chicken fettuccine I'd prepared for dinner when the phone rang unexpectedly. Mom didn't get many calls; it seemed that she, like me, kept a limited social circle. Most of the time she went out to dinner and movies alone, though occasionally a member of her book club or a fellow employee joined her. In the few weeks I'd been home, I could count on one hand the number of times the phone had rung. That evening, we both jumped at the noise, looking at each other in surprise.

"It must be Shane," I concluded, as I pushed back from the table and stepped into the hallway by my bedroom to catch the call. "Hi, sweetie," I answered, fluffing my curls for a man who could not see me.

"Already I'm *sweetie?*" a female voice teased me.

"Nova?" I ventured, slightly disappointed it wasn't Shane. I slumped against the textured wall. He hadn't called me for days.

"Yep," Nova said. "I hadn't heard from you, so I wanted to make sure you didn't lose my number." The confusing chatter of her children played in the background; the loud screech of the television competed with them. It was good to hear her voice again. After our meeting at Dr. Fisher's office I had hesitated to call her, fearful I'd misread the apparent ease of our reconnection, that she'd only been so friendly to me out of a sense of politeness. I'd fallen out of practice communicating with other women. I hadn't had a friend like Nova in San Francisco; I'd never found someone I felt comfortable opening myself to. There was always too much to explain about who I was, why I didn't talk with my family. I kept my relationships pretty much on the surface, going out for drinks and movies and other things friends do together, but never moving past the basics into deeper emotional territory. I was afraid that even if Nova were the friend I remembered, I might not remember how to be the friend I had been to her.

"So, when are you coming over?" she asked me.

I hesitated. "Are you sure it's okay?" A loud crash erupted through the phone, followed by the high-pitched wailing of a child.

"James, honey," Nova soothed, "I'll be right there."

"Is he okay?" I inquired, sitting up from the wall where I had been leaning.

Nova sighed. "Yeah, but he bit the dust off the couch and whacked his head on the floor. I should go. But come over tomorrow, okay? I won't take no for an answer." She quickly reeled off the address and basic directions. I agreed to come, then hung up, returning to the kitchen only to find my mother gently cleaning up Jenny's hand and face. "Who was it?" she inquired.

"Nova," I said flatly. "You don't have to do that." I stepped over to take the washrag from her. If she wasn't going to offer her help, then I sure as hell wasn't going to let her think I needed it.

"I know I don't *have* to," she said, letting me take the rag. She began clearing the table. "Old habits die hard."

You could've fooled me, I thought as I finished cleaning Jenny up. "We're going to see Nova tomorrow," I told my sister, ignoring my mother altogether. Jenny's eyes lit up at the sound of Nova's name. I touched her nose with the tip of my own and smiled. "We're going to see our old friend."

*O*n the way over to her house the next day, I considered telling
Nova about what had happened that night so many years before.
What my father had done to Jenny. What he continued to do for
several years. The times he hit her—those were the nights he'd go
into her room. Nova knew about my father's physical violence;
she'd even seen him hit Jenny a few times herself. But I wasn't
sure what Nova was ready to hear, what kind of support she
would provide. From our brief interactions at Dr. Fisher's office
and on the phone, I was fairly sure she'd react with compassion,
but then again, maybe she'd be disgusted that I hadn't done
something to stop my father—the same way I was disgusted with
myself. Terrified by the thought of being judged for my inaction,
I had long ago vowed never to talk about the sexual abuse to anyone. But being home, being in the same room and hearing the ancient squeak of Jenny's bed every night as I laid her down had
reached into my heart and lodged there like a splinter. I could not
ignore its sting much longer.

After years of schooling on the subject, my psychologist's

mind knew that men like my father, men who felt weak in their own lives, often resorted to sexual abuse as a means to exert power over those who made them feel most powerless. That it wasn't about sex—it was about control. I understood that my father felt lost in the life that having Jenny had created for him; I understood that her disabilities overwhelmed him, made him feel inadequate as a man for having created her. To be the father of a retarded child is to have failed. Sperm malfunction. You are told by men in white lab coats with official-looking certificates on their walls that it is impossible to say what caused your daughter's retardation. They say it is nobody's fault, but you feel it deep in your bones that you made it happen. All the pot you smoked in college, the bad LSD trip you took only a year before your girlfriend got pregnant and you knew the only thing to do was marry her. You are deficient, broken, not a real man.

Worse, still, is that you cannot do anything to fix her. Every day you don't know the name of her disease you are ground a bit deeper into a hole. Every day as your wife wheels her into the kitchen for a pureed breakfast, you see your child's sagging mouth and startled, wide eyes and you are reminded how you have failed this child, bringing her into the world malformed, unable to experience the joy of being alive. Your child does not live; she is simply maintained.

You ache for a life without medical bills and doctors' appointments and a wife who cries herself to sleep almost every night. You long for family barbecues with the neighbors without the bright, uncomfortable chatter and polite inquiries as to your daughter's health. The sliding stares that glance over her but never truly see her. The stare that is becoming more like your own. Your inability to see her anymore, the detachment you are attempting so that maybe, if you can open your eyes and she isn't there anymore, you can leave. Or maybe your wife will finally decide to place her in a home where they are trained in maintenance. You want her to leave so that you can have a normal life. If she isn't going to leave, you will have to.

I halfway thought I decided to study psychology in the first place so I could I find a way to understand all this about my father, and though I did, I could not forgive him. Would not forgive him. What he had done was unforgivable.

I looked over to Jenny, who sat next to me in the car, a twenty-five-year-old strapped into a booster seat that was designed for children, yet even with her weight gain fit her perfectly. She stared out the window, hands quiet in her lap, entranced by the bright lights in a stereo store's display. I gripped the wheel a bit tighter.

"How you doing, sweetie?" I asked her, but she did not look at me, seemingly lost in her own thoughts. What were those thoughts? I often wondered. Was she communing with God? Conversing with angels? I could not believe her mind was a blank, as so many doctors had told us over the years. I saw such life behind her eyes; I imagined piles of words in her brain, laid up like a logjam desperate for release. The language we shared was a gift, a link between sisters. I believed that when I heard her voice within me, one or two of those jammed words managed to slip through whatever held the rest back. Whatever disease threaded through her brain, it had not touched her soul.

Nova lived near Alki Beach in a sky blue rambler with a daylight basement. "It's the one that looks like there's a yard sale going on," she had laughed over the phone. True to this description, I pulled up in front of the address she had given me, a little taken aback by the mess on the lawn. Piles of brightly colored plastic toys littered the grass along with a few scattered lumps of clothing. There were a swing set off to the side of the yard and a Big Wheel and three open bags of sand on the parking strip. I had to move the car a little farther down to make sure there was room to get Jenny out and into her wheelchair.

Nova saw me through a small window over the garage and waved. Her three older children ran out the red front door and down the stairs toward us. "They're here! They're here!" they screamed. "Mama, they're here!"

My eyes widened at the small onslaught of tiny bodies clambering around me as I tried to maneuver Jenny out of the car. Nova came rushing down the stairs, her wavy hair frizzed and loose around her shoulders. She was barefoot and wore a

brightly colored East Indian–style wraparound skirt that empha-
sized her fleshy hips. Her white V-necked T-shirt was hiked up
on one side over her breast, an appendage to which Layla was
firmly attached. Nova appeared unfazed by nursing in the middle of the street, as if she were simply holding her child's hand. I
admired her comfort with such a seemingly intimate act. It told
me she did what she thought was best, despite what other people
might think. It told me she was still the woman I had known.

"Hey, Buster Browns," she sweetly addressed her brood.
"Give 'em some room! Remember what we talked about?"

Isaac and Rebecca nodded; their little brother, James,
watched them and followed suit, his head bobbing vigorously in
agreement. Nova smiled. "Okay, then. Back off." She smiled at
me, too, a bright and beautiful thing. "We're working on the
personal-space issue."

"Gotcha." I leaned down and forward, wrapped my arms
around Jenny's waist and hiked her into a standing position.
"Ow!" I touched my twinging back.

"You okay?" Nova asked, concerned, but still watching her
children race around the front yard.

"Yeah, just not used to all this lifting. She weighs a ton." I
stopped myself and hugged Jenny. "I'm sorry, sweetie. You don't
weigh a ton. You're just right."

I managed to hoist Jenny and her wheelchair up the few stairs
into Nova's house. Her living room would have given Shane a
heart attack. Toys everywhere, magazines and books spread
across the floor like a second layer of carpet. I immediately noticed a plaque that hung above the fireplace that challenged you
to LOVE ME, LOVE MY MESS in Gothic black letters. The air
smelled of cinnamon, something taken fresh from the oven, then
set on the counter to cool.

Nova swung out her arm. "Welcome to my humble abode.
Make yourself at home." She set Layla carefully in the baby
swing that sat next to the couch and hollered out the front door.
"Time to play in the backyard, buddies, okay?" They seemed to
ignore her. "Hey!" she bellowed. "Did you hear me? Backyard,
now!"

The threesome scrambled through the house and out the back door without so much as a glance at their mother. She sighed in relief and plopped down on the navy blue leather couch, motioning me to do the same. "Ah, peace." She screwed up her pretty face. "For the moment, at least."

I maneuvered Jenny's chair next to us so she could watch Layla in the swing. My sister's gaze attached itself immediately to the infant, seemingly enraptured by her. I wondered if Jenny understood the connection between Nova's child and the baby inside her; I wondered if she was even *aware* of what was happening within her body. I could infer a bit from what I picked up from her thoughts, but really, there was no way to know for sure what Jenny understood about her pregnancy. I settled in the opposite corner of the couch, a spot worn in deep and comfortable by another person's regular use and smiled at Nova. "So," she began, "how *are* you?"

"Hanging in there," I replied, which was as short a summary of the truth that I could manage. I could not hear myself telling her how I felt like the seams of a too-tight pair of jeans, ready to burst at any second. How my breathing became shallow and panicked every time I allowed myself to consider all I had taken on. How the smell of my childhood home made me ill and the sound of my sister's bed pushed me to tears; how my mother treated us like strangers. How I thought the man I loved might be the wrong man altogether and how afraid I was of letting him go for fear of never finding another.

But instead of relaying all of this and making her reconsider inviting me back into her life, I inquired politely after her. "How are *you?*"

"Oh, you know. Fine. Fucked up, Insecure, Neurotic, and Exasperated."

I laughed. "Excuse me?" I had almost forgotten how funny she could be.

"That's what 'fine' stands for. F.I.N.E. That's how I am." She grinned.

"I'll have to remember that one."

There was a sharp knock and a man stuck his head in through

the front door. "Hey, Nova," he said, his voice low and smooth, like melted chocolate. The sound of it made me want to roll my tongue around in my mouth.

"Hey, Garret. Come on in. These are a couple of old friends of mine, Nicole and her sister, Jenny."

Garret stepped into the room. Tall and broad shouldered, he wore faded blue jeans with a tucked-in, thin black sweater. His black hair was wavy and full, falling down to one side in front of his hazel eyes. His expression was warm, his smile genuine and deep as he waved in greeting with one hand and pushed his hair away from his face with the other. The tips of his ears poked out from his head in an endearing fashion. He looked like a cross between a supermodel and an elf. I returned his smile, sure I was showing too many teeth. I wished I had taken the time to put on some lipstick.

"Where's Gracie?" Nova inquired, glancing around his legs.

"Already out back with the other munchkins. We heard them halfway down the street." He smiled again and I noticed his front teeth slightly overlapped each other. "She took a pretty good nap, but refused to eat any lunch. I think she's having peanut butter issues." He screwed his smile into an amused expression.

"No problem. We'll see you later."

"Thanks again," he said, then directed his attention to me. "Nice to meet you, Nicole. Maybe I'll see you again." He smiled at my sister and then addressed her. "You sure have pretty eyes, Jenny." My stomach jumped at his speaking to her; most people felt uncomfortable when they first met Jenny. I wondered if he had had experience with other handicapped people.

Jenny perked up at the mention of her name, pulling her gaze from Layla. She bestowed a beautiful smile upon Garret in return for the compliment.

After he left, I widened my eyes at Nova, fanning my hand in front of my chest. "Whew! Who was *that?*"

Nova grinned wickedly. "He's my neighbor. I watch his little girl for him in the evenings while he's at work. He owns a restaurant down on the strip. Quite the charmer, eh?"

"I guess! What about his wife?"

"Divorced him. Moved to Palm Beach."

"*Why?* Was she nuts?"

"Come on, now, what about your laundry fanatic?"

I sighed, flopping my head back against the couch. "Who knows?" I could not keep the resignation from my voice.

Nova leaned in, touched my hand. "Okay, chick. Now I mean it. How *are* you?"

I closed my eyes against the tears that too readily filled them. I shook my head, unable to speak. Nova moved to wrap an arm around me.

"Hey, hey. It's okay. Come on, sweetie." She kissed my forehead, smoothed back the hair from my face. "Look at me."

I shook my head again, fearful of what might come out if I opened my mouth, but desperately relieved someone had finally noticed that I was drowning.

She placed both of her soft hands on my cheeks. "You can talk to me, Nic. Remember? Please, tell me what's going on."

I lifted my eyelids, blinking away the tears. Her familiar blue eyes gazed back at me so fragile and open, ready to accept anything I had to say. I took a deep breath, the tightness in my chest beginning to loosen as the words began to tumble out. I opened my heart and finally, gratefully, told someone the truth.

"Why do you think your mother is acting like that?" Nova asked me as we moved from her living room to the kitchen. We had been blessed by an uninterrupted hour of conversation before Isaac came into the house moaning that his stomach was empty and he might die if he didn't get food pretty soon. I had told Nova everything that had been bubbling within me, starting with the first night my father went into Jenny's room and ending with my mother's odd detachment from us. She was shocked by the news of my father, disgusted and sad that I had carried its burden alone for so many years. I felt relieved, as well as thankful that she'd reacted with the love and understanding that I'd expected from her.

As Nova pulled out a glass bowl filled with cooked spaghetti from the refrigerator and set it in the microwave to warm, I slid

Jenny's wheelchair up to the light oak farmhouse-style kitchen table, rummaging through my bag to find her bib and vitamins. Nova's kitchen was a rectangular space edged in long white tile countertops. The walls were painted pale lime green, trimmed in white. The refrigerator was covered in children's art projects: mostly macaroni-glued paintings sprinkled with glitter. By her sink I noticed a mug that proclaimed WELL-BEHAVED WOMEN RARELY MAKE HISTORY.

"I'm not sure," I said. I adjusted Jenny's tray and helped her to take a sip of juice from a specially designed cup with a built-in straw. "I thought that once Jen was home she'd warm back up to the mother she used to be. I was *counting* on it." I looked at my sister. "What about it, Jen? Do *you* get what's going on with Mom?"

Jenny blinked once, twice, then closed her eyes to us completely as she continued swallowing her drink.

"Well, if she does, she obviously doesn't want to talk about it," Nova said with a laugh as she tossed butter and Parmesan cheese in with the warmed noodles. "I think you just have to talk to your mom about it. Confront her."

"Ooo, that should be fun," I said mockingly. " 'Gee, Mother, why are you being such a bitch?' "

"It'd probably be a good idea to word it a bit more tactfully than that." Nova stuck her head back into the living room to check on Layla, who was still sleeping peacefully in her swing, then looked at me with sharp blue eyes. "You're a therapist, right? You'll figure something out."

"I *used* to be a therapist."

"Close enough. What would you tell a client who was going through this with her mother?"

That was a good question. "You know," I said thoughtfully, looking at her with admiration, "I hadn't thought of it that way. Have you *always* been this smart?"

She grinned at me. "Of course." Walking over to the back door she yelled, "Kids! Dinner!" She moved to the cupboard next to the sink and grabbed a handful of small, plastic plates, setting them haphazardly on the table, along with several plastic cups, then filled each plate with small servings of pasta and green beans.

"No silverware?" I inquired.

She shrugged. "They don't use it, so I don't bother. Less to wash this way."

Four small heads popped up the stairs and ran to sit at the table. A dark-haired, fairy-looking child I had not seen before plopped down on the bench next to Jenny's chair. This had to be Gracie. She was small-boned and pale, with her father's pointed ears and a charmingly pretty, lightly freckled face. Her petite frame was clad in hot pink bike shorts and a bright yellow T-shirt, and on her tiny feet were fluorescent green saltwater sandals. I wondered if Garret had picked out this startling ensemble or if Gracie took pride in dressing herself. She didn't speak, but glanced at me with animated hazel eyes before sticking her fingers into the pile of noodles in front of her and holding up her meal to Jenny. "Want some?" she asked my sister, moving her gaze to Jenny's face, then shrugging to me. "She says she doesn't like cheese. It gives her a bellyache."

"How'd you know that?" I said, a little surprised. I looked at Nova. "She's allergic to dairy."

Gracie shrugged again, her mouth full of wiggling pasta. "She told me."

Nova smiled. "I swear kids are telepathic." She set plain buttered noodles on Jenny's tray, along with a pile of steamed green beans. "Gracie, especially."

"Here you go," Gracie singsonged to Jenny as she removed the green beans from her own plate to my sister's tray.

"Uh-uh, Miss Gracie," Nova corrected. "Put those back; they're yours. Jenny already has some."

"But she *wanted* them," Gracie reasoned.

"Nuh-uh," Isaac piped up from his spot across the table. "You just don't *like* green beans! You said they taste like poop!" All the children tittered.

"Enough!" Nova barked, clapping her hands together. "Eat and then it's bath time, you hear me?" There was an edge to

Nova's voice that must have caught their attention because miraculously the children obeyed.

After dinner, I held Layla while Nova managed to bathe four children, get them into their pajamas and then to bed in less than half an hour. The feather-soft weight of Layla in my arms stirred up dry places in my heart and moistened them with juicy feelings I could barely name. From the beginning of our relationship, Shane had made it clear that he certainly didn't want children and I had thought I felt the same way, but I couldn't believe how precious this child felt to me, how intensely I wanted to inhale her baby smell. It was richer, more intoxicating than any drug I had ever tried. I immediately thought of Jenny's baby, wondering if I'd ever hold it this way. If anyone would. Would it end up in an orphanage somewhere, or maybe a foster home? Just the idea of abandoning her baby the same way I'd abandoned Jenny wound my stomach into a complicated knot.

I looked at my sister, who sat next to me on the couch, her blue eyes firmly attached to the sight of Layla in my arms. Her expression was tender, and to my surprise she suddenly lurched toward me, letting her lips fall against Layla's tiny head in a wet kiss. I instantly wondered if this meant that she knew of the baby inside her. I hadn't seen her around other babies; I didn't know if this was a typical reaction. She slowly moved her head back and forth in a gesture of affection, then pulled back, smiling softly, as though she harbored a secret. Careful not to disturb Layla's sleep, I looked at her, amazed. I leaned over and brushed my lips across Jenny's forehead. "That was very sweet, sis," I told her, my chest full of restrained tears.

A moment later, Gracie tiptoed lightly into the living room, Nova following close behind. "She insisted on giving Jenny a kiss good night," my friend explained.

Gracie stepped over to the couch and climbed up on Jenny's other side. I choked up at the sight of this elfin child's lips touching my sister's cheek with such tenderness. She patted Jenny's arm. "Night-night, little girl," she said in a sweetly soft voice as Nova directed her back to Rebecca's bedroom.

"Wow," I said when Nova rejoined us. "What an angel."

"I know," she agreed as she sat in a nearby rocking chair. "Garret's a great father, but I don't think that's all of why she's so sweet, you know? Some kids just have that nature."

Like Jenny, I thought. *She's always had the angel in her.* Maybe that was why Gracie connected with her so quickly; she recognized a kindred spirit. I considered whether Jenny's baby would carry the same sweet temperament, if it was something that could be passed down from mother to child. "Is Gracie a lot like her mother?" I asked Nova as Layla's tiny head turned toward my chest. Her mouth opened and soft, snorting noises began to ripple out.

"Not at all," Nova said. *So much for that theory,* I thought. Considering my own mother, I should have known better. *She* certainly hadn't passed on any angelic genes to Jenny or, for that matter, to me.

Layla let loose an insistent, high-pitched wail and Nova stood up, reaching for her child. "She's rooting for the boob, hon. Better hand her over." Reluctantly, I did. My arms felt strangely deserted, suddenly anxious for an infant's weight to return and fill them up, as though they had finally discovered what they'd been made for in the first place. The sensation was a little bit frightening.

"Why exactly did Jackie leave Garret?" I asked, oddly curious about the man I'd met so briefly.

"You want the short or long version?" Nova inquired as she settled Layla at her chest.

I shrugged and put my arm around Jenny's small shoulders, hugging her to me. "Whichever."

"Well, they moved here just before Jackie was due with Gracie. The woman bitched about being pregnant a *lot.*" Nova raised her thin blond eyebrows and frowned briefly, considering something before continuing. "Not that *I* didn't complain when I was pregnant, but this was different. One of the first things she said to me was how she felt like the baby was a parasite. Sucking her dry."

"Yikes," I said, pulling Jenny's hands gently down from her mouth, where she had been gnawing on them. Did Jenny feel anything like that about the baby inside her? Maybe this was all too much for her to handle; maybe we were making a huge mistake letting her go through with the pregnancy if seemingly normal women like Jackie had such a difficult time with the changes in their bodies. It was too late now, of course. There was no turning back. I let my sister lean more tightly against my chest, where she rubbed her face and blinked heavily. It was getting close to her bedtime, as well.

"Yeah, yikes," Nova agreed, bobbing her head. "I think all mothers go through some degree of that feeling, but it didn't leave Jackie, you know? Even after Gracie got here. And it wasn't like she was a difficult baby. She was sweet then, too. You should have seen Garret with her. He used to strap her in the front pack and take her everywhere he went, even the restaurant." She shrugged and set her feet up on the coffee table, crossing one ankle over the other, careful not to disturb Layla. "I just think Jackie couldn't handle what being a mother demanded of her. She stuck around for a couple of years, then left. Garret took over and Gracie's a fabulous four-year-old."

I was silent, considering how overwhelmed I had felt the past few weeks, caring for Jenny—the guilt that filled me every time I allowed myself to feel even an ounce of resentment toward this person who could not help needing me so much. How my mother must have felt at some point every day of the fifteen years she cared for Jenny at home. It dawned on me that perhaps she was keeping herself distant from caring for Jenny now so she wouldn't have to go back to those feelings. I said as much to Nova.

"That could be," she agreed. "But still. She's Jenny's mother. I have a hard time understanding how she could just turn her feelings off like that." Looking down at Layla with a tender expression, she ran a light hand over her baby's head. "I know I couldn't."

"It's possible," I said softly, nuzzling my face into Jenny's hair so Nova would not see the guilty tears that filled my eyes, but the cracks in my voice betrayed me. "I did it for ten years. I basically pretended my sister didn't exist. What kind of person does that make me?" I lifted my gaze to Nova, whose eyes overflowed with compassion.

"The kind of person who made a mistake, Nicole. It makes you human. At least you're here, doing something about it. You're trying to make up for your mistakes. Your mother isn't."

The back of my neck bristled at the sound of disgust in Nova's last words and I felt the odd urge to defend my mother. "Maybe. But she's at least visited Jenny over the years. She's been here. I haven't."

Nova carefully switched Layla to her other breast and set her feet back on the floor before speaking. "There's a difference between being there physically and being there emotionally, don't you think? Being physically in the house with you two hasn't meant shit so far. I still think you have to talk to her."

Her words stood in front of me like a brick wall I didn't have the strength to climb. It was easy for Nova to say I should just talk to my mother; she wasn't the one who'd have to do it. I knew the conversation would bring up truths I hadn't had the courage to tell Nova—truths that would knock on doors to rooms I wasn't sure I was ready to enter. Doors that once opened could never be closed again.

When my mother had come home from her trip to Portland, I could not find the words to tell her how my father had gone into Jenny's room. She guessed correctly about the mark on my sister's face and while I hid with Jenny in her bedroom, our parents screamed at each other in the kitchen.

"I can't believe you *hit* her! You bastard! What kind of a father *are* you?" I imagined my mother standing in front of him, fists clenched, her thin body shaking, her face scarlet with anger. I knew my father's hair would be standing out from his head in fiery licks of red and gold, stretched to their limit by his angry, raking fingers. His sapphire eyes would flash in warning, daring Mom to make him angry enough to flee the house. I wrapped an arm around my sister, whose pale skin illuminated the angry bruise on her cheek like a floodlight.

"The kind who thinks his daughter needs to be in an institution!" he said loudly. "I've told you a hundred times, Joyce, we can't handle her here." The defensive note in my father's voice twisted my stomach into a thick knot. He knew what he had done. He knew what kind of man he was. I hugged Jenny tighter to me. I wanted to envelop her, to cover her tiny body with my own and never let anyone hurt her again. And yet I knew that no matter how hard I tried, I'd fail. My inability to protect her left an atrocious taste in my mouth, as though I'd been chewing tin foil.

Scared.

"Me, too," I whispered in her ear.

"You mean *you* can't handle her," my mother hissed. "If anyone has the right to lose it with her it's me, Mark. *I'm* the one who spends every waking minute with her. I dress her and feed her and wash the shit from her body every day. I deal with her screaming and you just run away. You haven't earned the *right* to be at the end of your rope."

And yet when the next screaming fit came, and the next and the next, so did my father's frustration. It flew from his fists to my sister's body with terrifying ease and intensity. Our mother reached out to protect her each time, but did nothing to prevent him from doing it again. "Get us out of here!" I longed to scream. "Get us away from him! Don't you know what he's doing?" Each night after he lost control of his fists, I heard him slip into Jenny's room, the low murmur of his voice mixing in dark harmony with the aching squeak of her bed. I tried to work up the courage to tell, to make it all stop, but I could not. My voice was a tangled fishing net in my throat, silencing me. I punished my cowardice by forcing myself to peek out the door as he went into Jenny's room, to bear witness to what I did not have the strength to end.

One night when I was fifteen, after a particularly bad screaming episode, I slowly opened my door to see him move into her room. Out of the corner of my eye, I noticed a different shadow flash in the doorway that led to the kitchen. It was the slight form of my mother hiding behind the corner, the ruffled edge of her white nightgown giving her presence away. In the reflection of the light of the full moon, I saw her eyes shiny with tears, watching her husband sneak into her helpless daughter's room. She *knew.*

How could she know and do nothing to stop it? My own fury

rose up in me then, stronger and fiercer than anything I had ever known. It oozed into the space around my heart like wet cement, hardening with each breath, forming walls that anesthetized me, completely paralyzing my ability to feel. Walls that two years later allowed me to walk out the doors of Wellman, leaving my sister at the mercy of strangers; walls that had kept me from her for a decade; walls that I knew would someday have to crumble if I was ever going to find the strength to forgive.

After our conversation the morning of Jenny's first appointment with Dr. Fisher, I had left Shane several bright-sounding messages on our machine in San Francisco, all of which he had ignored. The morning he finally called, I had just settled Jenny in front of a videotape of baby animals and was trying to straighten up the house and get lunch ready for us both. Nova was expecting us that afternoon; she had rummaged through her maternity wardrobe and wanted to see if anything she had might fit Jenny. I thought the call would probably be from her.

"Hey, babe," Shane said when I answered the phone in the hallway by my bedroom. Instead of waiting for me to respond, he immediately continued. "I'm really sorry it's taken me so long to get back to you, but I've been waiting to hear from the lawyers I called up there. A guy named Jack Waterson is going to get ahold of you, okay? I talked to quite a few lawyers, and if I were you, I'd go with him."

"What did he say when you told him about it?" I inquired, keeping my tone tight so he'd know I was angry. I couldn't believe he was being so casual with me. He hadn't called me once since I'd been in Seattle. I could see him in his office, standing by his perfectly organized filing cabinet, tapping his shiny Kenneth Cole loafer against the hardwood floor. His hair would be slicked back, his face freshly shaven, and his suit pressed as smooth as butter. It struck me how easily his life moved forward without me there, how little my absence affected him. Did I mean anything to him at all?

"He said it sounded like a pretty straightforward case," Shane answered. "Wellman will probably settle to avoid the publicity."

I poked at the already chipping baseboard with the tip of my shoe; a few flecks of paint fell to the rug. "What about an investigation of their hiring policies?"

"I don't know. You'll have to ask Jack about that. He's checking out what's going on with the criminal prosecution, too. Has anyone from the Seattle PD contacted you?"

"I called them a few days ago, but the detective working on the case didn't have much to say. They're still looking for the guy."

"He's probably long gone."

"Gee, honey, you think so?" I stopped picking at the wall and stood straight. I heard Jenny giggle in the living room as "Old MacDonald" began to play on her video; I wished I were with her instead of having this conversation.

Shane's breath was heavy in my ear before he spoke. "Have I done something wrong, Nicole? Where's this attitude coming from?"

"My attitude? What about yours? You haven't returned any of my calls. It's been two weeks."

"I was waiting until I had something to tell you about a lawyer."

"You can't just call to see how I'm doing?"

"I'm busy, Nic." He was obviously annoyed. Too bad. I wasn't going to let him off the hook.

"Busy with what?" I demanded.

He sighed. "I've got like ten cases going on at once down here. The D.A. is riding my ass like you wouldn't believe. It's an election year. I'm sorry, okay? I know you're going through a rough time." His voice softened a bit with those last words and I felt a small twinge of compassion rise up in my chest.

After a moment's pause I returned the apology. "I'm sorry, too." I fought the tears that thickened the muscles in my neck and twisted the springing, beige phone cord around my index finger. "I just miss you. I miss Moochie and Sunday mornings in bed with the paper. I never thought . . . I guess I thought I knew what it took to take care of my sister by watching my mother do it, but actually doing it—"

"Exactly why we don't want kids," he interrupted.

In protest, the memory of Layla in my arms the other evening immediately filled my mind, but I didn't say anything, trying to maintain the fragile reconnection we'd made.

He spoke again, apparently finishing his last thought. "Especially if your sister's problems are hereditary. There is no way in hell I'd be up for that."

I tried to digest this statement without choking on it. My voice cracked and I cleared my throat. "I've got to go, Shane. Jenny needs to eat. Thanks for your help on this."

"Sure. Sorry it took me so long. I'll try to be better about calling."

I hung up and went back into the living room. Jenny rocked in time with the video's music while I paced back and forth in front of the fireplace, unsure why I felt anger flowing in my blood like fire. I agreed with Shane, or at least I thought I did.

One of the reasons I figured I wouldn't have children was my fear of ending up with a handicapped baby. A baby like Jenny. I was terrified of it. Terrified of landing in the life I had watched my mother live, giving up my freedom, becoming so completely enmeshed with another human being that my own identity became a hazy memory.

It suddenly struck me that perhaps *this* was why Mom hadn't wanted Jenny to come home. Maybe, after ten years of being away from it, the fear of landing back in that life was enough to keep her from being the mother she used to be. She was terrified of losing herself again.

I stopped my pacing, unsure what my mother might be feeling and even less sure what was going on with me. I dropped to the couch, clutching a pillow to my chest, one question stacked precariously on top of another. Was I changing my mind? Did I want to be a mother? What was I now? What had I been in San Francisco? A failed therapist? A pastry chef? A pet owner? The girlfriend of a man who seemed to love his career more than he loved me? Was this the valuable identity I'd lose?

I pulled the pillow over my face and screamed my frustration into it. Feeling a little better after the outburst, I tossed the pillow to the end of the couch and looked over to the recliner at Jenny's swelling pregnant body. Oblivious to my emotional turmoil, she was happily gnawing on her fingers, her dark hair pulled back from her face with a silver barrette, her bright eyes glued to the frolicking farm animals on the screen.

Not for the first time, I considered why I had been avoiding calling Social Services to ask about placement for her baby. I knew I'd have to eventually, but something was keeping me from it. I suspected it was the same something that made me want to strangle Shane for not being desperate to have a baby with me. God, I was confused.

I stood up and walked over to my sister, kneeling down in front of her in order to see her eyes. I took her hands from her mouth and held them in mine. "Am I going crazy, Jen?" I asked her, afraid she might just answer me.

"Arhemmm," she murmured, leaning to one side so she could see around me to the television.

"Thanks," I said wryly. "That was very helpful." I glanced at the clock and went back through the kitchen and into the hallway. I dialed the bakery, hoping Barry hadn't gone home yet. Our brief conversation reminded me that there were happy aspects of my life over the past ten years and I experienced a brief stab of homesickness. An ache for the ease of my routine, the comfort I found in my relationship with Shane, even if we didn't share a terribly deep, emotional connection. I missed the deliberately nurtured lack of complication in my life. I realized that in San Francisco, my life had been held together by the powerful adhesive of denial. Here, with my sister and mother in the house where the hardest part of my life occurred, the illusion of contentment I had created was fading fast, leaving nothing but the raw nerves of reality in my path.

After a quick lunch, Jenny and I headed over to Nova's for the afternoon. As her kids napped and she and I worked in concert in her living room trying different maternity outfits on Jenny, I told her about Shane's apparent lack of concern for what was going on in my life.

"He's only called you once?" she said, obviously trying to hold back a look of shock from her face. "That sucks." She squatted down in front of Jenny to roll up the legs on a pair of too-long maternity jeans. Most of Nova's outfits were way too big for my sister, but as long as the ankles and sleeves were rolled up, a few of the knit ensembles seemed to be working well enough on Jenny's smaller-boned frame. The month away from Wellman's starchy menu had served her well; though she hadn't lost any weight, her flesh had relinquished the puffy look of an unhealthy diet. The shadow of the angel I knew in childhood had become more apparent.

I dropped to Nova's couch, flinging my head back and looking up at the textured ceiling, arms flopped dejectedly at my sides. "It does suck, doesn't it?" I concurred.

"I'd kill Ryan if he didn't call me at least twice a week from the fishing boat." Nova looked at me, her hands on Jenny's feet, her glance at me slightly hesitant. "If you don't mind my asking, what exactly drew you to Shane in the first place?"

"His looks," I confessed a bit guiltily as I closed my eyes, imagining Shane's handsome, angled face and intense sky blue eyes. I told Nova about the day he bumped into me in line at the Starbucks near my then-office. We had chatted about the odd cold snap, our respective occupations, then ended up sharing a table in the crowded café. I couldn't believe he was flirting with me; he looked like he belonged on the cover of *GQ*. On my better days I felt cheerleader-cute at best, but his attention made me feel like the most beautiful woman in the world. Two months later, I sublet my studio apartment and moved into his Pacific Heights town house. I'd never had a man like Shane interested in me; he was not only gorgeous, but a well-established professional. He had a retirement plan. He was a homeowner. Everything in his life was efficient and organized in a manner mine never had been. "I guess in a way, being with him calms me," I said. "He's very predictable."

"What did he think of your career switch?" she asked as she gently pulled a swing-cut purple top over Jenny's dark head. "That couldn't have been very predictable."

I snorted, setting my heels on the edge of the coffee table. "He thought I was nuts. He still thinks it's just a phase."

Nova tilted her blond head at me and sat down in the rocking chair on the other side of the room, glancing at the baby monitor on the coffee table. Layla was sleeping in her room. "Is it?" she inquired. I appreciated how she didn't seem to pass judgment on me for the apparently rash decisions I'd made in my life regarding Shane and my career. I passed enough judgment on myself for the both of us.

"I don't know. Sometimes I miss the whole therapy process. Other times I can't believe I wasted six years of my life going to school when I could have just as easily been happy working at the bakery."

"I wouldn't exactly call getting a master's degree a *waste*," Nova countered. "I wish I'd finished college. How am I ever going to convince my kids they should?" Nova had been working toward a degree in early-childhood education when she realized she was making more money waiting tables than she ever would in a public school system. Then she met Ryan, got married, and decided that at least while they were young, her children would be her career.

"I don't know," I answered honestly. I looked at Jenny, whose head was lolling back against the couch. She was almost asleep. I considered telling Nova more of what I'd been feeling, the reservations I had about putting Jenny's baby up for placement, but couldn't quite find the words. Instead, I told her more about Shane. "Shane doesn't want any kids, so I guess I won't have to worry about getting them to go to college."

Nova's expression was matter-of-fact. "If you decide to stay with Shane."

I didn't look at her, fiddling instead with a loose string on my cotton sweater. "You think I shouldn't stay with him?"

A sharp cry arose from the monitor and Nova jumped up, tucking her sandy hair behind one ear as she spoke. "I didn't say that." She stepped over a jumbled pile of colorful wooden blocks. "But shouldn't it be you and not your boyfriend who decides if you want to be a mother?"

"Well," I began, and she held up her hand to stop me.

"Just food for thought," she said as she headed down the hallway to get Layla.

As if my thoughts didn't already have enough to eat, I said to myself as I stood up in order to get Jenny ready to go. I wanted to be there when our mother got home. I had something I wanted to ask her.

When Mom walked through the front door, Jenny and I had finished dinner and were sitting in the living room listening to NPR's classical hour on the radio. Jenny gazed at our mother, adoration shining in her face like polished gold. "Ahhh," she gurgled from her spot next to me on the couch as a smile blossomed with drooling lips. A small part of me resented how much my sister seemed to still adore our mother when it was I who was with her all of the time.

Mom sat down next to Jenny and ruffled her youngest daughter's dark curls. "Hi, sweetie. Your sister taking good care of you?"

You'd better say yes, I thought to myself, looking at my sister with warning in my eyes.

"Ahhh," Jenny responded happily.

Mom smiled. "Good." She unfastened the clip that held her hair in a bun, letting it fall loose around her face. I noticed her hair's roots, gray and thick across her scalp, announcing her age. She slid a slender arm behind Jenny's shoulders and hugged her. Such open display of affection had been unusual for her since Jenny had been home; I wondered if her defenses might be melting. I decided to take the chance.

"Mom?" I ventured hesitantly, sliding one foot under the opposite thigh and adjusting the rest of my body to face her.

"Hmmm?" She didn't look at me.

"Do you ever regret having us?"

"What?"

I leaned forward over Jenny, anxious for an honest response. "I just wonder if you ever wish you hadn't become a mother. If you ever thought about what you might have done with your life if we hadn't been born."

"For heaven's sake, what brought that question on?" She turned her face to me briefly, then looked back to her lap. She appeared oddly unnerved.

"Talking with Shane. He doesn't want kids."

"I thought you didn't, either."

"Yeah, well, maybe I'm not so sure anymore."

Mom sighed, pulled her arm away from my sister and rested her hands in her lap. "The grass is always greener, honey. I know it's a cliché, but it's the truth."

"That's a nice way to avoid answering my question." I should have known better than to try to talk to her about this.

"I'm not avoiding it. That is my answer. When you have kids, you wonder what it would be like to not have them. I'm sure that when you don't have them, you wonder what having them would be like. Regret isn't even an issue."

"Even with all that happened with Jenny? You never regretted having her?" My sister turned her dark head to me and poured her eyes into mine as I said this, quietly awaiting our mother's answer.

Mom was silent, the only sound in the room the faint classical rhythm still playing from the stereo. She breathed deeply for a moment before responding. The muscles of her face were tight, but a small twitch danced nervously beneath her right eye, suggesting the effort her restraint took. She snapped and unsnapped the clip she held with the tips of her fingers several times. I held my breath, waiting until she finally looked at me, her green eyes filled with tears.

"It's hard to explain when you haven't been a mother yourself," she whispered.

"Could you try, please? I want to understand." And I did want to. I thought if she could explain her feelings about having a daughter like Jenny, I might better understand what was happening with us now.

Mom stared at the mantel above the fireplace. "I don't regret having Jenny," she began. "The only thing I regret . . ." She trailed off and blinked away tears, then shook her dark head.

Jenny sat quietly between us, looking off to some unknown point toward the kitchen entryway. I reached out a tentative hand over my sister's lap, the tips of my fingers barely brushing our mother's own in reassurance. I was desperate to hear what she might have to say. "What, Mom?"

Her thin bottom lip trembled and she lifted her chin to steady it. She turned to me, her face full of a pain I didn't recognize, then finally spoke. "I regret not protecting her," she said quickly, as though she couldn't get the words out fast enough. Stunned, I opened my mouth to speak, but nothing came out.

She stood up immediately, pinching the bridge of her nose. "I've got a terrible headache. I'm going to bed."

"But," I began, reaching out to stop her from leaving. I had to know what she meant.

"I don't want to talk about it," she said, jerking her body away from my reach. Talk about what? *What* hadn't she protected Jenny from? The rape at Wellman? Dad's angry fists? Or was my mother admitting she knew about what else he had done?

"Good night," she said resolutely, stepping purposefully past both her daughters. She strode down the hall to her room, slamming the door behind her, leaving me with more unanswered questions than one person should be forced to carry.

"*D*o you want to know the sex?" the technician inquired as she slowly rolled her instrument over my sister's bare belly. Jenny lay stiffly on her back, hands clawed together nervously, unsure of what was happening to her. I had explained that we were going to see pictures of the baby in her tummy, to make sure it was healthy and happy, but as the technician helped me lay her down on the table in the darkened room, panic danced in Jenny's eyes.

I looked over to Dr. Fisher, who had what Nova said was the unusual policy of attending her high-risk patients' ultrasounds. "What do you think?" I asked my sister, my hand gently stroking her dark hair back from her face. I looked into her eyes. "Should we find out if you're having a girl or a boy?"

Jenny's gaze searched mine, and the word *baby* whispered through me. I smiled, a little surprised. Maybe she understood more than I thought. "I think we'd like to know." I knew I wanted to.

The technician maneuvered the wand over Jenny's belly

again. "I can't give you a hundred-percent guarantee, but if you've bought any blue clothes you might want to return them. This baby is as girlie as she can be."

"See right there?" Dr. Fisher was pointing at the screen. "The golden arches, we call them. Labia." She turned to the technician. "I can take it from here, Janet. Thank you."

After the technician left, Dr. Fisher helped me set Jenny upright and get her back into her wheelchair. My sister was groaning a bit, not unhappily so, but simply emitting the low, constant sound I had begun to understand as her way of releasing stress.

"So," I said, "a girl. Is everything all right? Did she look normal?" The image on the screen had been only a blur of gray-and-black static to me, though seeing the fluttering heart sent tears to my eyes in the same manner hearing its beat had.

"The baby looks fine," Dr. Fisher said. "The only discrepancy is that the fetus is measuring at twenty-two weeks, and we're pretty sure the pregnancy is at twenty-six weeks."

"What does that mean?"

"Just that she's a little on the small side. We'll keep an eye on it at our office visits." She paused, considering something, then nodded to herself, as though she had made a decision. She turned her sharp brown eyes to me, probing. "You're doing great with her, Nicole. How about with yourself?"

"I'm fine," I said, surprised by her show of concern. I wondered if I looked as worn-down as I felt. Then I laughed, thinking of Nova's explanation of what the letters of "fine" stood for. I told the story to Dr. Fisher.

"That sounds like Nova," she said with an uncharacteristic grin. It lit up her entire face and suddenly she appeared not only elegant, but very pretty. "I'll have to teach it to my other patients." She paused. "Have you called Social Services yet about placement for the baby?"

Terrified she might ask me the reasoning behind why I hadn't taken care of this seemingly simple task, I lowered my head and shook it. "I can't seem to pick up the phone."

"Are you considering keeping her?" Her tone revealed nothing of what she might think.

Panic fluttered in my chest as I whispered my response. "Maybe." I couldn't believe the word as it passed over my lips, and yet there it'd been, waiting to be spoken.

She seemed unfazed by this revelation. "Well, you have some time to decide." She stood up and went to the door. "I'll see you two next week, okay?"

"Okay," I said, trying to gather my rattled senses. "Um, thanks for coming, Dr. Fisher. I really appreciate it."

She waved in acknowledgment and then was gone. When Jenny and I were bundled into the car and I had started the drive home, something pulled me in a different direction, toward Nova's house. We hadn't seen her for a couple of days and I was dying to tell someone who'd be excited as I was about finding out Jenny was having a baby girl. I couldn't believe the anticipatory thrill I felt in knowing. From the moment the technician had told us, my mind was flooded with images of shopping for darling frilly pink outfits and teensy-tiny black patent Mary Jane shoes. Visions of cradling this child in my arms overwhelmed me: nuzzling her to my breast the way Nova did with Layla; kissing her toes and the chubby rolls of her thighs; drinking in the sweet nectar of her breath. The strength and immediacy of these images shocked me; I had not had them before.

I sighed, glanced over to Jenny, who was staring at me disconcertingly. "Your sister is losing it, Jen." It wasn't as if I would actually keep the baby, despite my shaky response to Dr. Fisher's question. But the knowing intensity of Jenny's gaze moved over me like a laser. I shivered and returned my focus to the road ahead.

The front door to Nova's house was open, so after I managed to get Jenny up the stairs, I walked right inside, calling out for my friend. "Hello? It's Nicole. Anybody home?" I heard a tittering explosion of laughter coming from the back bedroom as the door opened and out stepped Garret, looking nothing like the man I had met the night of my first visit to Nova's.

He was bedecked in a pointed fairy hat, complete with a trailing pink veil. His lips were painted bright red to match the circles of rouge on his cheeks and he wore a sweeping pink cape around his shoulders. He appeared a bit embarrassed when he saw me, but still smiled, his lips greatly exaggerated by their makeup.

"Hi," he said. "I've been shanghaied into playing castle. Come on back." The warm sound of his voice entered my bloodstream and the temperate, early-summer air suddenly seemed unbearably hot.

"Where's Nova?" I inquired as I gently guided Jenny's stilted steps down the hall to Rebecca's bedroom. Gracie and Rebecca were also in costume, jumping on Rebecca's bed and giggling ferociously.

"She took the boys and Layla to the beach, so I'm watching the girls." He swished his cape dramatically around his body. "Do you like my outfit? Gracie picked it out herself."

"Oh, it's gorgeous," I said, amused by his silliness. I backed Jenny up, carefully lowering her down on the cushions of the window seat.

Garret moved toward us. "Here, let me help you." He grabbed a couple of pillows from the bed and set them around Jenny, who was staring at his garish appearance with amazement. "How about you, Jenny? Do *you* like my outfit?"

Jenny blinked deliberately, turning her head away in a coy movement, a delicious smile lighting up her face. Garret sat down next to her, putting the cape between her fingers. "Here, feel. Isn't it silky?"

Gracie jumped off the bed and hopped over to her father. Her smooth cap of dark hair bounced haphazardly, a crooked rhinestone tiara nestled on the top of her head. She wore a long-sleeved lavender leotard with a bright orange, netted tutu. She patted Jenny's other hand. "Hi, little girl. Do you want to play castle?" She paused, then looked at me, the green in her hazel eyes bright. "She says yes. Can I dress her up?"

I stood back, shaking my head in amazement at this eloquent child. "Sure."

Garret retrieved the plastic makeup compact Gracie held in her little fingers. "Let Daddy help you, Peanut. Why don't you go find Jenny a hat?"

"I'll do it!" Rebecca cried out and she and Gracie raced out the door and down the back stairs to the basement.

"The costume trunk is downstairs in the playroom," Garret said by way of explanation for their journey.

"I see," I smiled. I paused, unsure what to say next. I finally settled on a compliment. "You seem so comfortable with Jenny. Have you been around other handicapped people?"

He nodded. "A kid in my neighborhood, growing up . . ." He trailed off, remembering.

There was a slightly audible pause, neither of us knowing exactly what to say. Once again, I picked a compliment. "Gracie's a great little girl."

"Thanks. She is pretty amazing. I can't believe sometimes that I helped make her. That she *came* from me, you know?"

"That must be amazing. I don't have kids, so I guess I can't know exactly how it feels, but I think you're doing a great job with her."

His smile was slow as he pulled the fairy hat off his dark head. "And I think what you're doing for your sister is great. Nova told me about your situation. I hope you don't mind."

I shook my head. "Of course not. She told me a bit about yours, as well."

"So you asked about me, too, then?" he inquired, a flicker of something terribly exciting in his eyes. Something I hadn't seen in a man's eyes for a very long time. I flushed, crossed my arms over my chest and looked down to the floor.

"Well, yeah. I guess I did. Gracie was just so sweet. . . ."

"Oh, so it was *Gracie* you were curious about?" He was teasing me and I couldn't believe how much I liked it. I switched to a safer subject.

"So, Nova said you own a restaurant on Alki?"

"Um-hmm. The Beach Basket."

"I'm a baker down in San Francisco. What kind of menu do you offer?"

"It's pretty eclectic. Seafood, pasta, sandwiches, salads. You name it, we've probably served it. We keep the entrees as healthy as possible, but I'm kind of a traditionalist when it comes to dessert. The more butter and cream you can stuff into a recipe, the better."

"I agree. Do you have a pastry chef?"

"Are you asking me for a job?"

"Are you always such a tease?" I countered, my stomach fluttering.

"Most of the time. Do you like it?"

"Some of the time."

He laughed. "You *are* Nova's friend, aren't you? Cut from the same fabric, I'd say."

"What kind of fabric is that?"

"Intricately woven." He directed his light brown eyes at me before finishing. "Beautiful."

Color rose to my face again, but thankfully the girls returned with Jenny's costume and saved me from making a complete idiot of myself by weeping in gratitude at the compliment. I could not remember the last time Shane had told me I was beautiful when we weren't about to have sex.

I watched Garret as he used the tips of his fingers to gently apply blush to my sister's pale cheeks and then adjust the purple jester's hat the girls had brought for her to wear. Jenny gazed at him with a smile in her eyes, happily patting her fingers together as the girls danced around her and pretended to laugh at the jokes my sister was supposedly telling them. When Garret jumped up to dance around with them, waving his arms and legs like a goof, the girls dissolved into puddles of laughter on the floor. I giggled along with them, the relief I felt washing over me like a river.

I tried to imagine Shane there, softly touching my sister's cheek and dancing with abandon to entertain her, but I could not. Shane would be the man standing in the corner, arms crossed over his chest looking upon Garret with amused disdain for so joyfully acting the fool. A month ago, I might have done the same myself. But there I stood, not quite believing the ease I felt with this man I barely knew. I had never met someone so sure of himself without it coming across as arrogance.

Later, when Garret and Gracie had gone home and Nova sat

with Jenny and me in her living room, I asked about him again. "Is he really that great, or is there some dark side I don't know about?"

"I know he's a perfectionist when it comes to the restaurant, and *boy howdy*, the man can be stubborn when he thinks he's right about something, but other than that I think what you see is what you get." She twisted her soft body toward mine on the couch. "What are you thinking?"

"I don't know, exactly. It's not like I need another complication in my life right now, but man, he's a hard one to ignore." I clapped my hands to the sides of my head. "I can't believe I'm even thinking about this. I love Shane. I want to work it out with him. My life is with him." Dropping my hands to my lap, I tried to mask my uncertainty with false-sounding conviction.

"Your life is with you," Nova said. "Whether you choose to live it with Shane is an option, not a requirement."

Slightly annoyed that once again she had insinuated my relationship with Shane might not work out, I wasn't sure how to respond. I decided humor was my best defense. "That's good advice," I said teasingly. "Are you sure *you* aren't the therapist?"

"Yep. I just watch a lot of *Oprah*."

"What would Oprah say I should do?"

"Pray, girlfriend. Oprah'd tell you to pray."

Jenny was awake most of the night following her ultrasound; after getting up with her for the fifth time, I wondered if she, too, was excited about the news of her baby's sex. When she finally drifted off into a deep sleep around six a.m., I found that I couldn't do the same, so I dressed and went into the kitchen to make a pot of coffee.

After setting it to brew, I stepped into the living room and saw that my mother was already awake. With the aid of the pale pink light of dawn that flowed through the front windows, I could see that dark circles bruised the soft flesh beneath her bloodshot eyes; her skin was taut and paler than usual. Her bare feet were tucked under her on the couch and a full ashtray rested on the side table, evidence that she had been there awhile.

Since her startling disclosure the other evening that she regretted not protecting Jenny, our interactions had been minimal. I was attempting to give her whatever space she might need in order to open up to me again, but it irked me to think that the tiny steps we had taken toward actually communicating might have been completely erased.

I walked in quietly through the entryway from the kitchen, sitting down in the recliner across the room from her. She glanced at me briefly, green eyes exhausted as she took a final drag before snuffing her cigarette out.

"Sorry," she said shortly, referring to her smoking. After I found her in the kitchen that first night Jenny had cried, she had promised that she'd keep her habit outside from then on, in consideration of Jenny's baby.

"It's okay," I said, pulling a rainbow-hued afghan from the back of my chair to cover my legs. It was already the first week of July, but the early mornings still felt chilly to my internal California-set thermometer. I looked at my mother and thought of what Nova had suggested, that I should try to see our situation as I would a client's. What would I say to my mother if she had come to me for help? I started slowly. "You couldn't sleep?"

Mom shook her head and jutted her chin in the general direction of Jenny's room. Earplugs or not, she had obviously been distressed by her younger daughter's cries. I wondered why, then, she couldn't bring herself to come and comfort Jenny. She pulled her knees up to her chin and wrapped her arms around her shins, turning her gaze out the window to the gold-rimmed, puffy white clouds that served as buffer to the bright morning sun. I recognized this classic defensive position and realized how vulnerable my mother must be feeling. Maybe my training hadn't been a waste, after all. "Jenny had an ultrasound yesterday," I revealed. "She's having a girl."

Mom's expression brightened momentarily, her color perking up, but then it faded dull again without so much as a word. Her eyes looked glazed and distant; it struck me that she might be seriously depressed. "Is something bothering you?" I asked her carefully. "Do you want to talk?"

In response to this question she stood up abruptly, grabbing the ashtray and looking at me warily. Her dark bob hung limp and tangled around her face. "No, Nicole, I don't. I want to get ready for work." She sounded as though this were the last thing she actually felt like doing.

I sighed in defeat as she brushed past me down the hall to her bedroom. I pushed the recliner back so that I might rest a little before Jenny decided to wake for the day. As the water began to rumble through the pipes for Mom's shower, I closed my tired eyes and considered the brief interaction that had just occurred. At least I knew I was right to quit practicing therapy. If I couldn't get my own mother to open up to me, how could I have ever expected to get a complete stranger to?

I curled up under the afghan, pulling it to my chin and holding it there with two tightly clenched fists. Maybe it was time to face the ugly truth that my mother and I might never heal the wounds between us, that I'd simply help Jenny through the pregnancy on my own, find placement for both her and the baby, then return to my life in San Francisco.

If it was a life worth returning to, I thought sadly, opening my eyes as the sun's long reach touched my face. If it was a life I wanted to live at all.

*O*n a Saturday morning a couple of weeks after Jenny's ultrasound, I was in the kitchen with my sister when Mom came through the door from the living room, yawning.

"Did I wake you?" I asked as I firmly pressed fresh raspberries through a sieve I held over a bowl. We'd barely been speaking; I'd given up trying to reach her.

"Kind of. It's early for seafood, isn't it?" She nodded toward the pile of peeled and steamed shrimp that sat next to the sink.

"It's for the barbecue at Nova's this afternoon. Right, Jenny?" I looked at my sister, who sat quietly watching me from her wheelchair. We had had a tough night. She was awake several times, moaning and crying off and on and though I managed to settle her back to sleep each time, I could not figure out what was bothering her. Her eyes were a blank page, no messages left for me to read.

She was up early in the morning, too. It was only seven o'clock and I had already fed, showered, and dressed her in one of the maternity outfits Nova had passed on for her to use. She wore a short-sleeved, pale lavender baby-doll top and matching stretch pants, tightly laced white tennis shoes, and a purple-and-white-checked headband in her dark brown hair. Despite her advancing pregnant state, the adult-styled outfit looked slightly out of place on her child-sized frame.

She sat near the kitchen table, staring off into space, bottom lip sagging, drool leaking onto her shirt. For some reason, this annoyed me. "Careful, Jenny! I want to keep that outfit clean! Mom, could you put a bib on her?" The tips of my nerves felt raw from lack of sleep, as though an evil carpenter had rubbed them with sandpaper in the night. The compounded pressure of caring for Jenny alone and getting little rest was taking its toll; I felt as though if anyone asked me how I was doing, I'd fall to the ground weeping.

Our mother reached for the bib on the counter and placed it around Jenny's neck, then kissed her on the head. The ease of her gesture bothered me. If she wasn't going to do the work involved in taking care of Jenny, why should she be entitled to the affection?

"What's the barbecue for?" Mom asked.

I tilted my chin down and looked at her over the end of my nose. "Sort of a late Fourth of July celebration. Ryan got home last night from Alaska, and since he hasn't met us yet, Nova wanted to throw a little party." I paused. "She told me to ask you to come, but I was pretty sure you wouldn't want to."

She reached for the coffeepot and poured herself a cup. "Why wouldn't I?"

"I don't know. Maybe because you haven't spent any time with us since we've been here. I guess I figured this wouldn't be any different." I opened a bottle of balsamic vinegar and carefully added a couple of teaspoons to the raspberry mixture in the bowl.

"Maybe you figured wrong." She lowered herself into a kitchen chair. "Will Star be there?"

"Yes," I said as I began to vigorously whisk the sauce. "I haven't seen her yet, either. She's been in Las Vegas and New York trying to get her jewelry line launched." I set the whisk on the counter and glanced at her briefly. "I'm sure she'd love to see you." This wasn't exactly true; Star and my mother had never been close, but because of Nova's and my friendship, they were at least always polite.

When we were children, Star made a point to invite our family to their holiday celebrations and summer parties even though we rarely accepted. My parents didn't understand the easy, open lifestyle Star and Orion championed. The Carsons touched readily in front of Nova, discussed politics and religion with her over dinner, and often took long walks around the neighborhood, holding hands and stopping to kiss every house or two, the love that flowed between them a palpable, glowing thing.

The only memory I have of my parents touching was the few times when my father came up behind my mother while she tended to Jenny or worked in the kitchen. He'd rub his face into her neck, his hands on her waist. I remember watching the look on Mom's face move from surprise to impatient tolerance, then finally disgust. "Mark," she'd say, her voice thick with warning. And he would walk away, shrugging his skinny shoulders as though he were trying to rid them of a heavy weight.

When I looked to the night sky, dreaming of what a marriage might be, I did not look for the story of my own parents in the stars; I watched for the constellation of Star and Orion.

As I began arranging the shrimp concentrically on a wicker, lettuce-lined serving platter, I thought about how much I was looking forward to seeing Nova's parents, knowing they would be equally happy to see me. I also knew Garret would be there and the idea of talking with him again made my stomach warm and fall in on itself like a deflated soufflé. Thoughts of him had often invaded my mind since our last meeting at Nova's house; I saw his easy smile, heard his chuckling laugh, felt the tips of his fingers brush mine when we parted. I felt like a teenager again, my belly full of twittering muscles and my mouth overcome by spontaneous, happy grins.

My attempts to quell these feelings fell heinously short even as my conversations with Shane increased. Feeling guilty, I'm sure, after our last phone call, he was calling me every night when he got home from the office, no matter how late that was, but after a long day with Jenny I found I had little to talk about with him. I knew he wasn't interested in hearing about Jenny's latest enema or crying jag; in fact, I was pretty sure he was thankful when I didn't bring her up. Since my days were full of such details, my end of the conversation was fairly limited.

Mostly, I listened to the difficulties he was having with a particular case or coworker and offered words of comfort or advice. He'd talk about restaurants we'd gone to together, plays or movies we might have seen if I'd been there, but oddly, I didn't feel as though I were missing anything. My life there almost seemed as though it hadn't happened, as if it might have all been a dream. I ended the calls feeling frustrated and empty. I considered whether our relationship had always been like this and being so close to him I had refused to see it. Once again I took Nova's advice and thought about what I might say to a therapy client if she was in a similar situation and found that I wasn't ready to hear my own advice.

"I'd like to come, if that's all right with you," my mother said, now, interrupting my thoughts.

"Of course it is," I said, trying to sound sincere while keeping the surprise I felt from my tone. "We're glad you want to, aren't we, Jen?"

"Ahhh!" Jenny screeched, angrily clapping her hands together. Irritated that I had to stop what I was doing and wash my hands, I inspected her from head to toe in order to make sure there wasn't a physical cause for her outburst.

"You're fine, Jen. Everything's fine." She was still tense, a balloon filled too full with air. When she quieted again, I went back to the careful work of finding the perfect balance of sweet and sour for the shrimps' raspberry dipping sauce, trying not to be too wary that Mom wanted to come with us to the barbecue.

A while later, after Mom had gone to shower and get ready for the day, the phone rang and I quickly ran my hands under the faucet to clean them off before grabbing the receiver. "Hello?"

"Nicole Hunter?" A man's voice, low and professional.

"Yes?"

"This is Jack Waterson. Shane Wilder gave me your number."

"Oh, yes. He said you'd be calling." So wrapped up in the everyday details of Jenny's care, I hadn't had much time to focus on the case against Wellman. Stretching the receiver's cord, I moved to stand in the kitchen's entryway so I could keep an eye on my sister.

"I'm sorry to bother you on a Saturday," Mr. Waterson said apologetically, "but I've just gotten off the phone with the D.A.'s office, Ms. Hunter, and they've informed me that the police are narrowing in on Mr. Zimmerman's whereabouts. What I need to know is—and I swear I'm not client chasing here, but Shane *did* tell me to call you—are you interested in going forward with a civil case against Wellman, and if so, do you want to have me represent you on your sister's behalf?"

I looked over to Jenny's belly and thought I saw something jump beneath her shirt. Could that have been the baby? My sister froze; the look on her face was one I had not seen there before. "Oh, my God!"

"Is everything all right, Ms. Hunter?"

"What? Oh, yes, everything's fine. Well, not fine, but right this minute, yes, I'm fine. Something just surprised me." I took a breath. "Sorry. I'm not really as scattered as I sound." Ha. Little did he know. "I am interested in going forward with the suit, Mr. Waterson, and Shane's recommendation of you is more than enough credibility for me. Do we need to discuss your fee?"

"I'm paid only if you are, Ms. Hunter. Forty percent of whatever you get. And let me say I believe this will be a fairly open-and-shut case. Wellman will most likely settle to avoid the potential negative publicity a trial would bring about."

"That's what Shane said. What kind of settlement are we talking about?" I twisted the phone cord around my fingers and stuck my tongue out at Jenny, trying to amuse her. She ignored me, her eyes locked on some unseen point behind me. She looked as though she were trying to leave herself, the soft outline of her spirit seeking reprieve from the body that imprisoned it. I shook my focus back to the phone. "I only ask because I need to find a new placement for Jenny and I guess I'm wondering what kind of money I'll have to work with."

"It should be a substantial amount. I'll ask for five million and we'll go from there."

Stunned, I almost dropped the phone. "Five *million*?"

"Five million what?" my mother asked as she walked back into the kitchen, once again reaching for the coffeepot.

I shook my head at her, pointing to the phone.

"Oh," she said. "Sorry." She poured the steaming liquid into a white mug, then sat at the table next to Jenny's chair, crossing one leg over the other. She wore blue jeans, sandals, and a baggy cotton candy pink sweater. The pastel hue made her usually translucent complexion appear washed-out. It made her look a little bit ill.

"Yes," Mr. Waterson continued in my ear. "Five million. We'll probably get it, too. After my fee and taxes, your sister will have more than enough for the finest of care. Have you visited anywhere?"

"No. I don't really know where to start." I dreaded this search, the inevitable wandering through places too horrible to even imagine visiting, let alone leaving my sister to live.

"I hope you don't mind, but on the chance that you did decide to hire me, I had my secretary research a list of the highest-rated homes in Washington State. They're all privately managed, small population group homes. Nothing state-funded, like Wellman. They're pricey and some have long waiting lists, but the sooner you start looking, the sooner you'll find something. Why don't you give me your address and I'll get it in the mail to you today?"

"That would be fabulous. Thank you so much." We set up a time to meet and I was still reeling from the amount he quoted for the settlement when I hung up the phone. Mom looked at me expectantly.

"Who was that?"

I stepped back to the counter and began cleaning up the mess I'd made. "The lawyer Shane recommended for the civil case against Wellman."

"I didn't know there was a case."

"Well, I'm filing one. They should pay for allowing that man to do what he did to her. They're responsible."

She nodded. "I agree."

I stopped wiping the counter and swung my head around to look at her, my mouth open in disbelief. "You *agree?* You're the one who wanted to leave her there to have the baby!" I could not believe what I was hearing. Was it the prospect of the money? I hadn't thought of this before, but because she was guardian to Jenny, the settlement would be under her control. Was this the cause for her sudden interest in spending time with us? I wanted to strangle her.

"I know. I was wrong, okay?"

"It's about time you admitted it." I could not keep the venom from creeping into my voice.

"What is *that* supposed to mean?"

I narrowed my eyes at her and threw the washrag into the sink. "You know exactly what that means." Living under the enormous weight of our unspoken history had simply become too much for me to handle. I realized that I had had enough of tip-toeing around; it was time to demand the truth.

"No, I don't. Perhaps you could enlighten me." She recrossed her legs and folded her hands over her knee. Her foot shook impatiently.

Jenny looked anxiously back and forth between us, moaning uncomfortably. The muscles in her face tightened almost imperceptibly before her entire body tensed and an ear-piercing shriek erupted from her mouth. She slammed her hands together, then violently shoved them between her teeth, as though trying to quiet herself. Panic rose in her blue eyes like a wave on the ocean.

I rushed over to her. "Jen, what's wrong? Honey?" My hands searched her body again for skin caught in a zipper, a waistband pinching too tight on her bulging belly. Nothing. She screamed again.

"Has she had any dairy this morning?" my mother asked, a tight edge to her voice. "It gives her terrible gas."

"I know that, Mom. Don't you think I know that?" My heart was pounding a horrible, remembered rhythm in my chest. My nerves throbbed. These fits had dissipated at Wellman. The doctors wrote them off as family-induced, emotional outbursts, never again searching for a physical cause.

"She hasn't done this in years," my mother said, anxiety wriggling its away across her face, moving like a fog over her green eyes. She set her coffee down on the table. "Has she been like this all night?"

Jenny shrieked again, her legs rigid and stuck out from her body in hard, straight lines. I knelt down in front of her and massaged them vigorously, the muscles like wood under my hands. "No. She was up a lot, crying, but not screaming." I looked up to my sister's contorted face, distress oozing through my own body like warm honey. I gripped her legs tighter. "Jen. Stop it, honey, okay? Would you please just stop it?" Any patience that might have remained within me had fled. I felt something dark rising up through my body, something ancient and angry, something that had been hiding in the shadows of my heart for years. Before I knew what I was doing, my fingernails dug viciously deep into the skin of her legs and I shook her, hard, pulling another scream from her throat. "Stop it right now!" I shrieked at her.

Surprise popped up on her face like runway lights. Fat tears rolled down her cheeks. *Why?* whispered in my heart and I let her legs go, looking at my hands as though they did not belong to me. They belonged to my father.

"Nicole," my mother said gently, reaching out to grasp my fingers. "It's all right."

"No, it's not. Did you see me? Oh God, did you see what I just did?" I looked at her, pleading, my hands raking through my red curls, another gesture that belonged to my father. I shuddered at the thought. "I don't know what's wrong with me. Can you help? Please, Mom, can you help me?" Tears strangled my words.

A strange calm overtook my mother's face and she looked at Jenny with a long-forgotten tenderness. Her expression softened; her entire body seemed to relax. It was like watching the mother I used to know move back into her body. "Has she had a bowel movement this morning? Maybe she's constipated."

I swallowed my tears, shaking with guilt. "No, her diaper was full when she woke up. I've been making sure she gets lots of fiber to balance the iron in her prenatal vitamins." I racked my brain, trying to pick what I had done wrong, what I had forgotten that was causing my sister so much pain. I felt like a child again, helpless and lost, watching my sister spin into a chaos she could not control. Then something hit me: the jump of her belly beneath her blouse. "Do you think it might be the baby? What if she's having contractions? Maybe I should call Dr. Fisher."

My mother rested her hands on Jenny's belly, settled them there for several moments. She shook her head. "I don't think so. Her stomach is relaxed. It's her legs that look tense." She squatted on the opposite side of Jenny's legs and we both rubbed them, my touch as tender and loving as I could make it. *I'm sorry, I'm sorry, I'm sorry* was the message I massaged into her flesh. My sister watched us both with contemplative eyes, quieting some as we moved our hands over her calves, her thighs, her feet. Then I remembered.

"Klonopin!" I exclaimed, jumping up to the counter where I kept all her medications. "I forgot to give her Klonopin last night." I broke the pill up beneath the flat side of a knife and mixed it quickly into some applesauce.

"What does that do for her, again?" My mother continued rubbing as she spoke, watching my sister's face for any relief she might feel.

I carefully spooned the small bites into Jenny's mouth. "It's for muscle spasms in her legs. The nurse at Wellman told me they're like double whopper charley horses. Do you think they're what made her scream all those years?"

"I don't know. It's possible."

Within minutes, Jenny's legs began to relax and a small measure of peace returned to her entire body. The screaming stopped, but Mom and I kept at her legs, moving the ache out of her body until she smiled at us both, joy sparkling in her eyes again.

How could she forgive me so quickly? I wondered. Did she forgive my mother? Could I? I hugged her and whispered more apologies into her ear, then turned to my mother, who had moved back to her seat at the table.

"Mom?"

"Um-hmm?"

"Maybe I shouldn't be doing this." I was overcome by the urge to escape again, though I had no idea where I'd go.

"Doing what?"

I dropped into a chair and threw my arm around the room. "This. Being here, taking care of Jenny. Maybe I should just find a place for her as soon as possible and go back home."

"Oh, honey, no. Bringing her here was the right thing to do. You're doing such a wonderful job taking care of her. Better than I ever did." Something hung heavy in her expression, black and unnameable.

I felt a small crack in the hard wall around my heart start to spread. "You took good care of her." I took a deep breath, gathering my courage. "It was Dad who hurt her, not you. Right?" I searched her face, desperate for her to say, *Yes, yes, it was him; I should have done something to stop him. That was my sin and I am sorry for it. This is what I regret.*

Tears glistened across the surface of her eyes. "I let him, though, didn't I?" She touched Jenny's cheek with tips of her fingers. "Mommy's sorry, baby. I did the best I could. I wish I'd done better."

A sob climbed up through the muscles in my throat, choking me. "Oh, Mom." I put my hand over my eyes, as if that would hold back the tears.

Jenny moaned lightly, anxiously watching the two of us. Agitation tightening the muscles in her face, she touched her hands together, once, twice. Standing up, I stepped over to her and grabbed them.

"It's okay, Jen. Everything's okay. Mom and I are just having a moment." I smiled hesitantly at my mother. "Right?"

She wiped her eyes and returned my smile. "Right." Then she leaned forward in her chair and took Jenny's hands from mine. "I'm going to try and do better now, okay, honey?" she whispered. "I don't know what's been wrong with me. I promise, I'll do better." She looked at me, her eyes begging for understanding. "Please, give me a chance to do better."

"You already are," I said. I saw her shoulders lift, and I realized that they had been bowed under much of the same guilt I had felt for years. It was then that the crack in the wall around my heart broke open and a huge piece of ache simply crumbled and finally fell away.

After we arrived at Nova's house for the barbecue but before I went outside to join the party, I pulled my friend aside in the kitchen and told her about our morning. Jenny's screams, the horror of how I reacted, what had happened with my mother. "It was like Jenny's fit was a call to action for the mother she used to be. Like that part of her had been sleeping and Jenny's screams woke it up. Then she just broke down. Then I broke down. It was a real mother-daughter moment, you know?"

Nova gave me a firm hug. "I'm glad. So you feel like things are worked out with her?"

I thought of her all those years ago, standing in the hall, watching my father go into Jenny's room. There was still more for us to resolve. "Sort of," I relented. "It was like a crack in the ice. Everything's still kind of frozen between us, but it felt like the beginning of something. A warm front moving through."

"That's great." She pulled back and held my face between her hands. "Okay, smile."

I did. "What for?" I asked, my cheeks smashed together by the pressure of her touch.

"You look great, so I didn't want you to ruin it with lipstick teeth."

"Ruin what?"

She rolled her blueberry eyes. "Please. Like you didn't ask me fifty times if Garret was coming today."

"It wasn't *fifty*!"

"Okay, maybe it was closer to forty-nine. But if you're interested, he asked if you'd be here, too."

"Really?"

"Yeah. He tried to be all sly about it, like it was *Gracie* who wanted to know if *Jenny* was going to come, but please. Like I'm stupid. He looks at you the way an alcoholic looks at a cold glass of beer."

I grinned, plopping down onto the bench by the table. "So I look great, huh?" I had worn a deep amethyst, V-necked blouse and paired it with the least worn pair of jeans I had brought from home. The temperate July air turned my bloodred curls into smooth coils that fell loosely around my face and I had even taken the time to paint my toenails to match the plum-hued lipstick I wore. I felt guilty as I dressed, knowing who I was preparing myself for, knowing it was not Shane.

"Yes," Nova said. "You look great. Glowing, in fact." She reached into the refrigerator and pulled out a platter overflowing with vegetables: carrots, celery, various brightly colored peppers, and plump green broccoli stalks. She popped a baby carrot into her mouth and crunched it. "Come on, my mom's dying to see you."

We moved into the backyard onto the sunny deck, where my mother had taken Jenny when we first arrived. She sat by my sister, holding her hand with a slight tentativeness that I was sure only I noticed. With their matching dark hair and heart-shaped faces, the relationship between them was clear. They looked as though they belonged together. She said something to Jenny that I couldn't decipher and my sister smiled. It made my heart sing to see her there, connecting with her daughter in a way I thought she had forgotten. *Mama*. Jenny's voice rang through my blood with happy relief. She felt the warm front, too.

The children were all busy climbing on the wooden play equipment, slipping through the tunnel slide and racing across the monkey bars. I saw Garret helping Gracie up a small ladder, his back to me. I smiled in spite of myself, then carried my platter of shrimp over to a table that was already overloaded with food. A blond man stood next to me, his fingers dug into a bowl full of potato chips. His stocky, muscular frame reminded me of a swimmer's. When he smiled at me, his sky blue eyes twinkled against sun-weathered, copper skin. "You must be Nicole, the long-lost best friend." He popped the chips into his mouth, chewed vigorously, then held up a weathered hand in greeting. "I'm Ryan, Nova's hubby."

"Nice to meet you. I've heard a lot about you."

"I'll bet. All good, of course."

"Of course." I jumped suddenly as a pair of strong arms wrapped themselves around my body from behind and hugged me, hard. "Oomph!" I exclaimed, turning my head over my shoulder to see who was accosting me. "Star, you're an amazon woman."

"Strong like ox," she joked, releasing her hold and allowing me to face her. She had barely changed; her blond hair was streaked with a bit of ash, perhaps, but it still hung to the middle of her back, tied with a small strap of leather at her neck. Her face crinkled a bit more when she smiled, but there was no more flesh on her lithe body than ten years before. She wore a silky, royal blue sheath, her arms bare save the stacked bracelets that traveled several inches up from her thin wrists. "How are you, sweet girl? How's your life? What have you been up to down in sunny California?" She exaggerated the state's name: "Califor-nigh-yah."

"Oh, you know, I'm fine. Busy right now, with Jenny, of course." I glanced over to Garret to see if he had noticed my arrival. He hadn't. I took Star's hand and squeezed it. "How are *you*? How's the jewelry biz? Nova tells me you're about to go national with your line?"

"Yup." She jangled the bracelets on her arms. "These babies are finally going to pay off. Some New York business scout discovered my booth down at the Market a few months ago and suddenly I'm the talk of the jewelry world."

"The Market?"

"Pike Place. I've been peddling my wares there for the past five years or so. Decent enough living, but now I'll get to focus on designing and let somebody else sweat the selling."

"That's terrific. I'm so happy for you."

Ryan piped up, his mouth now full of my shrimp. "Nicole, this sauce is amazing. All it needs is a beer to wash it down. Where's that father-in-law of mine?"

As if on cue, Orion emerged from the basement door, amber bottles in hand. It was definitely he and not Star from whom Nova had inherited her plump frame. He was a bear of a man, tall and burly with a bushy head of brown hair and matching woolly beard. He had thickened over the years; his belly hung over his belted khaki shorts in an endearingly grandfatherly fashion. He came directly over to stand next to his wife, pinching her rear end after handing a beer to Ryan. "Miss me, woman?"

Star pinched his rear in rebuttal. "A little. Maybe you should go away again so I can be sure."

"Ha!" he exclaimed, taking a swig from his drink. He wiped his mouth with the back of his hand, bottle still between his fingers. "Nicole Hunter! A little bird told me we might see you here today."

"Hey, Orion." I hugged him, feeling in his arms what I always wished I had felt in my own father's: love, acceptance, safety. He smelled faintly of patchouli oil and, if I wasn't mistaken, the heavy whisper of marijuana. "My mom's here, too. Over with Jenny." I motioned my head in the direction of my family members and both of the Carsons moved over to talk with them. Nova came up to stand next to me, Layla over one shoulder, cooing softly.

"Hey, sweetie," I kissed at the infant, my finger gently fingering the amazingly soft skin of her chubby arm. Again, I experienced a stab of unexpected want. I did not know what to do with it. "How *are* you today? I've missed you!"

"Little bugger was up all night nursing like a fiend. I should have named her Hoover. Could you hold her for a while?" Nova handed the baby carefully to my arms. "I've got to get the chicken ready for the grill. Ryan?" She poked her husband in the ribs.

"Uh!" He chewed vigorously, then swallowed, sliding over to put a thick arm around his wife's shoulders. "What do you need, baby cakes?" He kissed her firmly on the lips. "Um-um-um, I have missed you!"

Nova laughed, a light, happy sound. "Me too, monkey-man. Now, help me get the grill ready."

"Yes, ma'am!" He lightly smacked her on the lips again. The two walked to the other side of the deck, playfully touching as they walked. I sighed longingly, the heavenly scent of their youngest daughter filling my senses as I breathed. I found a comfortable lounge chair in the shade of the white-limbed birch tree that grew in the back corner of their yard and settled there with Layla resting against my up-drawn legs, her head supported by my knees. She looked up at me with a wondrous gaze, slightly distracted, seemingly fascinated with the shapes of my face and the dappled sunlight dancing across my skin.

I wondered what Jenny's baby would see when she came into this world. Would she have the alert, sparkling and curious eyes that Layla did? Would her cheeks dimple when she smiled? Would she recognize me the way Layla seemed to each time I held her close? Would she have any idea who I was? "Can you see me, baby girl?" I asked her. "What do you see with those little blue eyes of yours?"

"She sees everything," a voice said, and I looked up against the sun to see Garret's silhouette standing before me. He motioned to the chair next to me. "May I?"

"Of course." I took him in out of the corner of my eye. He was wearing blue-checked shorts with a white T-shirt and Keds with no socks. His dark hair was a scattered mess around his head and his skin bore the fresh rosy glow of an active day spent in the sun. He reached his fingers to brush across Layla's perfect cheek.

"I think they see everything, don't you?" he asked. "Their eyes are so wise, like they know every secret you've ever kept. Even the ones you keep from yourself."

I nodded. "Jenny's like that, too. When she looks at you, you feel like you've just stepped behind an X-ray machine."

"Naked, inside and out, huh?"

"Exactly. It's a little unnerving sometimes." *So is he,* I thought.

"I'll bet." He paused. "How is she doing?"

"Good. I saw the baby jump in her belly today."

"Isn't that cool?"

"And kind of scary. It's pretty odd to think of an entire human body moving around inside her. A body that's going to come *out.*" I shuddered in sheer amazement at the thought.

Garret chuckled. "Jackie was freaked out by the whole thing, too."

I backpedaled, not wanting to be anything like the woman who left him. "I'm not freaked out, exactly. It's more like amazement that it's possible, you know? More like awe."

Garret threw a glance over to where Jenny sat, now surrounded by children. With my mother's help, Gracie had managed to climb into my sister's lap and was softly resting her ear on Jenny's belly. "It's definitely amazing. Is she going to be able to have a natural labor?"

"I'm not sure. Her doctor isn't sure whether Jenny'll have a natural urge to push." I shrugged. "And even if she does, we don't know whether she's got the ability to make her body do what it needs to to get the baby out."

"What's going to happen to the baby, once it's out?" He stopped himself, held his hands up defensively. "I'm sorry. That's a pretty personal question."

"No, it's okay. I don't mind. I'm still not sure what's going to happen. I was supposed to call Social Services weeks ago, but—"

"Why?" he interrupted, then grimaced. "Yikes. Never mind. More personal than before."

I smiled, touched his hand with my own. I felt his skin's warmth travel through my own body until it rested in my lower belly, a spot normally reserved for Shane. Flustered, I pulled away quickly, reflexively, as though I had touched a flame. "Really, it's okay. I need to talk about it. You've got as good a pair of ears as anyone's."

He screwed up his face at me. "Gee, thanks."

I laughed. "What I mean is, I like talking with you." I paused. "Is that okay?"

"What, that you talk to me or that you like it?"

I socked him playfully on the shoulder, careful not to upset the now-sleeping Layla. "Oh, boy, here we go. More teasing."

"You're living with someone," he said. The light in his hazel eyes suddenly dimmed, his tone became serious. "I don't want to be the cause of any more complications in your life. I've got Gracie to think about."

I eased back, resting Layla over my left shoulder, over my heart. Nova told me the other day that women instinctively place their babies over their hearts so the child can feel the remembered rhythm of the womb. And in that moment, I wanted it. I wanted to be a mother.

I stared up through the sparkling coin leaves of the birch. A small breeze brushed at my hair. "I know. I appreciate that. But honestly, I don't know what exactly is going on with Shane right now. We're barely communicating. Everything feels strange since I've been here." I turned my head toward Garret and he held my gaze in his eyes as though it were something precious. He was listening to me with such intent that I went on, sharing more than I typically felt comfortable revealing. "I feel like my life in San Francisco isn't real, you know? Like my job, my relationships all belong to someone else. It's Jenny and her baby who are real. Nova, her kids, our friendship." I paused and looked down to my lap, fearful of what I wanted to say but going ahead and doing it anyway. "Meeting you is real."

"I know what you mean." He touched my hand with the tips of his fingers with the same gentle caress he had used on Layla's cheek, and this time when the fire found my belly I didn't pull away. "I guess that's why I'm concerned. I like the looks of the road, but I don't want to travel down it if it goes off a cliff. I'm too old for that." His tone held a hint of bitterness and I wondered whether he'd worked through his feelings about Jackie's leaving.

"How about we just take it a step at a time, then?" I suggested. "Just a couple of new friends taking a stroll?"

He grinned. "We can turn around anytime, right? Part ways if need be?"

"Of course."

Gracie chose this moment to tear across the yard to her father and jump in his lap. "Daddy!"

He kissed her neck until she squealed. "What is it, Bug?"

"I sat on Jenny's lap. Did you see me?" Her dark cap of hair swished excitedly around her elfin face.

"Yes, honey. How is she?"

"She's all right," Gracie said with a measure of a sage beyond her years. "Her baby is jumpy inside her. She likes it."

I shook my head, looked at Garret inquiringly as if to ask, "Did you tell her?"

He shook his dark head back at me and shrugged. "Gracie, how did you know Jenny has a baby inside her?"

"I just did." She granted me a full-watt smile. "Daddy wants to take you and Jenny to the park next week for a picnic. He makes good sandwiches. Do you want to come?"

Garret ruffled her curls. "You beat me to it, Peanut." He smiled at me. "I was going to ask you later, after you'd had a few."

"Figured your chances might be better if I was liquored up?"

He actually blushed. "Now who's the tease?"

"We'd love to," I said, Shane's image popping up in my mind. I blinked to erase it. "Just tell me what I should bring."

"Jenny wants to feed the ducks with me!" Gracie exclaimed as she jumped up and down in the air in front of my sister's wheelchair. "Daddy, can I have the bread crumbs to feed the ducks? I want to feed the ducks!" She wore a lime green shorts set with buttons shaped like strawberries on her shirt. The outfit caught the green in her hazel eyes like a fly in a web.

"Okay, okay, Peanut. Settle down." Garret handed her a plastic bag full of stale bread pieces that we had picked up at his restaurant before heading over to Lincoln Park. "Here, you need to put your shoes back on."

"No, I'm fine." Gracie wiggled her bare corn-kernel-shaped toes in the grass.

Garret made his expression stern. "Gracie, listen to Daddy. If you're going to walk by the pond, you need to have your shoes on. Do you want duck poopies all over your feet?"

"Ewww! No!"

"Okay, then. Give me your feet so I can put your shoes on."

Amused, I watched this exchange between father and daughter from the comfort of my shady spot on our picnic blanket. Spending time with Nova and her kids had made me much more comfortable with the previously unknown and overwhelming world of toddlers. I'd figured out that they were simply little versions of grown people; they only wanted their needs heard and respected. Garret seemed to understand this about his daughter perfectly.

The pond was only a few feet away from us, so I felt comfortable when Garret carefully rolled Jenny's chair to a spot near the water. He checked to make sure the brakes were set securely on the wheels and that Jenny's wide-brimmed straw hat was adequately shading her pale skin from the bright glare of the early-afternoon sun. Gracie solemnly set a handful of crumbs on Jenny's lap. "Here are your bread crumbs, Jenny, and here are mine." She held up the bag for Jenny to see. "I will share more with you, if you want, but only when yours are all gone."

Garret plopped gratefully back next to me on the blanket, then called out to his daughter. "Gracie, you stay away from the edge, you hear me?"

"Okay, Daddy!" She took a deliberately large step backward and turned to see if Garret approved.

"That's great, Peanut."

"She is such a good kid," I remarked, sipping at the remainder of my iced tea. "Does she ever disobey you?"

He snickered. "Oh God, yes. You should see her at home. She's on her best behavior today, trying to impress you."

"Well, it's working. She's exactly how I dream a child should be." I paused, for effect. "Then, of course, there are Nova's kids."

Garret laughed outright. "They're a handful, aren't they? Managing four is much, much different than one. I don't know how she does it with Ryan away so often."

"Do you want more children?"

"If I find the right woman to be their mother, then yes, definitely."

"You seem to be doing fine on your own with Gracie."

He sighed, straightened his shorts, and then sat up to look at me, his forearms resting on bent knees. His baseball cap shrouded his handsome face in a dark shadow, making it almost impossible to see his eyes. "I think she'd be happier with a mother."

I adjusted my position on the blanket, tucking both my legs to one side under me and leaning on a straightened arm. "Why? She obviously adores you."

"Well, sure. How could she not?"

"Ha-ha. So *modest*."

"One of my better hidden qualities." He grinned, then continued. "But to answer your question, she's always asking me for one. She wants to know why she doesn't have a mommy like Rebecca has Nova. I mean, Nova's terrific—she's as close to an adoptive mommy as I could find—but I just think she needs someone all to herself. Her own mother."

"But not her *actual* mother." I shifted position again, sitting cross-legged beneath the skirt of the floral cotton dress I'd chosen to wear. I rested my elbows on my knees, fingers laced loosely together in front of me.

"Absolutely not. Jackie was not cut out for the job of taking care of a child."

"What job was she cut out for?"

"Taking care of Jackie."

I sucked the air in through my teeth, nodding. "Oh. I see."

"She told me she got pregnant because she thought it was what you were supposed to do when you got married, like it was the next ingredient in a recipe."

"Add baby, stir well?" I ventured.

Garret laughed. "Exactly." Then he sighed, wistful. "I thought she was the love of my life. She was this perfect package of a woman." Here he smiled wryly. "I guess that would have tipped a smarter man off. She just had this way of making me believe she was everything I'd ever need. Then, *pow!*" He made a fist with one hand and popped it into an open palm. "Flattened my heart like a Mack truck."

I brushed a stray red curl out of my line of vision. "Ouch."

"Yeah."

"Does she visit?"

"She pops up now and then. She gave me exclusive custody in the divorce settlement and didn't ask for visitation rights. Not that that surprised me."

"Do you even *talk* about her with Gracie?"

"As little as possible." He adjusted his hat, then looked at me, sidelong. "I suppose you think that makes me a terrible father."

I paused for a moment, considering this. I knew a little about terrible fathers, and from what I'd seen so far, Garret didn't even come close to being one. "Not necessarily. Silence seems like it would be healthier than bad-mouthing her."

"I hope so. Especially since what I'd have to say would be less than complimentary." He shrugged, as if to remove something itchy and uncomfortable from between his shoulder blades. A small gesture, but one that hinted at the wound left inside him. "I mostly tell Gracie that her mommy just has to live in another state, like her grandparents do. That's usually enough to satisfy her. For now, at least. I guess someday I'll have to find a way to explain that not everyone can handle being a parent. It's a tough gig."

I nodded. "I'm getting a taste of it with Jenny. I think I'm going to go nuts sometimes from how much taking care of her demands of me. It never stops. Even when I get a break, I don't really get to relax since she could need something from me at any moment."

"That's how it is with babies, too. It does get easier, though, as they get older. Gracie insists on doing so much for herself these days. . . ." He paused. "Do you want kids of your own?"

I hesitated, taking a moment to stretch my legs out straight in front of me. "That's something I've asked myself a lot, lately. I can't give you a simple answer."

"So give me a complicated one."

"Do you want to hear something *really* complicated? Something I haven't even told Nova?" I couldn't believe I was actually considering telling him what I'd barely even told myself. There was just something about him, something that made me feel safe.

"Sure, if you want."

I swallowed hard, resting my eyes over on Jenny, who was joyfully watching Gracie fling handfuls of bread crumbs into the dancing group of ducks on the water. I couldn't believe she was already seven months along, that two months had passed in the blink of an eye, the moments bleeding into each other like watercolors on a page. I was running out of time.

"I'm thinking about adopting Jenny's baby," I said, hopeful that if I made the words quiet enough, they wouldn't hold as much power out loud as they did in my head. Oddly, after they were spoken, I felt stronger than I had keeping them so tightly under wraps.

Garret leaned toward me, squeezed my hand quickly, then let go. "I think that's great."

"You do?" I was amazed.

"Yep."

"You don't think I'm out of my mind?"

He tilted his dark head toward one shoulder. "Why would I think that? You're related to that baby. Her blood is your blood. Of course you'd think about keeping her."

"But I'm still not sure. I don't know whether I could do it. Don't you think I should be sure about something like that? I'm terrified something might turn up wrong with her, the way it did with Jenny. All the tests have been negative so far, but you never know what might happen. Jenny was basically normal for almost two years before her disabilities really showed themselves."

"First of all," Garret began, turning his body toward mine. He quickly glanced toward the pond to check on his daughter before turning his gaze back to me and continuing. "No one is ever really sure about becoming a parent. I wasn't. I was terrified when Jackie was pregnant. I played the 'what if?' game till I thought I'd go nuts. What if she's got Down's syndrome? What if she doesn't have any feet? You can't believe the crazy stuff I came up with."

"No *feet*?" I threw my hands up in the air, joking. "Give me *more* to worry about, why don't you?"

Garret sucked his lower lip under the top row of his teeth. "Oops. Sorry. I was actually trying to make you feel better."

I laughed. "I know. It's all just really overwhelming, any way I look at it. The idea of being a single parent . . . Well, then I see you and Gracie and you seem to manage everything so smoothly, parenthood, career." I paused. "The restaurant is fabulous, by the way. I don't think I told you that. I really liked the feel of the place."

And I had. When we'd stopped there earlier to pick up the lunch he had prepared the night before, Garret had given me a quick tour. It was right on the beach, all of the tables had a view of the water through walls made entirely of sliding glass doors. The tables themselves were naked wicker with glass tops, their centers adorned by dew-fresh, bursting bouquets of sun-yellow roses and purple freesia. The chairs were high-backed, wicker as well, though heavily padded, looking to be the kind that were difficult to convince your body to move from once you were settled in for a meal. The kitchen was well-spaced and efficiently planned, with shining stainless steel appliances and countertops. I confirmed Nova's assessment of Garret's expectations for perfection with a large sign that hung over the wait staff's station. It read IF YOU'VE GOT TIME TO LEAN, YOU'VE GOT TIME TO CLEAN.

He smiled, obviously pleased. "Thanks. I've worked hard to make it that way. But my life doesn't go smoothly all of the time.

If I'm not taking care of Gracie, I'm taking care of some crisis at the restaurant. . . ." He threw his hands up in the air in a casual I-give-up gesture. "It doesn't leave much time for me. There are days I want to run away, screaming."

"What would you run away to?"

He shrugged. "I don't really know. Just away. Don't you ever feel like that?"

"Oh, yeah. It's a feeling I'm *very* well acquainted with. I've even indulged it a couple of times. That's how I ended up a baker with a master's degree."

"Daddy!" Gracie hollered in our direction, holding up the now-empty plastic bag. "We're all done!"

"Duty calls." Garret grinned, standing up and reaching a hand down to help me do the same. "I should probably get her home for a nap."

"I could use one myself." I rubbed my stomach. "You're a great cook. I am positively stuffed. I think I gained five pounds." We had eaten a glorious pasta salad filled with dark, juicy olives, roasted red peppers, and goat cheese, crusty French bread, plump purple grapes, and cream-cheese-swirled brownies. No crumbs remained.

"That's okay. I like a woman with some meat on her bones."

"Thanks a lot." I self-consciously sucked in my gut.

Garret moved the flat of his palm up and down my back, sending shivers to my scalp. I felt his eyes glide over my skin like a touch as he spoke. "I mean it. Any man in his right mind would be thrilled to curl up to someone like you."

I smiled shyly and tried to accept the compliment gracefully. "Well, thanks."

Garret kept his hand on the small of my back as we walked over to the pond. As we loaded Jenny and Gracie into his car and then for the entire drive home, a stupid grin plastered itself on my face. I knew it was silly, I knew I was stepping into dangerous emotional territory, but I simply could not help but savor that this amazing man had closed his eyes and imagined the feel of his body next to mine.

❖   ❖   ❖

The next morning I sat at Nova's kitchen table, my forehead resting in open hands. Jenny was in the living room on the couch watching a *Sesame Street* video; after all these years Grover still made her smile. Nova's older children played outside while Layla slept in the swing near Jenny, her chubby infant neck squished against her chest in a way that made me worry she'd have a hard time breathing. But Nova assured me that the baby was fine, that all babies slept that way until they gained better head control.

"What am I *doing* with this guy?" I groaned to my friend. I had barely slept the night before, replaying the time I had spent with Garret at the park. I was giddy as a schoolgirl.

"What do you *want* to do with him?" Nova asked wickedly as she reached for a couple of coffee mugs from the cupboard above the stove and poured us both a cup. She was barefoot and wore a scoop-necked ocean blue linen dress, princess cut and tied in the back to accent her hourglass shape. The rise of her fleshy bottom pushed at the material as she moved, swishing the skirt around her legs in a fluid motion. Her lush figure looked like something to aspire to; it made me proud to be a woman.

I groaned again. "That's a horrible question. Not that you don't already know the answer."

"Hmmm, let me see." Nova tapped her index finger to the side of her face in mock contemplation. "What would you possibly want to do with Garret? Go grocery shopping with him? Do his *laundry*, perhaps?"

I wadded up a napkin and threw it at her. "Stop it."

She grinned as she set a steaming cup of black liquid in front of me, then poured in a quick shot of half-and-half. I watched the cauliflower explosion of cream with great interest, waiting until the drink became the perfect shade of taupe. There was something comforting in having her know the exact color my coffee should be. Whatever part of me grieved for the loss of a normal sister relationship with Jenny also thanked the stars for blessing me with Nova.

I blew on the hot fluid, then took a small sip, holding the cup with both hands. "So, am I just indulging a childish fantasy?"

"I don't know. Are you?" She stood at the counter, one ankle crossed over the other, sipping at her own drink.

"Could you stop asking me more questions and give me some advice here, please?"

"What do you want me to tell you, that it's okay to sleep with him because things are shaky with Shane?" She shrugged. "Sorry, chick. Not gonna happen."

I set down my coffee. "I didn't say I want to sleep with him. . . ."

Nova held up her hand to stop me. "Please."

"I didn't! It's just— We had such a great time yesterday. He listens to me. He barely knows me and he's interested in how I feel and what I think and what I want. It's very flattering."

"Hmm," she murmured, contemplating.

"I found myself picturing him holding our baby, for Christ's sake. I've never *once* done that with Shane. I feel like I'm already cheating on him and I haven't even *done* anything."

"So now you not only want to sleep with him, you want to have his baby?"

I paused, stuck my finger in my coffee to stir it around. "Maybe not his baby." I looked up at her. "Maybe Jenny's baby."

Nova set her cup noisily on the white tile counter and came over to sit by me, her expression a blend of confusion and concern. "I thought motherhood wasn't in the plan for you."

"I thought so, too. I'm reconsidering, I guess." I swallowed before continuing. "I just can't stand the thought of handing her over to some stranger to raise. She's my sister's child, you know? I can't stop thinking that I'm supposed to take care of her."

"The way you wished you'd taken care of Jenny before you left?"

I paused, considering this. "Maybe. I don't know."

Nova puffed up her cheeks and exhaled loudly. "I wish you'd stop feeling like you have something to make up for with Jenny. You have been busting your butt the past couple of months."

"And that makes up for years of neglect?"

"You neglected me and I don't feel like you need to make up for anything."

I sighed. "That's different."

She shifted on the bench, leaning her back against the edge of the table as she crossed her legs. "Why?"

"It just is. I didn't abandon you in an institution where you ended up getting raped." I shook as emotion welled up in the muscles of my chest and took control of my words. "And for what? What is so extraordinary about my life that my sister had to be raped for it?" Tears threatened my voice. "And I just can't stop thinking about it, you know? How she must have felt, what she must have been thinking with that horrible man on top of her. . . . How it must have reminded her—" A shuddering breath escaped me. "Did she cry? Did he hold his hand over her mouth so no one would hear? God, how it must have *felt* to her with no one to protect her. No one to tell what had happened. *Again*." I was weeping now and Nova grabbed my hands, her eyes glazed with tears.

"Listen to me," she said, her round chin trembling. "You can't control the world. The men who hurt her are not your responsibility. Punishing yourself is not going to make up for what they did. And adopting Jenny's baby just to relieve your guilt is a pretty empty reason for becoming a mother."

"I know," I agreed, pulling my hands from her grasp. "But I can't get it out of my mind that I'm supposed to do it." I wiped my eyes with the back of my hand and sipped nervously at my drink. "Do you have any chocolate? Caffeine isn't cutting it."

"Does the Pope have a Bible?" She jumped up and opened the freezer, pulling out a quart of double fudge ice cream. "Bowls?"

I shook my head. "No."

She grabbed a couple of spoons from the drawer beneath the sink and set the tub between us on the table, glancing out the back door. "If the kids catch me doing this, I'll never hear the end of it. It's barely nine o'clock."

I dug out a bite and slid it into my mouth, the cold strangely pleasing after the heat of my coffee. After a couple more bites and several deep breaths, the tension that had rattled my core slowly began to dissipate. I looked up to see Nova staring out the window, checking on the kids as they played in the backyard. I found myself suddenly envious of her life. "What made you realize you were ready to be a mother?" I asked her.

She moved her gaze back to me, took a bite of ice cream, then smiled, her mouth still full as she spoke. "The stick turned blue when I peed on it."

I choked on the ice cream as I laughed. "Really. I want to know."

"It's true!" she insisted. "With Isaac, at least. If you remember my telling you, he wasn't exactly planned. Ryan and I wanted to be married a while before having kids, but a couple months after the wedding I started feeling pukey in the mornings and voilà: Welcome to parenthood."

"What's it like?"

"Being a mother, you mean?"

I nodded, quickly dipping the next bite of ice cream into my coffee for a touch of mocha flavor.

"It's the absolute greatest thing that has ever happened to me. All the clichés you hear about it having the biggest rewards and the most difficult challenges?"

I nodded again, my mouth full.

"Absolutely true. There are moments of utter joy balanced only by hours of excruciating terror."

"Terror? You? Come on. You're great with your kids."

"Not all the time, babe. It's not a pretty sight when I lose it. However passionately you love your babies, there are moments you dislike them just as much."

"So you're saying it's not easy."

"Far from easy. But let me tell you, the other moments, the ones when you're rocking them to sleep and they look up at you with your own eyes and smile . . ." She shook her head fondly. "There ain't nothing in the world like it. Then they reach up for your hand when you're taking them for a walk and they don't even look up to see if your hand is there. They just know it will be. . . ." Nova's words sputtered a bit as she spoke and a fine mist veiled her eyes. She waved fluttery fingers in front of her face. "Oy. Look at me. All worked up."

"I'm sorry."

"No, no, it's okay." She scooped another bit of ice cream into her mouth. "It's the best thing I've ever done, Nicole. I wouldn't trade it for the world. Even on the bad days." The patter of feet on the back steps interrupted us, and Nova rushed to return our dessert to the freezer.

Rebecca stomped in through the door, her eyes hawklike on her mother. "Can I have some ice cream too, Mom?"

Nova looked at me like, "See what I mean?" then shook her head at her daughter. "Sorry, honey."

"How come you get to have it and I don't?"

"That's the way of the world, my sweet. You can have a yogurt."

"I don't want a yogurt. I want ice cream." Rebecca stubbornly stomped her sandaled foot. I tried not to laugh out loud.

"Well, I want to be a size six, but that just ain't gonna happen, now is it?" Nova reached into the fridge and pulled out a carton of lemon yogurt. "Do you want this?"

"No!"

"All right, then. Do you want something else?"

"Ice cream."

"Oh, all right. Fine." She snatched the container back out from the freezer and handed it to her daughter, along with three spoons. "Take it outside, then, and be sure to share it with your brothers, you hear me? I don't want to hear any fighting over this or I'm putting it away. Okay?"

Rebecca lit up on her tiptoes, smiling widely. "Okay, Mama! Thank you!" She rushed over and hugged her mother's legs in a quick motion before racing back out the door.

"Way to stand your ground there, Nova." I teased.

"Yeah, well, lesson number one of motherhood: choose your battles. This was one I didn't feel like fighting."

"And lesson number two?"

She reached into the freezer, pulled out another container, and dropped it between us. "Always—and I mean *always*—have more ice cream."

*J*ack Waterson's office was on the fifteenth floor of the Columbia Tower. At his request, I arrived for our first official appointment with my mother and Jenny in tow. He wanted to meet Jenny, whom he called his "true client," as well as the guardian of whatever settlement monies he managed to get from Wellman.

Mr. Waterson greeted us at the double doors of his private office. A ruddy-skinned man with an average build, he wore a slightly rumpled blue suit with no tie. When he smiled, wiry black brows pushed toward a receding hairline. His handshake was firm and reassuring and I was heartened by his approach to Jenny, how he carefully rested his fingers on her forearm and said hello. "Please, make yourself comfortable. Can I have my assistant get you anything? Water, coffee?"

"No, thanks," Mom and I said at the same time.

Mr. Waterson settled into the well-padded burgundy leather swivel chair behind his cherry wood desk, resting intertwined fingers on the blotter in front of him. The room was unapologetically male, full of dark wood walls, oil paintings depicting Eng-

lish fox hunt scenes, and the distinctive scent of Old Spice. It encouraged you to sit down with a good cigar and sip a well-aged
Scotch.

"Well," Mr. Waterson began, "thank you for coming. I have
good news to begin with. The police believe they have found Mr.
Zimmerman's last residence in Portland. He left there only a
week ago. They're pretty sure he'll be found soon."

"That is good news," I said, watching Jenny for any reaction
to her rapist's name. I wondered if she knew who he was, if she
remembered what he had done to her. Her eyes, however, remained riveted on the deer head mounted above the small brick
fireplace on the other side of the room and I could not tell what
she was thinking.

"Do you have any idea how much time he'll get?" my mother
asked, leaning forward in her chair, her foot wiggling nervously.
Since the day of Jenny's screaming fit she'd reached out more
often to my sister but seemed uncomfortable being involved in
anything further than giving Jenny a shower or feeding her dinner. I figured she still felt guilty about not fully admitting what
she knew my father had done.

"Unfortunately, no," Mr. Waterson told us. "There's just no
way to tell ahead of time what a judge will decide about sentenc-
ing. It's a complicated case. Even when they do find him, there's
the matter of proving that it was him who did this to your daughter. Since she can't be a witness, the prosecutor will have to rely
on more technical evidence to back up what we already know cir-
cumstantially: that he was the only male with regular, unsuper-
vised access to Jenny at the time she became pregnant."

"What kind of technical evidence?" I inquired.

"DNA, most likely, after the baby is born. If the baby is a
match to Mr. Zimmerman, that'll pretty much end the defense's
case."

"I see." I nodded. "Will we be notified when they find him?"

"The detectives working the case will call me and I'll contact
you immediately." He pushed his round head forward, urging his
body to follow. Forearms resting on his desk, he shuffled through
a stack of papers. "Now, about the civil case. Negotiations are

going well; I started our claim at seven million and Wellman's lawyers are up to four already. I'm required to present their offer of this to you, but honestly, I think they'll go higher."

"Four million dollars?" my mother gasped. "They've already offered that much even though Mr. Zimmerman hasn't been proven guilty?"

"Oh, yes. They know their institution will be held liable no matter who committed the crime. If it was one of their employees, they're liable. If they let a nonemployee gain access to Jenny, they're liable. They, as an institution, are guilty, and they know it."

"What about their hiring policies?" I asked. "Can we insist on an investigation?"

"That can be part of the settlement, yes. But I have to say on their behalf, they've already stepped up to the plate for it. They hired an outside firm to go over their background check routine. The fact remains, however, that even after close scrutiny, Mr. Zimmerman came up clean. His recommendations as a caregiver were glowing from every other place he worked. What happened with Jenny was either a first-time occurrence or Mr. Zimmerman was extremely good at hiding his offenses."

My blood heated in my veins. "What a bastard."

"Well, yes," Mr. Waterson agreed. "So, I just need you both to sign some paperwork today and I'll continue the talks with Wellman. Is there a specific amount you'd like to see Jenny get?"

"I wouldn't know what would be realistic to expect," Mom said. "I just want her to be well taken care of and not have to worry about the cost ever again."

Mr. Waterson nodded, gravely. "Of course. Have you been to visit any of the homes my assistant researched?"

Mom looked at me and I shook my head. "I've called a couple but their waiting lists are years long. We need something by September, October at the latest."

"Oh!" our lawyer exclaimed. "I almost forgot. I know that you, Mrs. Hunter"—waving his hand toward Mom—"are the guardian to Jenny right now, but have you thought about what you'd like to do when you no longer want or are no longer capable of managing her trust?"

"I'd like Nicole to take over as guardian," Mom said, glancing at me hesitantly. "If that's all right with you."

I paused for just a moment before speaking. I'd come this far in caring for my sister; it made sense for me to take this next step. "Okay with you, Jen?" I said, reaching out to place my hand on her gnarled fingers.

"Arrugh," she said, a positive lilt to the sound. She still stared at the deer head as though it might jump off the wall and come say hello to her.

I nodded at our lawyer. "Where do I sign?"

Mr. Waterson smiled with genuine indulgence. "All right, then, we're all set. I'll go back to Wellman with an asking price of six million, which I'm pretty sure they'll agree to. If not, I'll go to five, assuming, of course, that that amount is acceptable to you both."

After Mom and I agreed that this was a more than acceptable amount, we signed the necessary paperwork and headed home. The sun was masked by a thin stretch of clouds, though it was still bright enough to demand sunglasses. The heat was a heavy thing, a lid pressing down on the city. A sure sign of an impending storm.

"He seemed like a trustworthy man," Mom remarked as we drove up and over the West Seattle Bridge.

"Not what you'd expect from a lawyer, huh?" I answered.

She laughed. "Well, my only experience with lawyers was with the ones who managed my divorce, so I guess my frame of reference is a bit limited."

"Did Dad make it a difficult process?"

"Not really. He agreed to alimony and continued support of Jenny's care, which is more than I expected." She sighed, crinkling her almond eyes as she changed lanes to take the Admiral Way exit. "I've called him several times, you know, to tell him about what's happened, but he's never answered."

"What a surprise," I remarked blandly.

"Anyway!" Mom said brightly, obviously wanting to change the subject. "Can you believe what we'll be getting for Jenny? Five million dollars! Less than that, of course, after Mr. Waterson's fees, but how wonderful it will be to not have to worry about the cost of her care!"

I sighed. "Yeah, it's wonderful." What wasn't so wonderful was the task that lay ahead of me now. It was time to find Jenny a new place to live.

*T*he drive to the home in La Connor would take over an hour from Nova's house, so by nine in the morning she, Star, and I had strapped Jenny and Layla into their respective car seats in Nova's minivan, leaving Ryan with his other children for the day. We last saw him loosely tied to the red cedar in their front yard with Rebecca leading her brothers in a war dance around their smiling prisoner. Since Mom had to work, I had asked Nova and Star to come along with me for moral support. I also wanted to bring Jenny, to gauge her reaction to this home as best I could.

The Sunshine House was the last on the short list Mr. Waterson had given us. There was a larger home in Spokane with an opening, but a six-hour drive was farther away than Mom wanted her, so I hadn't even bothered going to visit it. Despite the bits of help Mom was providing with Jenny at home, she was still leaving the search for a new placement up to me. She asked only that Jenny be as close as possible to home. "I trust you," she had said. "You'll find something."

I resented having this daunting task left entirely up to me; part of me wanted to demand that she just keep Jenny with her at home. Money wouldn't be an issue; she could quit her job at the bank. Then the rational side of my brain pointed out that taking care of Jenny wasn't just a financial matter. It was an emotional and physical drain, and as I'd realized before, my mother had already gone through the complicated process of disentangling herself from enmeshment with Jenny; I doubted she wanted to go through it again.

I took on the search for Jenny's new home with deliberate intent. Earlier in the week I had visited the one residence on the list that was within the Seattle city limits. It had seemed the most promising; when the director gave me the historic Fremont District address I felt hopeful, picturing a quaint home trimmed in black filigree ironwork, a yard edged with antique roses and towering, century-old rhododendrons. I was not far off in my physical estimate. When I pulled up in front of the home, I was immediately drawn to its Victorian style. *What a perfect place for Jenny,* I thought, as I entered through gleaming white French doors. The walls in the entryway were bright but classy with a mural depicting a field of wildflowers. The furniture was all plush and clean, the windows open to let a fresh breeze blow through the gauzy white drapes.

I stepped a short distance into the living room, where the flash of cartoons played noisily on the large television set, around which sat three wheelchair-bound individuals, their eyes glazed and empty, their hands twisted together like tree roots. One girl had a small patch of macaroni and cheese upon her chest waiting to be wiped up. Unable to help myself, I went over to her and picked the noodles off, setting them on top of the television. I smoothed her light brown hair back from her face and one side of her sagging mouth lifted into the hint of a smile.

"Excuse me, can I help you with somethin'?" a loud voice boomed from across the room.

I whipped around to face a large black woman with an abundance of long beaded braids. "I'm Nicole Hunter," I stated firmly. "I spoke with Ms. Perlman about the placement opening?"

"Ms. Perlman's the director. She don't come in 'cept on Monday mornings." She pointed to the discarded pasta. "What's that up there?"

I straightened my spine. "This girl had it on her shirt."

The woman nodded and came toward us. She pulled a rag from her pants pocket and wiped the girl's face with what seemed to me a rough motion.

"So," I said, anxious to get on with things, "Ms. Perlman told me I could visit anytime."

The woman looked skeptical. "Is that right?" But after a brief pause, a small light went off in her eyes. "Wait a minute. I think she might have said somethin' 'bout your comin'. You got a sister?"

"Yes." I glanced down a hall that seemed to lead to the kitchen. "Are you the only staff person at the moment?"

"Yup. My name's Irene." She checked on the girls in their chairs, wiping the drool from one's chin and sniffing another's lap for evidence of the need for a diaper change. Apparently satisfied with their respective states, she turned back to me. "Let me show you around."

I followed Irene through the house. There were three bedrooms with two hospital beds in each tight space; two of the beds were occupied with the curled, silent figures of the other residents. The walls were painted white with a few colorful *Sesame Street* posters tacked here and there in the hallway. The one bathroom was clean but crowded and the kitchen was a skinny rectangle, its countertops scattered with unwashed dishes. There was a chart on the refrigerator marking the residents' medications as well as a sparse schedule of planned activities, which I noticed hadn't been updated since the month of May.

Everything was clean enough, but I got such a feeling of emptiness as I looked around. There were no family pictures, no evidence of any of the girls' personalities. Despite its warm exterior, the house seemed to lack a heart. Also, with room for six residents, it seemed to lack sufficient staff.

"Irene?" I called out.

She lumbered into the kitchen. "Yes, ma'am?"

"Are you a registered nurse?"

"A nurse's aide, ma'am."

"How many people are employed here?"

She lifted her chin and counted silently to herself. "Six, altogether, including me."

"And how often are you alone with all of the residents?"

"Just during the lunch break for the rest of the staff."

"Every day?"

"Yes, ma'am."

"I see."

"This here's a hard job, takin' care of these girls. Hard to find good people for the pay." She sounded defensive.

"I'm sure." I held my hand out for her to shake. "Well, thank you. I've seen all I need to."

"Should I tell Ms. Perlman that you'll be callin'?"

I turned down the hallway to the front door. "No, Irene. I wouldn't tell her that."

I'd wept a little when I told Mom about the house, knowing it was on par with most of what was out there. "It was just so impersonal," I said dejectedly. "I'm afraid it'd remind Jenny of Wellman." After this, Mom couldn't meet my gaze, the guilt she felt for putting Jenny in a place where she ended up getting raped stifled the air between us. I wondered if that was the only abuse she felt guilty about.

That night I had dreamed of my niece in an institution like Wellman, lying helplessly alone in a metal-barred crib, crying out for someone to hold her, busy nurses rushing past, too overwhelmed by the weight of their profession to stop and give comfort.

I saw myself standing next to the crib as this infant wept—her tiny form a dark-haired, blue-eyed miniature copy of my angel sister. Her petal-pink lips moved in slow motion, forming a word that my heart immediately recognized. "Mama," she cried, her eyes glued to me, as though she had finally given me my rightful name. But when I reached my arms out to lift her to my chest, an unseen hand dragged me away.

I was unable to touch her, unable to claim this child who so obviously needed me. With this image I awoke and my heart ached with such great force, such intense longing that I was afraid it might fall right out of my chest. The dream stuck with me on our journey to La Connor, to the home that I hadn't visited first because of the drive.

"Now, this place has a staff nurse, right?" Star inquired, as we drove along, the morning light bouncing off the many silver strands that hung around her neck. She wore a loose dress the color of flax and a bright red pair of Birkenstock sandals. Her toenails were painted fluorescent blue.

"Three, actually," I replied, scanning the map for the exit to Anacortes the home's director had told me to take. "One of them is always there. Plus there are five part-time aides, so with only three residents, the ratio is pretty good." I folded the map. "I think we're supposed to get off here."

"Do they have an opening for Jenny?" Nova asked as she signaled to leave the freeway.

"No, but one of the current residents is in the hospital right now, not doing very well. Her doctors aren't very optimistic. I feel terrible checking the place out on the chance that she might not make it, but—"

"If you don't, someone else will," Star commented.

"What about a waiting list?" Nova asked.

"There isn't one. It's a fairly new home. The director told me that very few people know about it. I guess Mr. Waterson's assistant knew someone who lives in La Connor and told her about it when it opened last fall."

"Kismet," Star commented. "Honey," she continued, addressing her daughter, "turn left up here at the light."

"I see that, Mom. There's a very large sign that says LA CONNOR. But thanks." She rolled her eyes toward her hairline.

Star saw the movement in the rearview mirror and tapped the back of Nova's seat with her foot. "Be nice," she instructed, her voice edged in warning. The air suddenly felt tense, as I sensed the same unease between Nova and Star that I often felt with my own mother.

"Still hate backseat drivers, huh, Nova?" I joked, trying to lighten the mood in the van.

"Backseats are only good for one thing," Nova said, smiling. "We learned that in high school, right, Nic?"

"Along with a few other things," I answered.

Star covered her ears. "Please. I don't need to hear this." She grimaced. "I may be hip, but I'm still your mother."

"Please. Like you don't know how I ended up with four kids."

"I'd rather not think about it, thank you."

"How *did* you end up with four kids?" I asked, laughing more.

"Easy. I'm a slut." Nova and I both roared at her joke and even Star couldn't help but join us. Jenny giggled at us all, and Layla cooed and smiled, batting at the colorful toys that hung over her car seat. The tension in the vehicle had lifted, suddenly upbeat and oddly out of sync with the purpose of our trip.

I sighed, still laughing a bit. "I envy you, you know that?" I twisted to look at Star. "You, too. Both of your marriages are so great."

"Ha!" Star and Nova snorted at the same time, sounding so alike their relation suddenly became apparent.

"What do you mean, 'ha?' You and Orion have been together how long, thirty years almost? And you and Ryan seem so close, Nova. I don't know how you do it."

Star reached up to touch my elbow. "You don't think thirty years has been all candlelight and flowers, do you? Because it definitely has not."

"And popping out a baby every few months is not exactly fuel for the romantic fires," Nova added. "Seems like every time I'd actually get up the energy to do it, Ryan'd knock me up and *poof!* 'No Sex in the Suburbs.'"

I laughed again, wistful. "I know. I guess I just wonder how it is to connect—I mean *really* connect—with someone. The right someone."

"Seems like I saw some connecting going on with that Garret fellow at the barbecue," Star commented knowingly. I wondered what Nova had told her about us.

I blushed, tucking my curls behind both ears. "Well, yeah, maybe, but I guess what I mean is how do you make it last? How do you stay together through the times when you *don't* connect?"

My thoughts fled to Shane as I considered whether we had ever actually connected on any level other than the physical.

"I think it's really about expectations," Star said. "If you expect to connect all of the time, you're doomed."

Nova whistled. "Watch out, Dr. Laura. Star Carson is on the air." She followed the curve of the road onto the short main strip of downtown La Connor.

"Nova," I groaned, shifting my body to look at my friend's mother. "Star, that was very helpful. Thank you."

"It was, Mom," Nova relented. "I also happen to agree with you."

"Well, will wonders never cease?" Star smiled. She looked out the window. "Here's the street we're looking for."

"Okay, Mom!" Nova tooted the horn, obnoxiously. "Got it!"

"Just trying to help," Star said, crossing her arms over her chest, her tone defensive.

"Well, give it a rest," Nova said, turning the steering wheel. It was good to see another person get so easily annoyed with her mother. It almost made me feel normal.

We pulled up in front of a boxy, two-story gray house with white shutters and a wraparound porch. A wide ramp served as entrance to the double front doors, so Star and I didn't have any trouble getting Jenny inside. Nova stayed in the car to nurse Layla, promising to join us soon.

When we entered, a short, stocky woman of what I guessed to be Latino descent approached us from behind a small desk. She wore violet-hued polyester pants and a matching nurse's smock with sensible white orthopedic shoes.

"Hello," she said, sticking out her hand. "You must be the Hunters."

"Two of us are," I answered, introducing myself, Jenny, and Star.

She bobbed her dark head sharply in our direction. "Did you have any trouble finding us?"

I shook my head. I had been expecting the director. "Is Ms. Navarro here today?"

"I'm Natalie Navarro." Her "r's" had a slight purring sound.

She gestured to her appearance. "I'm also a nurse a few hours a day. Shall I give you the tour?"

"Please." I held my breath as she led us through the house, fearful that the next corner would reveal the darkness I had been expecting, the stench that I believed accompanied all residences such as these. But all I found was orderly, professional surroundings edged by personal touches of photo galleries and stuffed animals. The two other residents were female, both with their own rooms on the first floor. The other room would be Jenny's; it was a small, square space with a large window that looked out into the backyard. There were two bathrooms, both well equipped with safety measures. Upstairs was Ms. Navarro's office, along with an extra bedroom and half bath for the nurses to share. The kitchen was set up family-style, a long white picnic table along the wall opposite the countertop and sink. The girls' wheelchairs would roll easily up to the table to eat. There was a television in the living room; one girl sat on the slightly worn couch watching a *Sesame Street* video. Nova joined us there; Layla slept peacefully in the sling. I smiled vaguely at her, and when she gripped my hand in her own, I did not let go.

"We encourage music therapy with movement," Ms. Navarro said as we came to a halt next to the front door. "Art therapy, too. There is a reading hour every day, as well." She stepped over to the resident on the couch and adjusted the pillows around her lolling head to be of better support, then kissed the top of the girl's head.

"Where's the other resident right now?" Star asked, her hand resting on Jenny's shoulder.

"Outside for physical therapy," Ms. Navarro replied. "We try to get the girls out for at least a couple of hours a day if it's not raining."

We followed her down a narrow hallway out the back door, then down another ramp to a covered patio area. A small grass area edged the cement and a high wooden fence lined the entire yard. There were several thickly padded mats on the ground, one of which had a resident on it. A nurse worked the range of motion for the girl's legs. Her touch seemed efficient, but gentle.

Jenny looked at the girl with awe. She had clawed hands similar to Jenny's and a head that drooped forward to her chest while the rest of her body looked like a tightly bound pile of rubber bands. "What do you think, Jen?" I asked nervously.

"Ahhh," she groaned, perhaps with a touch of apprehension.

"It's not quite what I expected," I said.

"I'd imagine not," Ms. Navarro concurred. "I know the flaws of most other homes; we aspire to a much higher standard of care. Residents are always supervised here, never left alone except when they are sleeping."

"What about male nurses? Or visitors?" Nova asked the question she knew I wanted to.

"We can't exclude male nurses from applying to work here, but so far, none have. My staff is very happy and I don't expect to replace anyone anytime soon. As for visitors, no man is allowed to be alone with any resident except the one he is related to." She tucked her hair behind her ears. "Would you like to join us for lunch?"

We agreed to stay, though I spent less time eating and more reading Jenny's reaction to her surroundings. She seemed to relax around the table, emitting short, happy yelps along with one of the other girls. It was almost as though they were holding a conversation. By the time we left, I was emotionally exhausted but fairly settled on placing her there. I told Ms. Navarro to let me know when a room became available, and she assured me, sadly, that it looked like it might be soon.

We were a quiet bunch as Nova drove along until Star spoke up. "It wasn't exactly a beautiful place, but I don't think you could do much better. The staff seems very caring."

"I know," I sighed. "It's just so hard, imagining leaving her again."

"You're not leaving her," Nova observed. "You're moving her to a place where she'll get the kind of care she needs and you can continue with your life. You can go see her whenever you want."

"I'm going to have to," I said, something rising up in me, filling me with resolve. "I'm going to have to take the baby to visit her."

Nova shot me a stunned look before wrenching her attention back to the road. "Excuse me?" she exclaimed, hands gripping the steering wheel.

"I'm going to adopt her baby." My eyes filled with tears, my heart bursting with the knowledge of doing the right thing. "I'm going to be a mother." I looked back at my sister as I said this, but she was already asleep, tired from the unusual exertion of the day's outing.

"Nicole!" Star exclaimed. "That's wonderful! How long have you been thinking about this?"

"I don't know." I shrugged shakily. "I guess some part of me knew I'd do it since the day I got here." I looked at Nova, who was darting probing looks at me while negotiating traffic. She was smiling deliriously even as a hint of apprehension danced in her eyes. "I promise," I went on, "I've thought about it long and hard and I'm not doing this out of guilt. I want to be this baby's mother. I think I just needed to know that Jenny would be okay before I could decide for sure, you know? I knew I couldn't take care of them *both*." I laughed a little before continuing, a slightly hysterical edge to the sound. "It's so strange, but I feel like I already know this kid. Like she chose Jenny to carry her so I could be the one to raise her. She's been talking to me." I told them about my dream, then swallowed to push down the tight knot in my throat. "Is that the craziest thing you've ever heard?"

Nova wove through the lanes to the shoulder of the highway. "No, it's the most *beautiful* thing I've ever heard! Oh, sweetie! I'm so happy you decided to do it. I knew you would." After shifting the van into park, she unbuckled her seat belt and threw her arms around me. "You are *such* an amazing woman." She turned teary eyes to Jenny in the backseat. "Do you know what an amazing sister you have, Jen?"

Still asleep, Jenny appeared unimpressed.

I laughed. "Well, we'll see how amazing I am."

"What do you mean?" Nova asked, wiping at her eyes.

"I still have to tell Shane." I sighed, leaned my forehead against the cool glass of the window, and pictured giving him the news. And try as I might, the only vision that filled my head was of his back as he walked away, leaving me for good.

I was sixteen the first time my father left us. I came home from school one Friday afternoon to find my mother bent over the kitchen table, her long dark hair hanging around her face like a shroud. Her shoulders shook silently. The cheerful sounds of *Sesame Street* sang loudly from the living room, where Jenny usually sat this time of day.

"Mom?" I said hesitantly. I set my backpack on the floor and moved over to set my hand on her back. "Mom?"

She looked up to me, her eyes red-rimmed and swollen with tears. The corners of her lips dug deep into the flesh of her chin as she tried to speak. "He . . . he's . . ."

My insides rattled against each other. "He's what, Mom?"

She tried again. "He's leaving."

"Who's leaving?" She shook her head and gestured to the hall connecting their bedroom to the kitchen. I stepped slowly, deliberately to their doorway, saw the closet open and half empty; a stray red-striped tie lingered alone on a hanger. It was the tie I had given him for Father's Day when I was eight and didn't know yet that most redheads couldn't wear red. My father stood next to the bed, stuffing a suitcase with fistfuls of underwear. He stopped when he saw me, his expression wild and scared.

"What are you doing, Dad?"

"Packing." He directed his attention back to his task, scanning the dresser for anything he might have missed.

Oddly, panic, instead of elation, danced in my belly. "Do you have a work trip?" He sometimes traveled to other cities to work on housing developments.

"No." He looked at me again, his pale skin flushing brightly pink.

"What, then?"

"Ask your mother."

"But—"

"I *told* you to ask your mother."

I went back to the kitchen, my heart rolling over in my chest.

I stood by the sink, tapping my foot on the worn linoleum. "What happened, Mom?"

She shook her head again, face in her hands. It felt as though a huge purple elephant was sitting in the middle of our house, crushing the rafters, knocking over walls, tearing down the very foundation of my family's home, and still she was silent. I wanted to yank the words from her throat, to be given some sort of explanation. I thought I deserved at least that.

When Dad came into the kitchen a moment later, he carried two suitcases and a duffel bag was slung over his shoulder. He set the luggage down next to my mother, stood tall next to her, staring at a spot above the refrigerator, not at his wife. "You're sure, Joyce? This is what you want?"

She shot him a look brimming with anger and pleading. "It certainly is not what I want. It's what you want. It's always been what you want. I want you to stay. I want us to be a normal family."

"That's not possible. There's nothing more we can do for her."

My mother grabbed his hands. "We can be her parents. We can love her. You love her, Mark. I know you do."

My father's intensely blue eyes—the eyes that he had passed on to the daughter he could not stand to call his own—were blank. His silence said more than any words ever could. It wrapped up his resolve and handed it to my mother like a broken gift. He gently extricated his fingers from her grasp and picked up his luggage. He didn't even look at me as he walked out the back door.

My mind bubbled with questions. What would we do? Where would we get money? Would my mom get a job? Would I have to quit school and stay home with Jenny? I looked to my mother for answers.

"What are we going to do, Mom?" I felt a strange mixture of excitement and terror at my father's departure: the child in me curled into a dark corner, whimpering for her daddy, the adult who had only begun to blossom in my being shouting a thankful hallelujah. I was not sure to whom I should listen.

My mother stared at me, wiped at her wet cheeks with the back of her hand. "We're going to do what we always do. We're going to make dinner." She stood, tucked her hair defiantly behind her ears. "Could you please go get your sister?"

And so I did. We made dinner, ate it, cleaned up, and went to bed. Life went on as usual for weeks. But for however much I despised my father, our house felt empty without him in it. I hated the part of me that missed him, the part that loved him despite everything I knew him to be. Or maybe it was everything I knew him *not* to be. I hated the searching look Jenny gave to his favorite chair, the murmur of *Daddy?* that flowed through my blood every day he was gone. How could she possibly miss him? I knew my mother did. She was unusually quiet, caring for Jenny and the house in her typical way, but seemingly disjointed, uneven, uncomfortable in her skin.

I did not know if my parents spoke during this time. I only knew that a month later, I came home one morning from spending the night at Nova's house to find him back in his chair, reading the paper as though he had never left. He crunched the paper down into his lap, smiled at me, and I felt the urge to growl like an angry dog, protecting her turf.

No matter how much I pressed her, my mother would not tell me why he had come back or, for that matter, why, knowing what he was doing to Jenny, she had let him. And I hated her for it. The wall around my heart grew thicker.

For a while, everything remained calm in the family. My father worked, came home early, joked, and smiled with us, even got down on his knees to dance cheek to cheek with Jenny each night before she went to bed. The joy on her face as our father held her was a radiant beam, warming the air around her.

" 'You made me love you,' " my father sang to her, his hands on her shoulders. " 'I didn't want to do it . . . I didn't want to do it!' "

Jenny grinned ferociously, and I sat on the couch, arms crossed, watching their exchange with equal measures of disgust and envy. He was trying; I had to give him credit for that. But later that night, when Jenny's screams pulled me from my room and I watched his frustration return in a lightning flash of anger and fist, I was glad that credit was all I had given him. I was glad I had not found it in my heart to forgive him, as my mother and sister seemed to have done. Whatever part of me had rejoiced at my father's return was smothered by the enormous weight of once again seeing his back move into her room, the sound of her bed drowning out the silent screams that filled my blood like an aching disease—a disease that, like my sister's, had no cure.

*T*he house was dark when Jenny and I returned from our trip to La Connor; I figured Mom must have gone out for a movie, thinking we wouldn't be home until late. Although we had worked out a sort of schedule with Jenny—taking turns going to her in the night and switching off caring for her on the weekend days—Mom still didn't seem entirely comfortable being around us on a regular basis, spending time together as a family. I supposed that after eight years of living a fairly private, solitary life, having both your daughters back in your house wouldn't be the easiest thing to get used to, even without all the complications of our particular situation. So even though part of me was bothered by her absence, I tried to be content that my face no longer tightened with anger each time she entered a room. We had come further than I ever imagined we would.

Once I got Jenny settled in the living room on the couch, I sat down next to her. After her nap in the car on the way home, she was alert but quiet. The room was lit in a dim yellow mist from the fireplace; the radio played softly in the background. I put my arm around Jenny's shoulders, my cheek resting on her soft hair, and took a deep breath. I had thought that telling Shane about my decision to adopt the baby would be my biggest challenge, but as we drove home, it dawned on me that the true challenge lay in finding out if my choice was okay with Jenny. She was, after all, the baby's mother.

Still unsure of exactly what she understood about what had happened to her, I didn't want to adopt the baby only to have it remind her of the rape. I lifted my head and pulled my arm out from behind her, shifting to the floor and kneeling before her so I could see her eyes. "Jen," I began haltingly, tucking my springy curls behind my ears. I was strangely nervous about what her reaction might be. "I have a question to ask you."

Her angel eyes stayed open, not blinking, her hands patted together softly just above her swelling belly. She was quiet, waiting for me to go on.

"You know the baby inside you? The one you told Gracie was jumpy?" I smiled fondly, remembering this moment at the barbecue. "Well, when she comes out of you, she's going to need someone to take care of her. I know you'd do it if you could. . . ."

"Ehhhh," Jenny groaned in agreement, and her hands stopped their gentle dance and rested on her stomach. The baby kicked, lifting Jenny's arm just the slightest bit, and my sister's mouth blossomed into a wondrous smile.

Baby.

My heart jumped at the word. "That's right—that *was* the baby." I inhaled before continuing, searching her eyes for any hint of what she was feeling. "I want to be the person who takes care of your baby, but only if it's okay with you." I searched her eyes. "Is it okay for me to adopt her, Jen? I need you to tell me."

Jenny's eyes sparked at me, her smile fading from one of wonder to content. *Love. Baby.* I wondered if this meant she had been waiting for me to ask, if my adopting the baby was what she wanted but she hadn't had a way to tell me. I reached up my hand, using the tips of my fingers to brush her dark bangs away from her eyes.

"Thank you," I said. "I promise I will love your baby with

everything in me." I moved my gaze from her eyes to her belly, tentatively lowering my head, pressing my cheek against its soft warmth. My sister lifted her hands and set them softly on the top of my head; the gesture felt like a blessing. "Hi," I whispered, speaking not to Jenny, but to the child within her. "It's me. I'm going to be your mommy." Would she recognize my voice when she was born? Would the part of her that knew Jenny know me in the same way? I waited a moment longer, and just as I was about to pull my head away, I felt a sharp jab against my cheekbone.

It seemed the baby heard me. She gave me a blessing all her own.

The next day I sat on the couch in the same spot I had watched my father dance with Jenny so many years before. Outside, my mother stood next to Jenny's wheelchair, showing her daughter the splendid summer roses that grew in the front yard, enormous as salad plates. Jenny's eyes were closed; she absorbed the flowers through her other senses, taking each delicate petal in with the tips of her gnarled fingers and the edge of her every breath. My mother spoke to her mostly with smiles and touches, though occasionally I would see her lips move, conveying some message to my sister, who stared at her mother with unabashed adoration.

When I had told her that morning about finding the Sunshine House and my decision to adopt Jenny's baby, she was thrilled. "Now you'll be a mother, too," she said, and I felt something deep and awe-inspiring rise up between us, something that speaks to a daughter only when she joins the mystical world her mother already belongs to. I clung to this new thread of connection, fearful of severing it with more truth from the past. And yet, as I thought of what my father had done, what my mother had not prevented, a deep-rooted sorrow rose up through my belly and into my chest where its branches spread, pricking at my tender flesh with thousands of tiny, angry thorns.

Rising from the couch, I moved outside to join them. It was a warm, early August day; the fading rhododendron leaves were slightly droopy in the wash of afternoon sun. Bright red and pink bunches of fragrant Sweet Williams announced themselves in the flowerbed at the base of the stairs; I picked one blossom and stuck it behind Jenny's ear so she could enjoy the scent.

"That looks nice," Mom commented. "Here, let me do yours." She snapped an abundant pink blossom and slid it behind my left ear, the tips of her fingers tickling my neck. Her touch felt foreign; despite the changes in our relationship over the past few weeks, she was still so much the stranger to me.

"Mom?"

"Um-hmm?" She carefully turned Jenny's chair to position her beneath the shade of a magnolia tree, then turned her attention to me.

"I have to ask you something."

"Okay," she said slowly, her tone carefully measured.

"It's kind of a difficult question."

She settled on the bottom step and adjusted the wide-brimmed straw hat Jenny and I had picked out for her because of its emerald ribbon, a perfect match for her eyes. Then she looked up at me. After an expectant pause, she spoke. "For heaven's sake, Nicky, just ask me. Whatever it is, we'll deal with it."

"I know, it's just . . ." I felt an odd kinship with her in the moment, the way I was making her drag the question out of me like she so often made me do with her stories. I tried to shake the similarity off. "Okay. I've been thinking a lot about Dad."

"Really? What about him?" She shifted uncomfortably on the step, reaching out to smooth an unwrinkled spot on Jenny's pink paisley maternity dress.

"I was thinking about how he used to hit Jenny." There. I said it. My sister snapped to attention, her blue eyes suddenly intent on my face. Perhaps she knew what I was going to ask.

Mom was silent, waiting. I plunged ahead.

"I was thinking more about how he used to go into her room at night the times after he hit her." I swallowed, stuck my hands deep into the back pockets of my Levi's and rocked on my heels nervously. "I heard him. I saw him go in. I saw you *watch* him do it."

"Watch him do what?"

I stared hard at the ground until the slender stalks of grass began to blur together into a green ocean. I wanted her to understand without my having to say it. I didn't know the words to use. "Go in there," I finally said. "You had to know what he was doing. You had to. I saw you standing there, crying."

She looked confused. "I knew he went in there, yes. I followed him." Her eyes searched mine. "I guess I don't understand what you're asking."

"How you could let him!" I exploded, throwing my hands up in the air and raising my eyes to plead with her. "That's my question. How you could watch your husband sexually abuse your helpless daughter and do nothing to stop it? How you could let him come back after he left us that first time, knowing what he did to her? How does a mother *do* that?" My voice shook with tears, the wall in my chest rattled, threatening to disintegrate.

"Sexual *what*? You've got to be kidding, Nicole. Your father never . . . How could you possibly *think* that?"

Emotion thickened in my chest, rose up through my throat, and battled against my voice. "I *heard* him, that's how. Jenny's bed, the noise it made. How long he stayed in there. I *heard* him!" I planted my feet firmly on the ground, trying to maintain control.

My mother's face wore a clear mask of shock, erasing her features. "You heard the bed? So you assumed he was . . ." She shook her head; I pictured words jumbled in her brain, trying to find a semblance of order. She looked at me, her green eyes soft and full of compassion. "Nicole. Honey. Your father went into Jenny's bedroom those nights to hold her. He sat on her bed with his daughter in his arms, rocking her to sleep."

I shook my head. "No . . . I heard the bed. . . ."

"The bed might've squeaked when he rocked her, yes." She stood, grabbed my hands. "I watched him, the first few times I knew he was going in there. He felt so horribly guilty. It was his way of trying to make up for hurting her. He loved Jenny very much. He just wasn't strong enough to stop himself. But he *never* did anything sexual to her."

I wrenched my hands from her grasp and stumbled a few steps back. "Then why were you in the hallway, crying?"

She sighed, then sat on the stair again. "Because I ached for his pain. And for mine. Because he was weak but wanted to be better. But he wasn't able to be. I was torn between the love for a husband and a child. And it was excruciating."

Thoughts spun in my mind like a top, dizzying me. I dropped to the grass, cross-legged, and moved my eyes to Jenny, who had been watching the conversation like a tennis match, her gaze a pendulum. She was thirty-three weeks along now; the baby twisted beneath her flesh every day, visible to us all. I could not believe I had been wrong about my father. "But I was so sure. . . ."

"I guess I can understand that. But I swear to you, if that had been happening, I would have known it." She smiled wanly. "I know you might not believe this, but your father had a great capacity for tenderness. He cried like a baby over his violence. I used to believe I could change him, erase the ugly side. If I couldn't cure Jenny, I could cure *him*." She laughed, a dry, barking noise.

I blinked heavily, still pummeled by the weight of my error. "Is that why you finally agreed to place Jenny at Wellman?"

"Yes. Fixing whatever was wrong with Jenny was just not going to happen. I eventually admitted that. I gave up. I gave in to his proclamation that there was nothing more we could do for your sister. I moved my hope onto him." She rolled her eyes more at herself than at me. "Not the smartest decision I ever made."

I looked at her accusingly. "Then why didn't you bring Jenny home from Wellman after he left for good?" My sister's gaze moved from my face to our mother's; she wanted the answer to this question, too.

Mom let loose a heavy sigh, full of despair. "At first, I wanted her home so badly I could taste it. But then, after your father left . . ." She trailed off, looking up to the sky, perhaps believing the answer lay hidden behind the clouds. She swung her gaze back to me. "I just didn't know how I'd do it, Nicky. I had to work; your father sent some money but not enough to pay for private care. It just wasn't possible." Her green eyes softened. "It still isn't." So she *had* thought about keeping Jenny with her after the baby was born. And yet I was right; she couldn't go back to a life limited by what caring for her daughter demanded of her. After months of caring for Jenny myself, I was beginning to understand why.

We sat in silence as I absorbed these new truths. My mind expanded and stretched, trying to wrap itself around all she had said. "Are you okay?" she asked after a while. "You look a little peaked."

"Well, this is all very hard to deal with. I've assumed for so long that he . . ." I trailed off, made a face of confusion. "I guess it'll just take some getting used to."

"*Life* takes getting used to," she said wisely, and she stood, urging me with outstretched hands to do the same. And there in our front yard, for the first time in years, I went willingly into my mother's arms, the love I felt there stronger than the distance that had pulled us apart.

I could not sleep that night, the discovery of my father's innocence nipping at my thoughts, cutting through the base of my entire belief system. So much of my life, my history, was built on a foundation that suddenly no longer existed. I did not know what to do with my feelings, the slow-burning embers of anger and disgust and guilt that had tainted every memory of my father, good or bad.

If he had gone into Jenny's room only to comfort her, to try to make amends for the sting of his open palm, if his fist was the only physical weapon he brandished against her, was he still a monster? Did he deserve as much hatred as had flowed in my blood for almost fifteen years? Or was he simply a man, disarmed by feelings of inadequacy and helplessness, a man, like so many others in this world, who was taught that the solution to overwhelming emotion is violence?

He loved Jenny, my mother had said. He had held her and wept, rocking her and begging for forgiveness. And then he had left, never calling or visiting, saving us from his fury, perhaps showing his love in the only way he knew how.

I sighed, rolled over in bed, and hugged my covers to the curve of my body like a small child. The moonlight spilled through my bedroom window and lay over me like a gentle hand, but did nothing to comfort me. It was as though my father were a puzzle I had put together all wrong, and now had to take apart and rearrange to make the pieces fit in a way that would make sense. And though I could not completely absolve him of his sins, at least I knew now that they were not as vile as I had imagined.

Nor were mine, as Nova had pointed out when I spoke with her earlier, relaying the conversation I had had with my mother. I hadn't failed to protect Jenny from his sexual abuse; the abuse had not occurred. The relief in this discovery was deep, an unexpected gift.

As I tossed and turned beneath the sheets watching bloblike shadows ooze across the wall, my mind wandered from my father to Shane. I had not yet worked up the courage to tell him about my decision to adopt Jenny's baby. Our conversations only skimmed the surface of our growing separate existences: he told me about his cases, I told him about the adorable things Nova's kids did or said each day. Something inside me was beginning to let go.

The reasons I was drawn to him and the predictable life we led together no longer seemed important. I didn't need his organized nature to stabilize me; I had stabilized myself. I no longer saw things through his eyes; I was seeing them through my own. I didn't want what he wanted: money, success, notoriety. I wanted peace. I wanted family. I wanted to go deeper. I could *feel* again; coming home had allowed that part of me to blossom. I felt ripe with emotion and suddenly life on the surface wasn't enough. It struck me that perhaps I didn't love Shane for who he was; I loved him for how he made me feel about myself.

I sighed again, rolled over onto my back, wishing I could talk to Jenny about all this. I needed a sister's advice. I longed to hear her voice the way I used to long for it when I was a child, aching for a sister who not only listened to my stories but told me hers as well. There is a mourning that comes along with having a sister like Jenny, the loss of the relationship that might have been.

Because of her disabilities, I knew the connection between us was immeasurable, something rare and precious and strong, but there were always those moments, moments like tonight, when I would have given anything to be like other sisters I had known. I wanted a sister who could tell me what to do.

As the minutes passed slowly on the clock, I felt edgy and loose; my heart pounded in my chest like a jackrabbit's foot. Even though she was quiet, my body urged me to check on Jenny several times. When she finally did cry out around midnight, I went to her, but I was distracted by all the thoughts that were trying to find a place to rest in my head and could not seem to settle her. I wondered if she sensed the stress I felt after that afternoon's conversation with our mother and couldn't go back to sleep because of it. "Hold on, Jen," I told her as she looked at me with tired eyes. "I'll get Mom." I moved through the dark house to our mother's room, rapping softly on her door. She appeared a moment later, her dark hair tangled; creases in her pillow had left sharp red lines on one of her cheeks.

"What?" she mumbled. Her slanted green eyes sagged with fatigue. "It's not my night with her, is it?"

"No," I said, feeling guilty for bothering her, but knowing I was in no shape to give Jenny the attention she needed. "But could you please come take care of her? I need to go for a drive or something. Clear my head."

Mom sighed, holding the doorknob with one hand. "All right," she finally consented. It was still difficult for her getting up with Jenny; sometimes I had to remind her it was her turn. I don't think she resented doing it. I think it was more that she had fallen out of the habit. Feeling another stab of guilt, I quashed the urge to tell her to go back to bed, knowing I desperately needed to take this brief escape.

I followed her through the house. "Are you sure this is okay with you?" I asked her as we stepped into the bedroom hallway.

She moved past me to my sister's door. "I'm already up," she pointed out. "Go."

I went back into my bedroom, pulled on a pair of jeans and a T-shirt, grabbed the keys, and headed out. The night was still, only a few cars moved along the streets, their headlights bright eyes in the dark. I drove down California Avenue through the Junction, marveling at the changed storefronts. What during my childhood used to be a collection of small, family-owned shops had metamorphosed into a conglomerate of big business: Bed, Bath, & Beyond, the Gap, and Restoration Hardware to name only a few. Marshall's Drugs remained on the corner, and I wondered if the pharmacy still handed out a wooden token good for a small ice-cream cone at their fountain while you waited for your prescription.

I found myself changing directions to head toward the beach. Nova's house was dark, and though I craved a conversation with her, I thought better of disturbing a rare moment of family peace. A glance at the stars might do me some good, I thought, so I drove slowly toward the strip, parked right on the beach and looked for hidden messages in the sky. Messages that would tell me what to do about Shane, how to make him understand my choice to adopt Jenny's baby. I barely understood it myself. It wasn't something I felt I could explain, but the decision was firmly rooted within me. It was instinct—a voice in my heart that was not my sister's but my own. A voice I hadn't heard in years but recognized in the deepest levels of my soul. A voice I knew spoke the truth.

I still hadn't decided what I would do after the baby was born, whether I would take her back to San Francisco or stay here and try to build a life. I knew Shane wouldn't move; he had gone too far in his career to make a change now. And if I was honest with myself, I didn't miss much about my life there; I couldn't see myself going back. Every sign pointed to the end of our relationship, the brightest of these my feelings for Garret.

I sighed, reaching to pull the seat lever so I could recline all the way back. I rested my hands behind my head, elbows pointing out, contemplating the pinpoint dots of the car's interior ceiling. I counted them, as I had always counted things, to gain some semblance of mental control.

Was I giving up on Shane because it was the right thing to do or was I indulging a whimsical attraction that would simply pass with time? Shane's reaction to the adoption would be the deciding point for our future, and though I felt as sure as I possibly could about the baby, I was shaky in my resolve to end what had been a comfortable relationship. A safe relationship.

I was used to being safe, cutting myself off from conflict and turbulent feelings. Adopting a baby, staying in Seattle and pursuing a perfection-minded single father was definitely not safe, but the idea of it made me feel more alive, more like the self I had always longed to be. It made me feel strong, authentic. Like my soul had finally settled inside my flesh.

After returning my seat to the upright position, I fired up the car again, thinking it was time to head back home. But before I realized what I was doing, I had driven a couple of blocks down to park in front of the Beach Basket. A soft light glowed in the back of the restaurant and I saw the silhouette of Garret's dark head popping around in the kitchen. I debated with myself only a minute before carefully observing whether anyone lurked in the doorway, ready to attack, then sprinted to the front window and rapped on it with my knuckles. I saw Garret jump in surprise, his hand over his chest as he strode to unlock the door. I smoothed my curls, realizing how wild they must look after hours spent tossing and turning on a pillow.

"Hi," I said meekly, stepping inside. "Sorry if I scared you."

"That's okay. Who needs a regular heartbeat?" He latched the door behind me. He wore Levi's and a plain white T-shirt. "What're you doing out this late?"

"Ever have one of those nights where your body wants to sleep but your brain has other plans?"

"I'm right there with you. Jackie called tonight." His face carried a strained look I had not seen before.

"Oh," I said. He hadn't mentioned his ex-wife in a while. "Wow. Tough conversation, I take it?"

He shrugged, indifferent.

I tried again. "When was the last time you talked to her?"

"It'd been a while." His expression was closed, his tone clipped. I was dying to know why she'd called him, but I decided not to push for details. If he wanted to tell me about it, he would. I hoped.

He gestured toward the kitchen. "Anyway. That's why I'm here. I don't know how to get my mind clear other than work. Pitiful, huh?"

"Not at all." I'd spent six months in the bakery doing the exact same thing.

He took my hand. "Come on back. I'm experimenting."

I followed him. "So Gracie's still at Nova's?"

"Yup. Friday night sleepover with Rebecca."

The kitchen gleamed beneath the fluorescent lights. Garret moved over to the stove, where he resumed whipping a magical-smelling concoction in a heavy-bottomed saucepan. I hopped up onto a stool by the counter, legs dangling. "What are you working on? It smells luscious."

"A sauce for the chicken special this week. Champagne, butter, heavy cream, and a little garlic with sweet grapes."

"Sounds like a Weight Watchers entree."

"Oh yeah, we take out all the fat and calories. Just a little customer service we provide."

"I thought you said you tried to keep the menu light."

"The menu, yes. The specials, no." He stuck his finger into the sauce, then his mouth. "Umm-mm. Want to give me a second opinion?"

"Sure." I jumped down, walked over to stand next to him. I reached for a spoon, but before I could find one, he stuck his finger back into the pan, then held it up to my mouth, his other hand cupped under my chin to catch the drips. I licked my lips and opened my mouth, pulse pounding in my belly. *Oh God, what am I doing?* I thought as his finger rolled slowly on my tongue, filling my mouth with an exquisite flavor.

His gaze never left my eyes, and as he started to pull his hands back, I grabbed his wrists and touched his palms to my face. His eyes questioned only for a moment before leaning in, soft lips against mine like the touch of a feather, then firmer, more insistent. I closed my eyes and matched my breath with his, our lips moving in what felt like a remembered dance. My hands found his waist and I rested them there. His entire body pressed against me, and I felt like I had finally come home.

"Wow," he breathed when we parted.

I smiled softly, my insides gooey and loose. "Definitely what a girl likes to hear after she kisses a boy."

"I thought it was me who kissed you," he said, grinning. A sharp, ugly smell suddenly rose up next to us. "Shit!" He yanked the pan from the burner; the tender cream base blackened and bubbled. "There goes that batch."

"I wouldn't worry about it." I wrinkled up my nose. "You stuck your drooly finger in it, anyway."

He laughed. "You're probably right. Want to help me make some more?"

I clapped my hands, rubbing them together. "You bet. Got an apron?"

We passed an hour in front of the stove, chopping and stirring, testing for the quality of champagne by sipping at the bottle. Eventually, we rested in the dining room in facing chairs, my feet in his lap. The position felt oddly comfortable, as though we'd been doing it for years.

"Nova tells me you've decided to go ahead with the adoption," he said, his hands cupped over the toes of my shoes. He jiggled my legs. "How's it feel?"

"Honestly?"

"Of course."

"Scary as hell."

"Are you still afraid there'll be something wrong with the baby?"

"Sort of. More that I won't be able to *handle* something being wrong with her. That I'll chicken out and leave her the same way I left my sister. Is that terrible of me to say?"

"Not at all. Sounds like you're being honest with yourself." He paused. "It's obviously not the same situation, but when Jackie left us I had some heavy doubts about whether I'd make it alone. At one point, I even called an adoption lawyer."

"Really?" I couldn't imagine him even considering such a thing. "What stopped you?"

"Gracie told me she loved me for the first time. I also realized I'd basically been parenting her by myself anyway, even with

Jackie there. So I just took a deep breath and decided to do it. I still feel shaky, some days, if that makes you feel any better."

I grinned halfheartedly. "Not really." I reached up, tucked my hair behind my ears.

We were quiet for a moment until his gaze drifted to the floor and he asked, "How does Shane feel about the whole adoption?"

I ducked my chin to my chest. "I haven't exactly told him yet."

Garret lifted his eyes from the floor and raised his dark eyebrows in genuine surprise.

"I know, I know. I'm a wimp. Let's just leave it at that." I didn't know how to explain all that was spinning in my mind. I wasn't sure I was ready to tell him just how heavily my feelings for him were weighing in my decision process about Shane. I didn't want to scare him out of his wits.

"Whatever you say." He sounded doubtful, but then continued in a lighter tone, glancing toward the kitchen. "Hey. Want some coconut ice cream? The cook whipped up some this afternoon. It should be frozen by now."

I shook my head. "I think I reached my cream limit tasting that sauce."

"Are you sure? It's yummy."

"Yummy?" I poked his stomach gently with my foot. "You are such a dad. No childless man would ever use the word 'yummy.' "

"So? 'Yummy' happens to be a good word. Very descriptive of this particular ice cream. But if you're sure you don't want any. . . ." He batted his eyelashes at me in an exaggerated fashion.

"Oh, what the hell," I said, pulling my feet from his lap and slapping my palms against the tops of my thighs. "It's two in the morning, right? Perfect time for ice cream."

Garret jumped up and rubbed his hands together conspiratorially. "All right! I knew you'd give in." He made a stop sign with an outstretched palm. "Stay right here. I'll go get it."

My heart jumped in my chest as I watched him basically skip into the kitchen, marveling over how ridiculously happy I felt. Shane would rather be dead than caught skipping. The thought of him washed over me in a waterfall of guilt and I glanced around as though he might be standing in a corner, watching me. *I shouldn't be here*, I thought. But that *kiss*. Oh, my. I stood up just as Garret returned from the kitchen, two bowls in hand.

"I'm really sorry," I said, "but I should probably get going."

He stopped, set the bowls down on the table next to him. "Everything okay?"

"Yeah, I think so. Just feeling the guilt thing, you know?"

He moved over to me, took my hands in his. "Shane?"

I nodded, my eyes glued to his face. "I need to make some decisions. Take care of a few things before . . . Well, just before."

"Did I step over the line, kissing you? I thought you wanted me to."

I squeezed his hands. "Oh yeah. I wanted you to. That's not all I wanted, which is probably why I should get the hell out of here." I paused, tried to read his expression. "Are you angry?"

He smiled. "Just at myself."

"What for?"

He pulled at my arm playfully. "You know exactly what for."

I shook my head. "No, I don't."

He leaned forward again, his lips against mine before I realized it was happening. My breath caught in my chest when he pulled away.

"Feel that?" he whispered.

"Oh yeah," I exhaled.

"That's why I'm angry. That I might lose my chance at this. Having it happen with you."

Tears tickled the corners of my eyes and I smiled at him. "Take a girl's breath away, why don't you?"

Garret took my hands, held them against his lips as he spoke. "Just give me the chance, Nicole. You won't know what hit you."

As Jenny napped the next afternoon, I decided I'd better do the same. My birthday was later in the week, but since it was Saturday, Nova had a small party planned for that evening. I wanted to appear well-rested. I knew Garret would be there and the simple thought of him curled my lips into an indulgent smile. Burrowing under a light blanket and pushing away the guilty feelings that nipped at my heels, I basked in the memory of the kiss we'd shared. Just as I was about to drift off, a sharp, insistent rap at the front door woke me.

"Mom?" I called out. She knew I was tired; she was still awake when I got home the night before and had gotten an edited version of my time with Garret. Mom had met him at Nova's barbecue, and though I hadn't told her of the feelings I had for him, I was pretty sure she suspected they existed. "Mom?" I said again, hopeful she would answer the door so I wouldn't have to get up.

When she didn't answer me, I assumed she hadn't heard the door, so I rolled reluctantly from bed and pulled on a green button-down blouse and my favorite jeans. As I entered the kitchen, I saw Shane coming in from the living room at the same time. Mom was right behind him. "Surprise!" he said as he strode over to kiss me. "Happy birthday!" I stood frozen.

"Shane," I started, finding my voice. "What are you doing here?"

"He came all the way from San Francisco just to surprise you," my mother piped up. She went to sit at the table, a half-eaten chef's salad in front of her. "I told him you were sleeping because you were up with Jenny all night." Her eyes were bright, trying to communicate something to me. She must have suspected my feelings for Garret; otherwise, she wouldn't be making such a point of not telling Shane the real reason I was so tired. I felt a twinge of kinship with her.

"You picked the wrong afternoon to nap," Shane remarked, his hand on the small of my back. Despite the warm weather, Shane was dressed in a typically impeccable blue suit, a yellow-striped tie knotted perfectly at his neck. "It's gorgeous out. I thought Seattle was perpetually wet."

"It's our best-kept secret, the summers here," Mom said. "Right, Nicole?"

"Uh, yeah. It's not bad during the summers. It's the winters you have to watch out for all the rain."

"Well, thanks for the weather update," Shane joked. His hand rubbed up and down my spine.

I moved from his touch, unnerved by the sensation. I gripped my hands on the back of a chair, locking my arms straight, bracing myself. "So! What a nice surprise! I thought you were swamped at work." He stepped over to hug me, and I felt stiff in his arms, a circle trying to fit into a square hole.

"I am," he said. "But I've felt so guilty about not coming and I wanted to make sure you knew everything was okay with us. Plus it's your birthday."

I sank into a chair, resting my elbows on the kitchen table, just as Jenny began to groan from her bedroom.

"I'll get her," Mom volunteered, pushing back her chair and stepping down the hallway.

"Thanks, Mom," I said, for the first time wishing she wasn't helping me with Jenny so I could've had a moment to gather my senses.

Shane sat down as well. "Aren't you happy I came?"

"Of course. Just surprised. And a little tired."

"Well, you'd better get some caffeine in you because I'm taking you out to dinner tonight."

"Uh," I said, the only witty response I could pull together on such short notice.

" 'Uh' what?" he inquired. "You don't want me to take you out for your birthday? I had to call in a favor for reservations at the Space Needle." Of course he had called in a favor; he couldn't just take me out for a burger. He had to make a *statement*.

"Well," I started, "Nova's planned sort of a party for me tonight—"

"Even better!" Shane boomed. "Now I'll get to meet all these people you talk my ear off about." *Me? Talk his ear off?* "What did you say her husband does?"

"He's a fisherman," I said weakly.

Shane paused, his manicured hands pressed flat against the table. "Ah. Well, I suppose we'll find something to talk about. Anybody interesting going to be there?" My stomach turned. Had I never noticed how truly arrogant he was?

"They're all interesting," I asserted in my friends' defense. "They might not all be *lawyers*, but they're wonderful people." I thought of Garret. Oh God, Garret. What was he going to think when he saw Shane?

Mom chose this moment to lead Jenny through the entryway. Shane rose from his seat and turned to look at her, a nervous, overacted smile played on his lips. "So! I finally get to meet the infamous Jenny."

My sister deliberately looked away from Shane, groaning lightly. She twisted her hands together in front of her belly, then slammed them hard into her mouth. Her distaste was obvious.

"Hello!" Shane boomed again. "I'm Shane!"

I looked at him, perplexed. "She's not *deaf*."

He reddened beneath his tan and sat back down. "I know that. I'm just happy to meet her."

Mom looked at me pointedly and maneuvered Jenny toward the living room. "We should get ready to leave soon." She paused, glancing at Shane. "That is, if we're still going to Nova's."

"Of course we're going," I said, with what I hoped sounded like enthusiasm. "I just have to shower." I stood, and nodded after my mother, who had stepped into the living room with Jenny. "They'll keep you company, all right?"

He looked at me with a suggestive spark in his blue eyes, grabbing my hands and kissing them in the same manner that Garret had only hours before. "I'd rather come keep *you* company." Something in me reacted to his touch, though I wasn't exactly sure what feeling was behind it.

I laughed nervously and pulled away. "Not here, okay?" I stepped into the hallway and headed to the bathroom, pulling the phone in with me. Sitting on the closed toilet lid, I dialed Nova's house.

"Hello?" Ryan answered, a tinge of impatience in his voice.

"Hi, Ryan, it's Nicole. Can I speak with Nova, please?" I heard the screech of children in the background, followed by a loud thump and a high-pitched wail. Next, Nova's muted yell: "That's it, young man! No TV for a week! And if you hit her again, your Gameboy is fish food!"

"Shit," Ryan swore under his breath.

"Troops restless today?" I inquired sympathetically.

"To say the least," he affirmed.

An idea struck. "Maybe we should postpone the party," I suggested, standing up to look in the mirror above the sink. With my crazy red curls and the smudged makeup I hadn't removed from the night before, I didn't *look* like a woman who'd have two men wanting to be with her.

"No way," Ryan said emphatically. "Nova's been cooking and cleaning like a wild woman. She'd go ballistic if it didn't go off as planned." He called for her, telling her who it was and she picked up the extension in the kitchen.

"Nova's Discount Baby House, one five-year-old boy, going cheap," she said, joking.

I laughed. "Oh, *that's* nice. Selling off your children, now, are you?"

"Some days, I tell you, it wouldn't be the worst idea." She paused. "You know I'm kidding, right? I adore them."

"Of course." I sat back down on the toilet lid, crossing my legs.

She sighed. "So what's up, birthday girl?"

"Shane's here."

"What?" she gasped.

I wiggled the phone cord and watched it dance. "He just showed up. He wanted to take me out for dinner but I told him about the party and now he's coming with us." The words rushed out of me in one breath. I paused for a moment before continuing. "He still doesn't know I'm adopting the baby."

"Oh boy. *This* should be fun." She knew without my saying that I was worried what Garret might think.

"I know." I reached to turn on the hot water valve for a shower. "What am I going to do?"

"Well, there's not much you *can* do. I would kick your butt if you didn't come and Garret would think something was hinky if I told *him* not to come, so I guess you're stuck just riding the wave, chick."

"Let's just hope I don't drown," I said sadly, and I hung up the phone to get ready for my birthday celebration.

When we got to Nova's house, Star and Orion had already arrived and were playing with Ryan and the kids downstairs in the family room. Mom settled with Jenny on the living room couch and I took Shane into the kitchen to meet my friend. The room smelled of roasted meat and various spices; the table was loaded with platters of food, over which hung a large poster, obviously painted by the kids that proclaimed HAPPY BIRTHDAY, AUNTIE NICOLE!

Nova was standing in front of the sink, washing dishes. She wore a sage green batik-print dress and, as usual, no shoes. Her blond hair was held back from her face with a dark green ribbon.

The running water muted her hearing and she didn't seem to notice that we were there. "Hey," I said to get her attention.

She turned to us in surprise, dropping the frying pan she had been washing into the sink with a loud clang. "Jeez! You scared me!" She turned off the water. Her eyes went immediately to Shane, sizing him up. She stepped forward and shook his hand. "Good to meet you, Shane. I've heard a lot about you."

"Likewise," Shane returned, flashing his most charming smile. "Nice place you have here," he went on politely, though I could tell from his tone he thought otherwise. Nova had definitely straightened up the usual messy state of her house, but it didn't come close to matching the cutting-edge luxury Shane was accustomed to being surrounded by. I was suddenly embarrassed for having brought him.

"Thanks." Her tone insinuated that she knew exactly what he thought of her home. She gestured to the table. "There are appetizers on the table and beer in the fridge. Help yourself." She turned her attention to me. "Nicole, can I show you something in the bedroom?"

I looked at Shane. "You'll be all right?"

He was already reaching into the refrigerator for a beer and nodded his head. "Sure, go on."

I followed Nova to her room and shut the door behind me. "What's up?"

She frowned. "I just wanted to tell you that I tried to call Garret and warn him that Shane was going to be here, but he wasn't home and I couldn't get through to him at the restaurant."

I nodded. "I left a message on his cell phone to call me, but he never did. I didn't know how to explain it on voice mail." I ran my fingers into my loose curls, dropping to the bed, elbows on my knees. "God, this is going to be horrible."

Nova patted and rubbed my back. "I know."

I laughed. "Thanks for the encouragement. I feel so much better now."

"Well, at least you look good," she offered.

"You think?" I stood and examined myself in the full-length mirror on the back of the door. I was wearing a chocolate-hued silk blouse and a matching bias-cut skirt. My red curls were loose, my face lightly made up. "We should get back out there," I sighed, tasting dread on my tongue like sour milk.

"I have to pee, first," Nova said. "I'll be right behind you." She paused before stepping into the bath that adjoined the room, considering something. "And don't worry. I told everyone else that Shane doesn't know about your taking the baby. They won't say anything."

"Thanks," I said, breathing a small sigh of relief. I moved down the hall to the living room, stopped dead in my tracks by the sight of Garret shaking hands with Shane in the entryway. My heart froze and it took Nova's hand on my back a moment later, urging me along, to get it started again. Garret's mouth was in a thin dark line across his face as he pulled his hand away from Shane's and looked at me with a tight expression. Mom and Jenny were gone from the couch; I assumed they had gone downstairs to join Nova's family. Gracie stood next to her father and ran over to greet me with an enthusiastic hug. She wore a lacy hot pink party dress, complete with a matching vinyl purse.

"Happy birthday, Nicole! We got you a present today. I helped Daddy pick it out. We shopped all afternoon!" She ran back over to Garret and I noticed that despite her frilly dress, she still wore her favorite white sneakers over bare feet. "Can we give it to her now, Daddy? *Please?*"

"Later, Peanut," he said, touching his daughter's dark head. "Why don't you go find Rebecca?" I couldn't read his tone.

"Okay!" she cried, jumping up and down, obviously too excited to be disappointed about my not opening the present. She tore down the stairs to the family room. Nova followed her.

"I should check how Ryan's doing with Layla," she said. "I'll be back in a minute." I looked after her longingly, then back to Garret.

Garret met my gaze, his hazel eyes dark with emotion I couldn't name. He looked incredibly handsome: his dark hair was slicked back from his chiseled features and he wore a cream-colored button-down shirt and khaki shorts. I thought of his lips against mine, the soft touch of his fingers on my face. I anxiously awaited the moment I could pull him aside and explain.

"So. I've met Shane," he said, lifting his chin almost imperceptibly in Shane's direction, a classic male gesture of uninterested acknowledgment.

Shane, unused to seeing me with children, had been watching my interaction with Gracie with relative surprise. But when Garret spoke, Shane stepped over to me and put an arm casually around my shoulders, the beer bottle he held cold against my bare skin. "Nic's mentioned you," he said. "She told me Nova watches your little girl."

Garret kept his eyes on me. "Really," he said flatly. "Is that all she told you about me, then?" The air in the room suddenly turned thick.

"Garret," I started, warily observing Shane's confused expression. This was not going well.

"You're right," Garret continued, swinging his gaze to Shane, as though I hadn't spoken. "Nova watches Gracie while I'm at the restaurant." He looked back at me, eyes probing.

"So you're a cook?" Shane inquired politely. My face burned hot, embarrassed by the condescension I detected in his words.

"He *owns* the Beach Basket," I said quickly. "It's a very nice restaurant on the strip." I glanced down the hall to the door that led to the basement. Wasn't anybody going to come and rescue me from this horrid conversation?

"Ah," Shane mused. "Have you eaten there, Nic?"

"Not exactly," I said weakly, looking down to the floor and nervously fingering the soft material of my skirt.

"What's the specialty of the house?" Shane asked Garret. "Maybe I'll take my girl out for dinner while I'm here." I suddenly realized I didn't know how long he was planning to stay.

"The champagne chicken is quite good." Garret's gaze had barely wavered from me. "The sauce is exceptional. Don't you think, Nicole?" There was a brief pause as the air became audibly thicker, seemingly more difficult to breathe.

"I thought you said you haven't eaten there," Shane commented, a hint of accusation in his voice.

"Er," I began.

"Saturday night's a busy time for the owner to be away," Shane went on, interrupting me. He shifted his arm around me farther in order to take a swig from his beer. "Your wife must be watching the place for you."

"Shane," I warned quietly, touching his forearm.

Garret held up his hand to stop me. "It's okay, Nicole," he said coolly, looking at Shane with slightly hostile eyes. "I'm a single parent."

Shane whistled. "Then I've got to hand it to you, man. Couldn't do the parenthood thing myself. Not even *with* the greatest woman in the world." He squeezed his arm around my neck, kissing my cheek.

Garret looked surprised, then pointedly at me, obviously understanding that I still had yet to tell Shane about my decision to adopt Jenny's baby. He moved toward the kitchen. "I need a drink." He sounded disgusted.

"Me, too," I said quickly, extricating myself from Shane's arm.

Shane held up his beer. "I'm good for now." He looked down the hall. "Think I'll go introduce myself to the rest of the party." He stepped toward the doorway that led to the basement.

I ducked my head down as I followed Garret into the kitchen. "Nice sign," he commented, glancing over to the table.

I touched his back and his muscles froze, repelling my fingers. I pulled them back as though they'd been bitten. "Garret, please," I started.

He snapped his head around to look at me, reaching out to grip the handle on the refrigerator door. "There's nothing to explain. I understand completely."

I reached out to him again, barely brushing the warmth of his arm. "No, you don't. I didn't know he was coming. I tried to call and let you know—"

"I'm sure you tried your best." Sarcasm clung to his words like static. He grabbed a beer and popped off the lid, taking a long pull on the bottle, then stepped back from me, out of my reach.

I tried again. "Please don't do this."

He looked at me, his warm eyes suddenly unrecognizable with

cold and indifference. "*I* haven't done anything." His tone stung like a whip. He pushed past me and left me in the kitchen, alone. I looked at my distorted reflection in the chrome oven door and frowned. "Happy birthday," I said ironically. "May all your wishes come true."

The rest of the evening passed mostly without event. Shane made polite conversation with Orion, in whom he had found a fellow golf enthusiast. Star and my mother reminisced about the birthday parties they'd thrown for Nova and me over the years, and Garret talked with Ryan, focusing on playing with Gracie and the other children while pretty much ignoring Shane's existence, as well as mine. Jenny watched everyone happily from her vantage point on the couch, her eyes sparkling with content. It wasn't until Nova brought the presents down to the family room that things became tangibly uncomfortable again. Shane stepped up to me and kissed me soundly in front of everyone, then smiled. "My presence is my present, babe. Happy birthday."

I laughed hesitantly, as everyone else glanced at each other, unimpressed by this pronouncement. I quickly opened my other gifts: a professional cookware set from Nova and Ryan; a set of silver-and-amethyst bangle bracelets made by Star; several pieces of artwork from the children; and a beautiful emerald green cut velvet scarf from Mom and Jenny. I had mentioned the scarf to my mother the week before when I'd admired it in a local dress shop; I was touched she'd remembered. I thanked everyone profusely. Then Gracie piped up, jumping from her father's lap, where she had been resting. "What about *our* present, Nicole? Don't forget ours!" She tilted her elfin face at her father. "Where is it, Daddy?"

Moving with slow deliberation, Garret reached into his shorts pocket and retrieved a black box that was topped with a small red bow. He handed it to Gracie without even glancing at me. I swallowed hard, watching Shane's face for his reaction. Anticipation hung heavy in the air, everyone watching me. Oblivious to the tension in the room, Gracie skipped over to me and held out the box. "Here! Open it!"

"How about you do it for me?" I offered, my heart pounding a nervous mix of excitement and trepidation. I had no idea what he might have gotten me.

"Okay," she agreed, pulling the lid off the gift. "I'll do the first part." Inside lay a black velvet jewelry box that Gracie pulled out with her tiny fingers and handed to me. "Now you."

I rested my fingers on the soft fabric of the box, eyes to my lap. What if it was a *ring*? I shook my head briefly. That was a ridiculous thought. Garret wouldn't do something like that after our conversation the night before. He knew I was still technically involved with Shane. Then why was he so angry with me for having Shane here? I told him I had some things to work out before we could—

"Open it!" Gracie cried out, interrupting my thoughts. She jumped up and down with her hands clasped in front of her chest, her dark brown cap of hair swishing around her freckled face. "Open it, open it, open it!"

"Gracie Mae," Garret said softly, reaching over to touch his daughter's small arm. "Settle down, please." The tenderness in his voice made my muscles quiver in remembrance of the night before; he had used the same tone with me.

I took a breath and opened the gift. Inside was a delicate silver strand upon which hung two tiny, jewel-studded rings, small enough to look like they might fit around Gracie's littlest finger. I pulled it out, admiring the necklace. "This is lovely, Gracie," I said, deliberately thanking the child and not Garret. "Thank you."

"One ring has your birthstone and the other has Jenny's," Gracie said importantly. "You can add the ba—"

"Birthstones of anyone else you like," Garret interrupted her. He looked at his daughter and she quieted, seeming to understand the warning in his words.

It was an incredibly thoughtful gift; I was terribly moved by the meaning behind it. The birthstones of the baby, Jenny, and me, forever linked, to wear around my neck. I longed to thank him, to kiss him the way he'd kissed me the night before. I longed to make this moment happen all over again without Shane in it.

"Nice," Shane said, reaching over to finger the necklace. He looked at Garret with a hint of challenge in his blue eyes. "Expensive."

Garret appeared unruffled. "Well, we cooks are paid pretty well these days," he said, taking a stab at Shane's earlier assumption about his profession. Shane responded with a cool look. Garret stood, taking Gracie's hand. "It's late, Bug. Time to go."

"But I don't want to," Gracie whined.

Nova stepped up and handed Layla over to Ryan. She prodded her other children toward the stairs. "It's bedtime here, too, Gracie Mae," she offered in support of Garret. "We'll see you tomorrow, okay?"

"I'm beat, too," Shane said, his eyes still smoldering at Garret. He took my hand. "Take me back to my hotel, babe?" His voice dripped with suggestion. Something inside me dropped another level. I felt as though I were sinking.

Garret shook hands with Orion and Ryan, then hugged Star and Nova, purposely ignoring Shane. He looked at me, a tinge of sadness shadowing the hurt in his light eyes. "Good-bye, Nicole." It sounded as though he was saying it for good.

"Bye," I whispered as I raised my chin, drawing on every ounce of self-control to keep from crying. His voice told me he had made his choice. He wasn't going to listen. No matter what I said, no matter how hard I tried to explain. Rejection oozed from his pores, and in that one moment, I realized we were over before we'd had a real chance to begin.

*A*fter dropping off Mom and Jenny at home, I went back with Shane to his hotel. In an oddly familiar motion, I pushed down my negative thoughts about him, ignoring all the reservations I'd been feeling about our relationship. It was surprisingly easy to fall back into the comfort of denial and it didn't take long for our bodies to be pressed together in the dark, reacquainting themselves. I felt less like his lover and more like a detective, searching his skin with mine for evidence of why we should stay together.

Afterward, I lay awake, covers pulled up to my chin, ashamed. I listened to the immediate postsex breathing of the man I had thought I would spend the rest of my life with, aching for the man I had only just met. I tried to push away these feelings for Garret but found them immovable, rooted somewhere deep within me. I didn't know how I'd ever let them go. Eventually, I drifted into a troubled sleep.

The next morning Shane woke me with a kiss. "It's my day with Jenny," I said, pulling my wrinkled skirt and blouse from the plush carpet and shaking them out before dressing. "I've got to get home."

He stretched out on the bed, twisting the covers between his long legs, yawning. "And I've got to get to work on an opening statement."

"You're going to *work*?" I asked, surprised. I flipped my hair up into a messy twist, fastening it with a silver clip I had in my purse.

"I'm not exactly on vacation here, Nic. I've got a pretty important case starting Wednesday morning."

I couldn't believe that after traveling all this way to see me he was going to spend the day in his hotel, working.

"Think I could work at your house?" he continued.

I considered this. "I don't think you'd be able to concentrate very well. Jenny can be pretty noisy." Actually, I knew he'd be able to work just fine around Jenny. And I'd lied—it wasn't my day with her; Mom usually took Sundays. I just didn't want to be around him. I wanted to go to Nova's and find out if she'd talked with Garret after he'd left. "How about you come over after you've made some progress?" I suggested, stepping over to the door. "For lunch, maybe?"

"Maybe we should go to your friend Garret's place. I'm sure he'd be happy to see you."

I paused, gripping the doorknob. "What's that supposed to mean?"

He slid folded hands behind his tousled blond head, elbows pointing to the ceiling. "I think you know."

My face flushed as I attempted to twist my expression into one of indignation and not guilt. "No, I don't." I didn't want to have this conversation.

"Come on, Nic. It seemed pretty obvious to me the guy is into you. He was all bristly and territorial, like he had something to protect. And that necklace he got you." He whistled. "Pretty impressive." He smiled at me. "I liked the way you thanked his kid so he wouldn't get his hopes up. You big heartbreaker." Obviously, my behavior had convinced him the attraction was one-sided.

I half laughed, half coughed in relief. "Oh yeah, that's it. Men falling all over themselves just for the chance at me." I shook my head. "Please."

After he agreed to be at the house around one, I grabbed a cab outside the hotel and gave the driver Nova's address. I knew it was early, but her brood typically got her up with the birds, so I didn't feel bad about not calling first.

She was in the kitchen with Ryan when I arrived, both of them still in their robes, sipping coffee and chewing on toast. The birthday banner still hung above the table; platters of half-finished appetizers were stacked by the dish-filled sink. The television blared noisily from the basement, where I assumed the kids sat eating their morning cereal. Nova didn't look surprised to see me.

"So," she opened, knowingly.

I dropped into a chair and Ryan busied himself pouring me a mug of coffee. "So," I sighed, shaking my head. "Garret was not happy."

"No, he wasn't." Nova shoved the plate of toast in front of me. "Here, eat. You want some eggs?"

I nibbled on the edge of the already-buttered raisin bread. "No." I looked at her. "Did you talk to him?"

"Uh-huh. I called him after you left."

"What did he say?"

"He told me he felt like you've been leading him on. That you rubbed Shane in his face."

"I didn't!" I exclaimed, knocking the table with my insistence, splashing the hot coffee from my cup.

"Think I'll go watch cartoons with the kids," Ryan said wisely, sensing this conversation would exclude him. "Want me to check on Layla?"

Nova smiled. "Please, hon. She's probably going to need to eat soon."

Ryan gave me a reassuring squeeze on the shoulder. "Hang in there, Nic. If either of these guys needs their ass kicked, you just let me know."

I gave him a grim smile. "Thanks."

Nova turned her attention back to me after he left the room.

"*I* know you didn't rub Shane in Garret's face. I'm just telling you what he *said*."

"Didn't you tell him what happened? That Shane just showed up?"

Nova shrugged her round shoulders as she set her elbows on the table, sipping her coffee. "I tried."

"Maybe you should have tried harder," I remarked, not without a shade of meanness.

"Hey, now," Nova warned as she set her cup down. Her blue eyes flashed. "Don't get all bitchy with me because things didn't go your way. The last time Garret really trusted a woman he got majorly screwed over. I'm sure your bringing Shane here last night just pushed all those old buttons. And I told you he's stubborn when he thinks he's right about something and he thinks he's right about this."

"That I was rubbing Shane in his face?" I sighed.

She bobbed her blond head. "Exactly."

"I guess he doesn't know me very well, then."

"Well, how could he? You two have barely spent any time together. I'm just playing the devil's advocate here, but for all he knows, you're just like Jackie, pretending to be something you're not just to get what you want from him." She looked at me over the edge of her mug. "Can you blame him for not wanting to go through that again?"

"No, but I'm not Jackie. And if he's too damn stubborn to see that, then tough shit for him."

"Tough shit for you, too, maybe?" She paused, sipped her drink. "You of all people should know it's easy to mistake how things appear for the truth. Think about how long you believed your dad sexually abused Jenny."

Though I hated to admit it, she was right. Of course, I didn't tell *her* that. I could be a little stubborn myself.

"Anyway," she continued, her expression assuring me that she knew her point was clear, "how did Shane take the news about your adopting the baby?"

I looked down to the table, fiddled with the place mat. "It didn't exactly come up."

"You're kidding me. You didn't *tell* him?"

"Nope. Your best friend's a big old wimp." I lifted my eyes to hers. "I slept with him, though."

"Really?" Her tone was edged in surprise and what I thought might be a hint of disgust. I couldn't blame her; I felt a little disgusted with myself.

"Yes," I sighed dejectedly.

"And how was that?"

"Weird. Like being with a stranger."

"Why'd you do it, then?"

"I don't know. Habit? Because sleeping with your boyfriend when he travels a thousand miles to see you is what you're supposed to do?"

"Um-hmm," she murmured, her mouth against the lip of her mug, her eyes like cattle prods, urging me to continue.

"I don't know," I said again, another sigh cushioning the words. "Mostly I think I just wanted to see what was left—if there *was* anything left, you know? Maybe it felt weird because we've been away from each other for so long. Maybe this whole thing with Garret was just to show me that Shane is who I'm supposed to be with." Even I didn't believe the words as they left me.

"But you still think he'll freak out about the baby, right?"

"Well, maybe he's right about that. Maybe I'm not cut out to be a mother." Self-doubt seemed to have taken over my thoughts and was now speaking for me instead of reason.

She squinted at me in disbelief. "Are you serious?"

"I might be." I threw my hands up in the air, leaned back heavily. "I'm scared, Nova, okay? I'm scared shitless. I know when I tell Shane it's going to be over and he's going to go back to San Francisco and I'm going to be all alone and I just don't know if I can take this on with no one to help me."

Nova set her coffee down with deliberation and pursed her lips before responding. "But you're not alone. You have me and my mom and your mom and *yourself*, Nicole. You told me your decision to adopt this baby was set in stone. You were completely sure this is what you were meant to do. Now you have some man trouble and you're letting it affect your sanity." She sighed. "What are you really afraid of?"

I stared at the speckled linoleum, tears filling my throat. "That she won't know me," I whispered quietly.

"Who?"

"The baby," I said. "What if she doesn't bond with me? How's she going to know I'm her mother when I didn't carry her inside me?"

"Breast-feed her," Nova suggested.

"What?" I asked. I had no idea if she was being serious.

Nova pushed back from the table and stepped over to the coffeepot, refilling her mug. The buttery early-morning light spilled through the window above the sink and bathed her round face in gold. "A friend of mine adopted a little boy from China a couple of years ago and breast-fed him. She said it really helped them connect." She shrugged, moved back to sit at the table. "It's just an idea."

I gaped at her. "I didn't know you could do that." I wiggled a little uncomfortably, and yet I was fascinated by the possibility.

"Not many people do." Nova paused and crossed her legs, looking at me. "Anyway, Nic, you've already started bonding with this baby. She's heard your voice for three months. You've touched her as you touched Jenny. You said yourself you feel like she chose you to be her mother."

"But—" I began.

"Who's in charge of your life, Nicole?" she interrupted.

"I am," I said, quietly disarmed by the strength of her words.

"*Who?*"

"I am," I said again, louder, more insistent this time.

"And what do you want from your life, right now, right this minute?" she challenged.

I let my heart answer. "I want to be a mother. I want to adopt this baby."

Nova nodded, shortly. "Okay, then. Focus on that. Get ready for it. Do what you have to do with Shane. Worry about Garret later. Stop waffling. It's time to get your goddamn priorities straight."

I sat there, stunned, staring at my friend. "When did you get to be such a hard-ass? I thought you loved me."

"I do love you. That's why I'm telling you the truth." She stood again and moved over to the stove. "Now quit your bitching and let me make you some eggs."

That afternoon Shane and I ate lunch with Mom and Jenny, then went to sit in the backyard beneath the shade of the pear tree. Small and hard green fruit lay scattered around our feet, rejected by the branches to make room for more healthy bounty. I rolled one back and forth under my bare foot, enjoying the smooth, cool sensation of its skin against mine. Shane held a few papers in his lap, reading them over and making notes in the margins. I thought about what Nova had said, how I needed to get my priorities straight and realized that Shane had already made his abundantly clear: work would always come first, before anything. Before us. Before a baby. By sleeping with him, by not telling him about the adoption, I had simply been putting off the inevitable. It was time for both of us to tell the truth.

"Did you mean what you said about being a parent?" I suddenly asked him, having planned a more subtle approach to the conversation, but unable to keep myself from this particular question.

He looked up at me, brows knitted together. "Hmmm?"

"Last night, at the party, when you told Garret you couldn't be a parent, even with me."

"Of course I meant it. Neither of us is cut out for it."

I contemplated the smooth edge of my shirt. "I don't know about that."

"Oh, come on," Shane rolled his eyes. "You've told me a hundred times that marriage and babies are not in the stars for you. Not after everything that happened in your family."

"I know, but—"

"You're changing your mind now?"

"I don't know. Maybe. Yes." I paused. "What would you say if I told you I was considering adopting Jenny's baby?"

Shane carefully set his papers on the grass before responding. "*Are* you considering it?"

I took a deep breath. "Yes."

He looked at me, eyebrows raised. "So. Does considering it mean you've already made up your mind to do it?"

"I think so, yes." *The paperwork is being processed as we speak,* I thought. I tried to make my voice sound sure, though every space inside my body was shaking.

Shane looked at me, expressionless. "What's this about? Is there something wrong with our life? I think we have it pretty good. A lot better than most people."

"There's nothing wrong with our life. It's just . . . Don't you ever feel like there's got to be something more? Something substantial and lasting and meaningful to live for?"

"So you're telling me we're not those things? That our relationship is insubstantial, limited, and meaningless?"

I sighed, folding my hands in my lap. "That's not what I meant."

"What did you mean, then?" His tone had fallen into lawyer mode; he was cross-examining me.

"I'm talking about finding more on an individual level. It's not about our relationship." I reached over to touch his hand with the tips of my fingers. "I feel like something is missing for me."

"Adopting a baby is not just about you," he interrupted. "It's about us. It puts our relationship in a place I don't want to go. A place you told me you didn't *ever* want to go." His dark eyes smoldered. "There'll probably be something wrong with Jenny's kid. How you could possibly want to take that on—I don't understand."

"There's no way to tell for sure if the baby will have problems. I'm hoping for the best."

He pursed his lips, shook his head in disbelief. "Nothing is missing for me, babe. I love my job, I love you." Once again, his priorities clearly stated, in case I needed the matter clarified.

"That's all I need to be happy," he continued. "If it's not enough for you, then I guess we've got a problem."

I dropped my eyes to the ground, watched an ant tackle the

mighty deed of scaling a blade of grass. I envied his determination. "I guess you're right."

We were both silent for a moment, lost in our own thoughts. It was I who finally spoke. "I'm sorry to drop everything on you like this, but being here has changed things for me. I didn't know it was going to happen. Being with Jenny reminded me that I'm good at helping people who can't help themselves. It's what I love to do. It's why I wanted to be a therapist."

Shane's gaze was cold. "You're not a therapist. You're a baker."

"I'm both. I'm just me, Shane. And now I'm going to be a mother."

He shook his head again, then stopped, raising accusing eyes to mine. "Is this about that Garret guy?"

"No." I sighed, frustrated. It wasn't about Garret; it was about me. And I suddenly realized that the man next to me didn't have the faintest idea who I was. Until recently, I'd barely known myself.

When Shane finally answered me, his voice was quiet, the hurt he felt cast over his face like a thin veil. He stared at the fence as he spoke. "You should probably call the shelter and have that dog shipped up to you, then, if you're staying."

"What?" I said, disbelieving, jutting my chin around to face him. "What did you just say?"

He looked at me, contempt etched across his handsome face. "I got too busy with work to manage him, so I boarded him at the shelter."

I gasped. "How long has he been there?"

"A couple months."

"I cannot believe you did this without telling me."

"Oh, well, arranging to adopt your sister's baby without telling me is a more forgivable offense?"

"That's not fair."

"None of this is fair."

I was quiet, silenced by the fact that he was right.

"Well," he said, his voice dark as a black mark against a white page, "this was fun. I'm so happy I decided to come."

"I really am sorry, Shane."

"Yeah, so am I." He didn't look at me. "I'll have your things packed and sent to you when I get home."

"You don't have to—"

"But I will." He finally smiled at me, ironically. "Don't worry. I know all the kitchen stuff is yours."

He waited for a moment, then stood. "I think I'll see if there's a flight out this afternoon."

"Do you want me to take you to the airport?"

"No. I've got the rental to return."

"Let me walk you to your car, at least."

He held up his hand to stop me. "I can take care of myself, Nicole. I just hope you've thought about whether you can do the same."

I spent most of the next week at home with Jenny, on the phone trying to tie up loose ends in San Francisco. I arranged for the shelter to board Moochie until the baby was due, then set up having him flown to me. Then, much to Barry's dismay, I let the bakery know I wouldn't be back.

"Well, chief," he said sadly when I told him the news, "I'll miss our talks."

I smiled. "Yeah, a couple of Chatty Cathy's—that was us."

"The best relationships don't always need words, champ. You know that."

I was quiet for a moment, letting my silence tell him how deeply I would miss him. Then I made him promise to visit Jenny, the baby, and me for his next vacation.

The next call I made was to Garret. I'd picked up the phone several times in the days following the party, but was unable to get my fingers to dial more than a couple of numbers before chickening out. Today, I managed to get all seven dialed, and before I could hang up, he answered.

"Hi," I said awkwardly. "It's Nicole."

He took a moment before responding. "Hi."

I inhaled deeply. "I just wanted to say . . ." I began, then trailed off.

"Yes?" he inquired, his tone indifferent.

"Just that I'm sorry about what happened. I never meant—"

"I know," he interrupted. "It's fine. I'm fine." There was another audible pause and I wished I could see the expression on his face so I could determine whether he was telling the truth. Maybe he *was* fine. Maybe seeing me with Shane confirmed the doubts he'd already had about having a relationship with me. Maybe I was the only one struggling with disappointment. Or maybe he, like me, was closer to Nova's definition of fine: Fucked-up, Insecure, Neurotic, and Exasperated. There was no way to tell for sure.

"Look," he continued. "I've got to get to the restaurant. I'm sure I'll see you at Nova's sometime." I couldn't believe how distant he was being with me. I guess I hadn't seen how deeply Jackie had wounded him.

"Okay," I said, the word small and quiet in my mouth. I hung up, disheartened, suddenly lonelier than I'd ever been.

The following morning, Jenny and I headed over to Nova's. Despite the turmoil I was feeling over Garret, I was anxious to observe my best friend in her role as mother, desperate for knowledge, desperate to believe that I could do with one baby what she did with four. When we got there, I immediately told her about my brief conversation with Garret.

"Give him some time," she suggested. "I'm sure he'll come around." I wanted to take her advice, but couldn't help hoping I'd get a chance to talk with him again, to try to salvage the friendship we had formed. I hoped he'd at least make room for that.

I laid Jenny on the couch, surrounding her burgeoning frame with pillows. At thirty-four weeks, she tired easily, the changes in her body making it difficult for her to walk around for more than a few minutes at a time. I played with Layla, watching as Nova whirled about the house with seeming ease, preparing meals during afternoon naps so she wouldn't have to think about it when the kids had their daily meltdown. "The whine with dinner hour," as Nova fondly referred to it. My friend spun like a dervish, cooking and dusting, mopping and scrubbing toilets.

"How did your mama ever learn to *do* all of this without Daddy's help?" I cooed at Layla, who gurgled happily as she stuck her fist between her pink gums. I couldn't believe how much the baby had changed since I'd first seen her at six weeks old. Again, I wondered what Jenny's baby would look like. Would there be any hint of the man who fathered her? Would she know how she'd been conceived? How would I ever tell her such a thing? I shook my head, reminding myself to take things on one challenge at a time, as Nova had suggested. My priority right now was to get ready for life with a newborn; I was here to learn whatever I could from my friend.

Nova, who stood with a sponge-mop in the doorway between the kitchen and the living room, grinned at the question I'd posed to her daughter before responding to it. "She learned quickly that if she didn't do it while she had the chance, it don't get done."

"Do you want some help?" I offered. "I could vacuum."

"Not while the kids are sleeping. They slept through the noise when they were babies, but not now." She wiped at the baseboard with her mop, scrubbing at a bright red marker stain, then leaned the mop against the wall. She stepped through the entryway and came to sit next to me on the couch, taking Layla into her arms and settling her down to nurse. Nova caressed her daughter's downy head, then watched me watching her. "Have you given any more thought to breast-feeding?" she asked, her eyes bright with interest.

I let my gaze stay on the child at her breast, immensely moved by the sight. "I've definitely *thought* about it, but I'm not too sure I'd be able to *do* it." Jenny snored softly next to me, her dark head lolled against the back of the couch. I smoothed her hair back from her face and her mouth curved into the hint of a smile.

"Are you uncomfortable with the idea?"

I shook my head. "Not really. I think it's a beautiful thing." I paused, not sure how to word all the fears I had. "I guess I'm worried it might hurt."

"It does, sometimes, in the beginning, but it usually goes away pretty quickly. It's really more of a tugging sensation."

"Okay," I said, nodding, considering this. "I suppose I just need to think about it some more. It's a pretty big commitment."

"Sure," Nova agreed. "But if you decide to go ahead, you'll have to try and get your milk started fairly soon. You can borrow my breast pump." The look of subdued horror on my face made her laugh outright and Layla accidentally popped off her mother's breast. Nova helped her latch back on as she spoke. "It's not the *only* way to bond, Nic. I only suggested it because my friend said it helped her."

I cocked my eyebrow at her, a little embarrassed. "How else do you bond with a baby?" I asked, sincerely curious. I felt like what I knew about babies you could fit on the head of a pin.

"Just holding her. Talking to her. Kissing her. Smelling her sweet skin." She looked down at Layla again, who met her mother's gaze and smiled back with a mouth full of nipple and milk. "Then, of course, you *could* go shopping. Buying clothes for your baby girl borders on being a spiritual experience." She smiled.

I returned her smile, lightly touching the small foot of Layla's pink rose-flowered sleeper. "The ultimate dress-up doll?"

"Better than that. You should go this afternoon," she urged. "I'll watch Jenny and you can shop. I've got baby equipment you can borrow coming out the ying-yang, but you really should get some clothes picked out for her."

My mind filled with images of red velvet dresses and tiny blue jeans, but the thought of Garret quelled any enthusiasm I might have felt. "Maybe tomorrow," I said. "I don't really feel up to it today."

"All right," she consented. "Tomorrow, then." She paused, adjusting her shirt and sitting Layla upright on her lap before continuing. "You know, Ryan and I were talking before he left this week. We were thinking it would be a good idea for you to stay with us after the baby gets here. We've got the guest room and bath in the basement—we're all set up for it."

"Really?" I shook my head. "I don't know. Wouldn't that be a huge inconvenience? I was planning to find an apartment."

"I know you were. But I figure you're basically going to be living over here anyway, so why pay the extra rent? You're going to need a few months to get on your feet. And even though you and your mom have worked out some things, I know you've had enough of living with her. My mom'd be lucky to be alive after four months under the same roof with me, God bless her."

"We *have* sort of used up our mother-daughter conflict management allotment dealing with Jenny's pregnancy," I relented, looking at my peacefully napping sister.

"Exactly. So I think you should stay here and I can help you with the baby and you can help me with the house and the kids. It'll be like frontier times: women living communally, waiting for the man to bring home the mastodon meat and all that good shit."

"Are you sure? Is it really okay with Ryan?"

She shrugged. "He thought it was a great idea. He figures with you around I'll have less time to think of reasons to bitch at him. Plus he loves you."

"Well, okay then." I hugged her. "You're the greatest person, Nova. The best soul on earth. You know that?"

"I can always use reminding," she smiled.

There was a sharp rap on the front door as she spoke and I held my breath, bracing myself to see Garret's face. Instead, a woman entered, her dark hair, pale skin, and annoyingly petite frame announcing her obvious relationship to Gracie. She wore a snugly fit, red linen sundress with matching sling-back sandals.

"Jackie!" Nova exclaimed. "What are you doing here?"

Garret's ex-wife smiled in a smooth, catlike movement. With her perfect makeup, sleek skin, and smartly cut, shiny black bob, she looked like she belonged on a nighttime soap opera, playing the vampy bitch everyone loved to hate. "Thought I'd surprise you."

"Well, you did!" Nova gestured to me, balancing Layla on one leg of her lap. "This is my girlfriend Nicole and her sister, Jenny."

Jackie looked at me with uninterest and I suddenly felt that I had done something wrong, offended her somehow with my too-big body and unruly curls. Her eyes brushed over Jenny's sleeping form as if she were simply part of the couch, then back to me. "Nice to meet you," she said.

I nodded, my tongue thick in my mouth. No way was this a coincidence. No way did she just show up out of nowhere after Shane's visit. Their phone call the night I spent with Garret in the restaurant must have been arranging for her to come; *that* was why he didn't want to tell me about it. Maybe they had discussed reconciling. What right did he have to get so angry with me over Shane when he was deliberately hiding what was going on with Jackie from me? Maybe *he* was the one pretending to be something *he* wasn't—an oxymoron: an honest man. I felt sick to my stomach.

"Can you come in for a while?" Nova asked politely, standing up and setting Layla in her swing as she spoke. "The other kids are about to wake up."

Jackie tucked a strand of hair behind her right ear, setting off the sharp angle of her cheekbone to its best advantage. "No, sorry. I just wanted to let you know Garret and I'd be home with Gracie tonight, so you're off the hook."

"How long are you staying?" Nova asked, glancing at me out of the corner of her eye.

"I'm not sure. We haven't discussed it yet." She tilted her head and raised her thin, penciled eyebrows. "You know how things are."

I know you abandoned your baby girl, I thought nastily.

"Well, thanks for letting me know about tonight," Nova said with false cheer. "Hope things go well."

"Oh, they will," Jackie purred. Then as quickly as she had appeared, she was gone.

Nova dropped to the couch, shaking her head. "Sweetie, I'm so sorry. I had no idea she was coming, I swear."

"Of course you didn't. Garret probably saw my car and sent her right over. Eye for an eye."

"No. He's stubborn, but he's not vindictive."

I shrugged, attempting nonchalance. "Oh, well. Who cares? It's not like I have a claim on the guy, right? It was just a passing thing. I should be on my own now, anyway. I've got enough to do with the baby coming." I looked at Nova, blinking quickly to push back the tears I felt threatening behind my eyes. "I need Rebound Boy, not Mr. Right . . . right?"

She hugged me. "Oh, hon."

I wiped my eyes, laughed a bit. "Skinny little bitch, isn't she? No tits at all."

"None that I've ever seen."

"At least I've got her beat in that department."

Nova hugged me again. "Believe me, chick. You got her beat in more ways than that."

Trying my best not to think about Garret and Jackie being together under the same roof three doors down, Jenny and I spent the next couple of weeks pretty much living at Nova's house, sprucing up the basement bedroom. The good-sized rectangular room was a horrid shade of pumpkin, chosen by the house's previous owners, so Nova and I spent several evenings after the kids had gone to bed repainting the walls a warm brick red. We left the trim around the large bay window that looked out into the backyard cream to match the Berber carpet and the heavy, room-darkening drapes. On the clearance shelf at Bed, Bath, & Beyond, I found a taupe-and-white-striped duvet cover to use on the down comforter Nova already had on the queen-sized bed. There was an old dresser and vanity table that I sanded down and painted a bright white, and with the extra crib and changing table Nova donated, along with several other sundry baby accessories, the room quickly morphed into a perfect temporary home for me and the baby.

During this time, I also took Nova's advice and left Jenny with her and the children for an afternoon so I could go shopping for the baby's wardrobe. Nova had plenty of basic clothes I could use, but I felt the urge to pick out something special, to say *this* is what I choose for my daughter to wear. *My daughter*. It was a phrase I had yet to become used to uttering. As I picked through the endless racks of adorable infant clothes, I chanted it to myself, hopeful that soon it would roll effortlessly out of my mouth, as natural as breath.

Several hours and Visa charges later, I pulled up in front of Nova's house with two shopping bags full of more outfits than any one child could possibly wear. Nova had been right; shopping for this baby girl made me feel as if I somehow knew her better, though I'd yet to hold her in my arms. As I walked around the car to open the trunk and retrieve the bags, the sound of Gracie's voice grabbed my attention. The little girl was tearing down the street, her dark hair pulled into jumping pigtails, her white sneakers pounding on the cement as she came in my direction. "Nicole!" she hollered. "Hi, Nicole!"

My heart started to rattle in my chest as I saw Garret following behind her. Unlike his daughter, he did not run; instead, he stepped deliberately, watching each foot as it hit the sidewalk in front of him. I grabbed my shopping bags and closed the trunk, taking a couple of deep breaths in an attempt to steady myself. Over the past couple of weeks, as Jenny and I arrived at Nova's each morning, I allowed myself one glance toward Garret's house, but saw neither him nor Jackie. Nova said she hadn't been watching Gracie, either; Garret was taking time off from the restaurant. I pictured him and Jackie sitting at their kitchen table, the morning sun washing over them as they sipped lazily at steaming cups of coffee, touching the tips of their naked toes together on the floor, laughing with wonder at the two years they'd wasted being apart.

I slammed the trunk shut and steeled my gaze on Garret's approach. His handsome face looked tired—due, I was sure, to the late nights spent reuniting with Jackie—and his dark hair was tucked under a baseball cap. He wore a black T-shirt and jeans along with brown Birkenstock sandals. I quickly tucked the necklace he'd given me under my blouse; I didn't want him to see me wearing it and assume that all was well.

Gracie ran up to me, jumping up and down. "Is Jenny in the car?" She stopped jumping in order to cup her hands around her eyes and peer in the tinted passenger-side window.

"She's in the house with Nova," I said, my voice tight. I didn't want to give Garret any hint of the turmoil I was experiencing. He approached slowly, his expression guarded.

Gracie turned to her father. "Can I go say hi to Jenny, Dad?"

Garret nodded his assent. "A quick one, Peanut. Your mom is waiting for us." My body tensed at this casual reference to his ex-wife and I looked at him with a challenging gaze, but waited for Gracie to dash up the stairs into the house before speaking.

"Things going well, then?" I asked, trying to sound as though I didn't care one way or the other. I self-consciously fluffed my red curls, happy I'd had the time to shower that morning. Knowing it was terribly immature to do so, I stood up straight, pushing my chest out a bit to emphasize the V-necked blouse I wore to its best advantage.

Garret looked down the street toward his house, then swung his eyes back to my face. "Things are fine." He paused, the tension in his body as obvious as mine. Hands shoved into the front pockets of his jeans, he dropped his gaze to the ground, focusing on digging the toe of his sandal into the parking strip.

"Well," I commented snidely, "I'm so happy for you. Jackie seems like your perfect match." I stepped toward the house, but his hand on my bare arm stopped me. His touch was electric.

"Jackie and I . . . ," he started, but then trailed off, his hand falling away from me.

"Jackie and you, what?" I prodded, the muscles in my neck thick with expectation. I dropped my shopping bags to the ground and waited. I figured he was about to tell me they'd decided to remarry and that he hoped I wouldn't hold a grudge and come to the wedding. Fat chance.

Garret's soft brown eyes searched my face before he looked away again, shaking his head. "Nothing. Never mind. Could you tell Gracie to get a move on, please?"

I nodded briskly. "Sure." I grabbed both bags and stepped resolutely toward the house, resigning myself to the fact that whatever might have been between Garret and me was over. Jackie's return was probably for the best. What had I come home for, anyway? I challenged myself as I ascended the front stairs. To fall in love? No. I came home to take care of Jenny, to assimilate the fragments of myself I had left behind ten years before, to become the kind of sister, the kind of *person*, I'd always longed to be. I didn't need Garret to do that. I didn't need a man at all. I'd spent way too many years trying to find approval in the circle of a man's arms. It was time to give up the search; it was time to finally approve of myself.

Thankfully, after this brief encounter with Garret, I continued to keep busy at Nova's and had little time to dwell on my disappointment. After a great deal of soul-searching and reading on the subject, as well as talking to Nova's friend and Dr. Fisher about it, I decided to give nursing the baby a try. Nova had offered the use of her industrial-strength breast pump, but something about a used breast pump didn't sit well with me, so I purchased my own, along with several lengths of thin tubing. When the baby arrived, I would tape the tubing next to my nipples as she suckled, drawing the formula she would drink as a supplement to my milk. To encourage my breasts to begin production, I sat twice a day with plastic shields attached to my nipples, the electric pump sucking away. My first attempt had not gone well; I ended up calling Nova into the bedroom to help, holding the tangled tubes up to her angrily, annoyed by the rhythmic whir of the pump. "This is crazy," I said, not caring that my breasts were exposed, my voice cracked with tears. "I can't get the damn thing to work."

"Here," she said, obviously unaffected by my naked state. She wet the inside of one of the shields with saliva, then moved it back over my nipple. "That'll help. The baby's mouth will be wet, right? Wet to dry creates suction." She detached the pump mechanism from the high tech-machine and began working it manually with all her strength. I felt a sudden tug at my breast and I gasped lightly.

"Okay, now. That just plain feels *weird*."

Nova grinned. "Get the other shield-thingy wet and get it on your other boob. We'll see if we can do both at once."

I giggled as I followed her instructions, imagining the odd picture we must make. "Good thing Ryan's in Alaska. What would he do if he walked in on us right now?"

"He'd probably grab a bowl of popcorn and sit down to watch."

"Yuck."

"Yeah, well, it's about as close as he'd ever come to seeing me get sexual with another woman."

"Like this is at all *sexual*." I snorted a bit, laughing. "What *is* it about that and men? Do they *all* fantasize about it?"

Nova shrugged as she continued pumping. "Probably. If they're straight."

"Well, I still can't believe you're sitting here pumping my breast for me." I batted my eyelashes at her prettily. "I feel so *special*."

She grinned again, then reattached the pump mechanism to the machine. "Don't get too used to it, chick. You are definitely going to have to figure this one out on your own."

And I had, after a few more tries with her assistance. As I sat there each night with the pump whirring away, I thought of ancient women who couldn't nurse, how other women—perhaps even their own sisters—took over feeding their babies and I felt a degree of female holiness that empowered me in a way I'd never experienced. Taking over the care of this child *was* a holy thing, the true reason my conscience had finally led me home. It was the reason Jenny and I were sisters.

"Isn't that right, Jen?" I asked her as we sat together on Nova's couch one evening, waiting for Nova to finish putting the kids to bed and come join us. Jenny gazed at me deeply, her indigo eyes full of our history, full of the truth.

Sister.

The word resounded through my blood like a thousand bells. I caught Jenny's gaze in my own, sending the word back to her with as much love as six tiny letters could possibly carry.

*I*t was the day after Jenny's thirty-six-week checkup when the call came. Nova's older children were wild—running through the house, bouncing on the furniture, pawing at their mother's limbs—while Layla mewled noisily in her bouncy seat on the couch next to Jenny.

"Awwrrgh!" Nova growled playfully, but with enough of an edge to make me realize she was reaching her limit. "Back off, turkeys! Give Mommy some room!" They scattered for a moment, leaving Nova to try to get dinner started, but within minutes they were back at her legs, whining and moaning about having nothing to do.

"That's it!" Nova announced. "Mama needs a break!" She stomped down the hall to the bathroom and slammed the door behind her.

"Is Mama mad at us?" Rebecca asked me solemnly.

"She's not mad, honey," I said. "She just needs a little time out."

"Did she do something bad?" Rebecca inquired. "I only get

time-outs when I do something bad. Three minutes on the stairs with no toys."

"No, Rebecca. She just needs a minute to herself. Can you guys please go outside in the backyard to play for a while? I'll call you when dinner's ready."

"Eww!" Isaac said noisily. "James is *poopy*! I can smell it all the way over *here*!"

James stood sheepishly by the couch, one chubby finger in his mouth as the other hand pulled at the pudgy rear end of his diaper. "I'll take care of it," I said, sighing. "Just go outside. Now." I kept my tone firm, mimicking the one Nova used with them when she meant business. Her "malevolent mama," she called it.

Amazingly, they listened. Maybe I'd make it as a mother, after all. I wrestled with an acrobatic two-year-old James on the floor, trying to get his diaper changed. Jenny was on the couch, watching my frustration mount with amusement sparkling in her eyes, her squirming belly resting heavily on her lap. It was the end of August and the warm days were fading fast, but Nova tried to make sure the kids squeezed every moment they could out of the sun. The phone rang four times before I could manage to secure James's shorts halfway up his diaper, then released him to join his siblings.

"Could you get that, Nic?" Nova called from behind the bathroom door. "I'm expecting a call from the boat." Ryan was due back from the season's final run to Alaska in a few days and it was obvious how sorely his presence was missed. I grabbed the receiver.

"Hello?"

"Yes, is Nicole Hunter there?"

"This is she."

"Nicole, it's Jack Waterson. I called your mother's work and she gave me this number."

"Mr. Waterson," I repeated. "What's up? More guardianship paperwork to sign?" Mom and I had been into his office several times to work with one of his partners to set up my adoption of Jenny's baby. I had gone through two interviews with Social Services and with the red tape mostly cut through, a month before Jenny's due date, the adoption was almost ready to be finalized.

"No, that's all been taken care of. It's Mr. Zimmerman. They've found him."

My organs froze in my body, seizing up with anger. I gripped the receiver, my knuckles turning white with effort. "Where was he?"

"In a hotel room in Eugene. They traced him there on his credit card. They think he charged the room on purpose so the police would find him." He paused, his breath heavy in my ear. "He hanged himself, Nicole. He's dead."

"He did *what*?"

"He left a note, too. Sort of a confessional for all the rapes he committed over the last four years in the institutions where he worked. I'm sorry to say that your sister was definitely not the first."

I was silent, tapping my foot against the green carpet, staring at Jenny as she smiled obliviously at Layla. Nova emerged from the bathroom, reaching to take the phone from me. I shook my head and pointed to myself, indicating the call was for me. I mouthed the word *lawyer*. Her brow wrinkled in concern at the look on my face and she took my hand. I squeezed it, thankful for her presence.

"Nicole?" Jack inquired. "Are you there?"

"Yes. Just a little shocked."

"Well, I'd imagine so." I heard the shuffling of papers and he spoke again. "I've got more to tell you, too. Are you sitting down?"

"Yes," I said, though I was not.

"Wellman settled with me this morning. I just need you and your mother to come in and sign the paperwork to make it official."

"Oh God." I sank to the floor, cross-legged, pulling Nova with me. "How much?"

"Six point five million. Give or take."

My voice caught in my throat, my mouth opened and shut silently, like a fish underwater. Nova took the phone. "Hello?

This is Nicole's best friend. She's a little overcome at the moment. Is there anything else I should tell her?" She listened, then thanked Jack before hanging up. She grasped my face in her hands. "You okay, sweetie? He said to call his assistant and set up a time for you and your mom to come in. What happened?"

Still in shock, I choked out the news: Jacob Zimmerman's suicide, his confession, and then Wellman's settlement. Nova jumped up, shook her curvy body with glee. "Ding-dong, the bastard's dead!" She went over to hug Jenny. "Did you hear that, hon? You're rich!"

I sat immobile on the floor, blinking my eyes heavily. "Oh God. I don't believe it. I can't believe he's dead."

Nova came back over to sit next to me on the floor. "It's good news, though, right? Now you don't have to worry about it anymore."

I shrugged, straightening my legs out in front of me, and smiled halfheartedly. "I guess part of me was hoping he would end up in prison with a very large, sexually angry cellmate. Preferably one with a handicapped sister. Death almost seems too easy."

"Arrwwhwa!" Jenny exclaimed, clapping her hands together in agreement.

Nova and I laughed. "Well," I said. "At least I'm certain now we can afford to keep her at the Sunshine House."

Nova ran her fingers through the mop of sandy waves that fell around her face. "Everything happens the way it should, Nic. Things with Shane, even Garret. Everything. You just have to listen to your heart and trust the Universe to take care of things."

"Go with the flow?"

"Exactly." An enormous yelp erupted from outside and Nova shook her head, despairingly. "And now, the flow directs me to the backyard, where I need to make sure my children are not murdering each other." She scooped up Layla from her spot on the couch and headed toward the back door. "Coming?" she inquired.

"In a minute. Jenny and I need to talk." She smiled, waved, then disappeared through the kitchen. I sat next to Jenny on the couch, my arm around her, and rested my face against her soft dark hair. It had grown in beautifully over the past few months, returning to the glossy curls I remember so well from our childhood. Her eyes glistened when she turned her head to look at me, silver-dipped blue irises that I prayed she would pass to her little girl. Our little girl. I leaned my head down and pressed my mouth against my sister's swollen belly. "Hi," I said. "How're you doing in there? I can't wait to meet you."

Baby. I felt the word dance inside me and I sat up to hug my sister close. "That's right, sweetie. Baby. It won't be long now." Jenny's checkup the day before had gone well; the baby's heartbeat was still strong, and Jenny's belly, though measuring a bit small, wrestled and jumped beneath Dr. Fisher's gentle touch.

Dr. Fisher was hoping Jenny could attempt a natural birth; our plan was to let labor occur on its own in order to see Jenny's reaction, but if she freaked out because of the pain, my mother had already signed the paperwork consenting to a cesarean section. We felt as prepared as possible under the circumstances.

Of course, circumstances have been known to change.

*J*enny was having a bad night. I was up to check on her several times, to reposition her in bed, shoving cushiony pillows between her knees, soothing her soft cries with the touch of my hand against her face. I checked her belly as well, feeling for the tell-tale tightening Ellen had instructed me to watch out for, but so far the muscles surrounding the baby were soft. She was thirty-seven weeks along, and thankfully, she didn't seem to be in labor.

"Ahhh . . . ," Jenny groaned. Her gaze bore into me, pleading for relief from whatever was tormenting her. Her eyes were jumping and shiny, carrying the look of an animal caught in a cage. I had given her all her meds, changed her diaper, tried to feed her a snack, and massaged her legs. Nothing seemed to help.

Desperate to comfort her, I dimmed the lights and curled up behind her on the mattress, nuzzling my body into hers. I rubbed her lower back with a gentle but insistent pressure. "Shhh, honey. It's okay. Everything's all right." I glanced at the clock: three a.m. I wondered if I should call Dr. Fisher.

Baby, murmured in my heart and I carefully rolled Jenny over onto her back, matching my gaze to hers, trying to gauge more of her thoughts. Her eyes were hectic, full of fear and confusion. "Is the baby all right, Jen? Is something wrong?" I pressed my fingers into the flesh of her stomach, waiting to feel the baby's usual responsive kick, but there was no movement other than the rapid rise and fall caused by Jenny's breath.

Baby, I heard again, more insistently. I moved my sister back to her left side and rose from the bed. "I'm going to get Mom, okay, Jen? Everything will be fine, I promise." I rushed down the hall and through the kitchen, then rapped sharply on my mother's bedroom door. Moonlight flooded the hallway when she appeared. She squinted at me, pulling her earplugs out and setting them on the dresser.

"What's wrong?"

"I'm not sure, but she's acting like something's really bothering her. I don't think she's in labor, but the baby doesn't seem to be kicking."

Mom grabbed her robe to accompany me back to Jenny's room. "Didn't Dr. Fisher say it's pretty typical for the baby's movement to decrease toward the end of pregnancy? I think I remember that happening with both of you."

"Yes," I said, a bit impatiently, "but there's something else. I just feel it."

When we returned to her room, Jenny was still groaning, her fists in her mouth, her eyes wild. Mom leaned over Jenny and checked her belly as I had. "There," she said, sounding satisfied. "I felt a kick. I'm sure she's fine. She's probably just generally uncomfortable. Things get pretty tight in there toward the end." She pushed Jenny's hair back from her forehead and kissed her there. "It's all right, honey."

BABY! veritably shouted within me; my heart bounced with the impact. "She's *not* just uncomfortable. Something's wrong. I think we should take her to the hospital."

Mom absorbed the look on my face, then nodded. "Okay. But why don't you call first and let her doctor know we're coming? I'll get dressed."

I went into the hallway and dialed Dr. Fisher's paging service.

"What's the nature of your emergency?" the operator inquired. "Is the patient in labor?"

"I don't think so." I briefly explained Jenny's special circumstances and my fear that something might be wrong.

"I'll have an obstetrical nurse give you a call, all right?"

"I'd rather you just called Dr. Fisher, if you don't mind. She's the only one familiar with my sister's case."

The operator paused briefly before responding. "Ma'am, I'm sorry, but we usually don't like to bother the doctor unless her patient is showing clear signs of labor, and it doesn't sound like your sister is."

I kicked the wall impetuously. "How would you know?"

"Excuse me?"

"I said, how would you know? Exactly how many handicapped women have you seen showing signs of labor?" My molars ground against each other, the gritty sound of sandpaper between my ears.

The operator was silent again. "Ma'am, I'm just following procedure, here. In cases like these, we call the nurse first."

"And I ask you again, how many cases 'like these' have you been involved with?" I sighed angrily. "Look, lady. I know my sister. Something is wrong, so I don't have time to play this little game with you. I am taking her to Swedish Hospital and I'll expect you to page Dr. Fisher and let her know we'd like to meet her there. Thank you." I slammed down the phone just as my mother emerged from the kitchen, dressed in dark slacks and a denim button-down shirt. She looked at me inquiringly.

"Is there a problem?"

"No," I said, moving into my room to throw on a pair of jeans and a sweatshirt. Mom stood in the doorway, watching me. "Unless, of course, you call ignorance a problem."

She looked confused and I shook my head. "Never mind. It's not important." I slipped a pair of tennis shoes over my bare feet. "Let's go."

"Shouldn't we get Jenny dressed?"

"They'll just undress her there, anyway."

The drive would have been silent if it hadn't been for Jenny's low, keening cries. Fear bounced around in her eyes like a rubber ball as we entered through the sliding doors of the brightly lit emergency room. The waiting room was deserted; the receptionist sat with her feet up on the desk, linking together paper clips into a chain, her gaze flickering intermittently to the blinking television across the room.

"Excuse me," I said to her. "My sister's almost nine months pregnant and I think something might be wrong with the baby."

She handed me a clipboard with a stack of paperwork without even glancing up. "Fill these out, please. Make sure you sign each page."

I dropped the clipboard noisily on her desk. "She's preregistered."

The girl finally looked up and saw my sister standing there, pregnant and drooling, my mother's arm draped around her shoulder like a protective cape. "It's *her*?"

"Yes!" I snapped. "Dr. Ellen Fisher is meeting us in Labor and Delivery, so we need to be admitted. *Now.*"

The receptionist, who wasn't wearing a nametag, dropped her eyes to the desk, awkwardly shuffling some papers. "Uh, is she in pain?"

"You know what? I don't need to be interviewed right now. Just admit her and get someone down here from Labor and Delivery."

The girl looked offended. "Well, I need to get the answers to this questionnaire before I can let you —"

"Arrrwgh!" Jenny screeched, slamming her hands together and into her mouth, her eyes flashing in warning. The girl jumped at the noise, looked hastily at me, then picked up the phone.

"Um, this is Shelley in the E.R. I need an admit clerk to come bring a patient to Labor and Delivery. Right away, please." She paused, tapped her long nails on the desk, then turned her head and ineffectually lowered her voice to a whisper. "She's *retarded.*"

"She's not the only one," I remarked loudly, and my mother smirked, still trying to calm Jenny.

Baby, baby, baby. The word pounded in my brain like a jackhammer. When the clerk arrived, we settled Jenny into a wheel-chair and headed up to Labor and Delivery. I clutched Jenny's hand, unsure whether it was she or I who needed the gesture more. A nurse led us to a small room, where we arranged Jenny on the examining table. Her muscles were tense, her eyes still wild.

Baby.

"What seems to be the problem with her?" the nurse inquired as she took Jenny's blood pressure, not even looking at my sister.

"She's been very agitated," my mother replied. "Which is very unusual for her. We just want to make sure everything is okay."

"I haven't looked at her chart—how far along is she?" The nurse spoke the words as if they left a bad taste in her mouth, looking at my mother and me as if we were lepers for allowing a handicapped girl to get pregnant.

"Just over thirty-seven weeks," I said, fuming. "Why haven't you looked at her chart?"

"We don't usually until we've spoken to the patient." She turned Jenny a bit roughly in order to wrap a monitoring belt around my sister's belly.

"Well, if you *had* read her chart, you'd see that this pregnancy was a result of rape, *Doris*," I said nastily as I located her name on the hospital identification she wore around her neck. "I'd appreciate it if you could increase your level of sensitivity a bit when dealing with her. Or is that a problem for you?"

Doris flushed, her lips pursed into a scowl. "I provide the same level of sensitivity for every patient."

"Well, if that's true, then I feel sorry for your other patients." I stood with my hands on my hips, tapping my foot angrily on the shiny linoleum.

She stared at me, her eyes flashing. "I'll just go get the chart."

"Why don't you do that?" I agreed. She left the room quickly. "God!" I exclaimed. "Some people!"

"I know," my mother soothed. "They talk like Jenny's a piece of furniture. I never quite worked up the courage to stand up for her." She rubbed my upper arm. "You're a strong woman, Nicole. I'm proud of you." The compliment sounded peculiar coming from my mother's mouth; I still expected her to find fault with me.

"Uhhwaa," Jenny moaned, turning her head back and forth on the crunchy-sounding pillow. Her dark hair was a mess; I hadn't thought to bring a brush. I went to stand by her, my hand on her cheek, until the nurse returned with Dr. Fisher right behind her.

"Hello," Dr. Fisher said, addressing Jenny as she checked the readout sheets of the monitor. She wore mint green scrubs and still managed to look regal. "What's going on with you?"

"She's been very agitated," my mother repeated. "Nicole thinks something might be wrong with the baby."

Dr. Fisher looked at me. "Why's that?"

"Her movement seems down and Jenny is bothered by it, I think. I just want her checked out, if that's okay. Just to be safe." I suddenly noticed the room was cold and shivered violently.

"Of course," Dr. Fisher agreed. "I'll get the ultrasound in here so we can take a peek, all right?" She asked Doris to bring in the machine, and after the nurse had left, she smiled conspiratorially. "So, I hear the sister of the pregnant girl in this room is a little edgy."

"Let me guess. Doris?"

"And the operator at the paging service."

"They're both idiots. Totally insensitive to Jenny's needs. . . ."

Dr. Fisher stopped me with her hand raised in front of her. "I know. I was just teasing you. You be sure to let me know if any of the staff gives you a problem. I inform them whenever I have a special case, but there's only so much a warning can do."

Jenny was groaning and watching us talk, her hands pressed between her teeth. When Dr. Fisher rolled the wand over her belly, Jenny moaned louder.

"Does everything look okay?" I asked, my breath a stone caught in the bottom of my lungs.

"Just a minute, please." Dr. Fisher spent another minute or two watching the blurry image on the screen, checked the monitor's readout sheets again, then turned to look at Mom and me as she picked up the phone next to the bed. "Hi, this is Dr. Fisher.

I need an OR set up for an urgent delivery. Who's on the nursing team tonight?" She paused. "That should be fine. Thanks."

"What's going on?" I asked, my heart rattling against my rib cage.

"The baby's heart rate is very low. So is Jenny's amniotic fluid."

"What does that mean?" Mom asked, coming forward from her seat to hold Jenny's hand.

"It means the baby isn't getting enough nutrition or fluids from the placenta. You were right to bring her in. Next week's appointment might have been too late."

"Dear God," my mother murmured.

"So you have to operate?" I asked.

"I don't think the baby would tolerate a natural labor. Of course a vaginal birth is always the ideal option for mother and baby, and we could try to induce Jenny and monitor the baby's response to the stress, but honestly, I'm afraid it might be too much for both of them." She rubbed my sister's arm, then continued. "As it is, I'm concerned about the baby's lungs being ready to work on their own. She's going to be fairly small, so there'll be a pediatric team in the operating room, ready and waiting. We can do a spinal so you both can be in there with her. It's probably going to be a bit scary for her, not being able to feel anything from the chest down, so I'll need you to try and soothe her as much as you can."

"I don't know if I should be in the room," Mom said, hesitantly.

I whipped around to face her. "Why not?" I couldn't believe she was backing out on me now, when I needed her most.

"I'm not very good with blood. I'm afraid I'd pass out and cause an uproar." She reached out for my hand over Jenny's body on the exam table. "It's your baby, anyway, Nicole. Yours and Jenny's. It should be the two of you." She sounded sincere; maybe she was right that it should be just Jenny and I bringing this baby into the world.

Dr. Fisher turned toward the door. "Whatever you decide is fine. I'll see you in a few minutes." Uncharacteristically, she winked at me before exiting. "Don't worry about Doris. She asked to be assigned to another patient. Surprise, surprise."

Mom squeezed Jenny's hand and touched her daughter's belly. "Did you hear that, Jenny-girl? The baby is coming very soon. Your sister is going to be with you and everything is going to be just fine."

I took a couple of deep breaths to calm the chattering in my chest, then dropped into a chair. "I can't believe this is happening. I'm so scared, Mom." My eyes filled when I looked at her. I never thought I'd need my mother's support so much. "What was I thinking? How am I going to do this?"

"You'll be fine. Look at all you've done already for your sister." She smiled wistfully. "Every woman in the world who has ever expected a baby has been terrified of it at some moment. Then she holds that little baby in her arms. Suddenly she realizes her purpose in life. You two were mine. This baby will be yours."

I sniffled, swallowed the terror in my throat, and tried to return her smile. "Thanks," I exhaled. "I should call Nova. She'll want to be here."

"I'll take care of that, okay? I'll have Nova bring all the gear you'll need and Jenny's overnight bag. You just focus on helping your sister through this." As she spoke, a different nurse entered the room, along with two strong-looking aides. The nurse smiled at us briefly, then walked over to Jenny's side.

"Hi, Jenny. I'm Emily. I'll be in the operating room with you, okay?" She was a slight thing, dark-haired and pale against her pink scrubs. She looked at my mother and me. "Are you both coming with us?"

"Just me," I said, standing up and stepping forward. "I'm her sister."

"Okay, Jenny, I have to start an IV for you so we can give you medicine if we need to. You're going to feel a small prick in your hand, then a little pressure. You just let me know if I hurt you."

Jenny watched Emily with wide eyes as the nurse completed the procedure, but didn't make a peep even as the needle poked through her skin. The two aides made sure she was secure on the bed before they maneuvered it through the door and down the hallway. Mom came with us to the OR's entrance, then hugged me after I slipped on a crinkling pair of scrubs. "You'll do fine, honey. I'll be right here waiting. For all three of you."

"Okay," I gulped. I followed my sister into the room, where, if all went well, I was about to become a mother.

The morning sun radiated through the hospital room's drapes, casting oddly shaped shadows across the slippery floor. A gift from Nova—a white porcelain vase spilling over with yellow roses, white freesia, and burnt orange tiger lilies—sat on the windowsill across the room from where I gently swayed in a rocking chair, a new life resting in my arms. Her delicate pink rosebud mouth worked diligently at my breast, pulling her meal both from me and the slim tube attached to the formula-filled baggie around my neck. The sensation was amazing, like nothing I'd ever known. For now, it seemed that nursing her would be a success. She was a wisp of a being—four pounds, six ounces—but otherwise, every part of her was perfect and in the right place. Ten fingers and ten toes and intensely blue, black-fringed eyes: the ghost image of my angel sister. She was eighteen inches long, but because Jenny's placenta had stopped supplying adequate nutrition, the baby was born with virtually no body fat. Her little rear end was flat as a board, her silk-soft skin, red and wrinkled. She resembled a crone from a fairy tale, a wise old woman entering the world under the guise of a child. On the first day of her life, I wondered already what lessons she would teach me.

Both she and Jenny had weathered her birth well; it had been I who wept in fear as the surgery progressed. Jenny had wriggled a bit as the spinal numbed her, but I spoke to her constantly, both in my heart and out loud, so that others would hear my telling her what was happening: that the baby she had carried was being born; that all her discomfort was going to disappear; and mostly, that I thanked her from the bottom of my soul for giving me this gift. When Dr. Fisher held the baby up for us to see and I heard her wail with vivid resistance at being pulled from the safe, wet warmth of Jenny's womb, my frightened tears melted into joy. The pediatric team checked her vital signs thoroughly before declaring her a healthy, strong little fighter and handing her, warmly swaddled and searching for a meal, to me. Her mother.

"Did you see what you did, Jenny?" I whispered as I rocked. "She's amazing. Thank you so much."

My sister lay in the hospital bed, sound asleep. They had placed us in a mother-baby suite, where Jenny would stay until she had healed enough to be transferred to La Connor. Ms. Navarro had reassured me that Jenny's place was secured and they were looking forward to her arrival.

I still ached with guilt every time I thought of leaving her there; I had become so accustomed to caring for her, seeing her every day, hoping for some sign, some blessing that might redeem me. Had I done enough? In coming home, had I made up for the years I had deserted her? I wasn't sure.

I considered it as I sat there cradling this fragile infant in my arms. A soft rap on the door interrupted my thoughts. "Come in," I said quietly.

Nova pushed the door open and came to sit next to me.

"Where are the kids?" I inquired.

"With my mom and dad. They all send their love." She smiled as she slid a finger over the baby's face. "How're you two doing?"

"We're great," I whispered. "She's glorious. Do you see how perfect she is?"

"Yes. She's a beautiful baby. Absolutely gorgeous." My friend turned her blond head to Jenny. "How's Jen?"

"She seems fine. Dr. Fisher said the hysterectomy went well, but she's drugging her up pretty good to make sure she's comfortable. She hasn't been awake very much."

"So your mother decided to go through with the hysterectomy, huh?"

I nodded. "We both thought it would be best. Just in case, you know. So we wouldn't ever have to worry about this happening again."

Nova tucked a stray curl behind her ear and moved her finger over the baby's face again. "Looks like she's eating for you."

"The lactation consultant said she's got a great suck reflex for coming a few weeks early. It took her a few tries, but now it seems like she's got it down." I carefully adjusted the supplement tube next to my nipple, then released a pent-up breath, leaning my head against the back of the rocker. "I have to tell you, I was terrified she wouldn't. All the reading I did made it seem like most adopted babies have a hard time getting started. I really didn't think it was going to work out."

"She knows who you are," Nova said simply.

I paused, looking down at the child at my breast, joy and fear and sadness rushing over me in one fluid motion. "God, this is amazing. I just want to savor it."

"I know exactly what you mean. I'll get going in a minute."

"I didn't mean for you to leave—" I started.

She smiled again. "I know. But you need this time together. God knows you won't have a moment's peace once you move in with us." She stopped as the door opened again and my mother came in, a basket full of fruit, bread, and cheese in hand. She held it up as she spoke.

"Another delivery. From your friend Garret. He's waiting at the nurse's desk." She set it on the table, then gave me a meaningful glance.

I looked at Nova, genuinely surprised. "Did you know he was coming?"

She smiled. "I thought he might show up."

Panic fluttered in my belly. "Well, he can wait. I'm busy."

Mom bent down to caress her grandchild's downy head. "And how's grandma's sweetie doing? You're a hungry bugger, aren't you?" Nova moved to the window seat that doubled as an extra bed and Mom sat down in the chair next to me. "Have you thought of a name for her yet?"

"I was thinking maybe Kyah."

Nova tilted her head thoughtfully. "What does it mean?"

"Forgiveness," I said, and my mother's eyes glossed with tears.

Jenny groaned a bit from her bed, her eyes fluttering open at the sound of our voices. She blinked laboriously, glancing around until her gaze rested on my face.

"What do you think, Jen? Is our daughter's name Kyah?" I

interpreted a wide, wet smile as her blessing before she drifted back to sleep.

"Okay, this is killing me," Nova said. "Can I tell Garret to come in?"

I softly fingered the pulsing spot on the top of Kyah's head. "Do you know what he wants?"

"Well, duh. He wants to see you. And the baby."

"Is Jackie with him?" I held my breath, waiting for her to answer.

"Jackie's gone."

I looked up to witness her smug grin. My heart banged a fearful rhythm behind my ribs, still unsure of what he might want. Knowing me well enough to take my silence as assent, both Nova and Mom left the room. Kyah was done nursing and had fallen asleep at my breast, her blue eyes closed, her tiny mouth open. I carefully adjusted my bra and blouse to cover myself, then continued to rock, breathing deeply. A moment later, Garret appeared. He had dressed casually, jeans and black T-shirt; his hair hung messily around his handsome face. He entered without a word, his soft brown eyes reflecting a trace of the same hesitance I felt.

"Where's Gracie?" I asked politely.

"With Nova's parents. She's very excited to see the baby, but I told her she'd have to wait for the next visit." So there'd be another visit? I pondered. What did that mean? Did he want to give us another try? Or did he just want to be friends?

Garret stayed by the door, stepping uncomfortably from foot to foot. He waited for a moment before bobbing his dark head toward Kyah. "She doing well?"

I nodded. "Perfect."

"How about Jenny?" He kept his voice low as he glanced at my sister's peacefully sleeping form.

"Her, too."

"I'm glad." He took in a deep breath, his hands linked behind his back, pausing a bit before speaking. "What's her name?" We were keeping the conversation safe; I felt the pressure of what we needed to talk about hanging over me like a rain cloud.

"Kyah," I told him, searching his face for what he might be feeling, the reason he had come. We were quiet for a moment, not looking at each other. I finally broke the silence, again choosing a safe topic. "Thanks for the basket. It's lovely."

"My pleasure." He looked down, fiddling with the fold of his jeans.

"Do you want to sit down?" I offered. He nodded his dark head and moved to the window seat, lowering himself slowly, then turning his gaze to me.

I shifted Kyah over my shoulder, one hand resting softly on her fragile spine, feeling her little body expand and contract with each new breath she took. The thought of the tense first weeks I'd spent not talking with my mother about what truly needed to be talked about convinced me it was time to jump right into the thick of things. No time like the present to get to the truth. "So," I said, "Nova tells me Jackie's gone."

He nodded. "She left a few days ago, actually."

"She stayed with you the whole time?" I tried to keep my words light, uninterested.

He paused, then nodded again. "Gracie wanted as much time with her mom as possible, so . . ."

"That was big of you."

He blinked at this comment, apparently offended. It seemed too complicated to try to explain that I'd meant it as a compliment. We sat in silence for several minutes, the only sound in the room our breath and the quiet whir of the hospital machines. "Well," Garret finally said, referring again to his ex-wife, "we had a few things to work out. She wants to see Gracie more often."

"That's why she came?"

"Did you think she was here for some other reason?"

"Of course," I told him, my words firm but quiet, so as to not to disturb Jenny or the baby. "You told me she called you that night at the restaurant. . . ." I trailed off, my face flushing at the memory of our kiss. His gaze was intent on me as I continued, driven by the anger that had been stewing in me for weeks. "Then suddenly she shows up after you had the gall to act offended by Shane's being at the party—"

"Wait a minute, now," Garret interrupted.

"You knew she was coming when you kissed me," I said before he could finish. "You had a few unresolved issues of your own."

He stared at me, his arms outstretched and hands cupping his knees, obviously contemplating what to say next. After a moment, he spoke. "You're right."

I squinted at him, unsure what I'd heard. "Excuse me?"

He shrugged, leaned forward to place his elbows on his knees, and laced his fingers together loosely. "I said, you're right. I knew she was coming to figure out her visits with Gracie. But as far as Jackie and I are concerned . . ." He paused. "Well, there *isn't* a 'Jackie and me.' "

My heart felt suddenly lighter in my chest, hope rising like a balloon inside me. "There isn't a Shane and me, either," I told him. "I ended things the day after the party."

"I know. Nova told me. I'm sorry for the way I reacted to him." He paused, sitting up straight again, his face open and sincere. "For the way I reacted to you."

I ducked my chin down, unable to look at him, fearful he'd see the hope in my eyes. I didn't want to scare him away. He went on.

"Nova also told me you're moving in with her for a while. Do you know what you're going to do for work?" Though his expression had relaxed, his eyes were still guarded. I met them with what I hoped was confidence in my own.

"I'm looking into getting certified as a therapist again." I had made a couple of calls and found it wouldn't take much to meet Washington's licensing standards. I was looking forward to starting a new practice when Kyah was a few months old.

Garret nodded. "Nova told me that, too."

"So you came to brush up on your already-held-conversation skills, then?" Hesitantly, I allowed a touch of playfulness into my tone.

He took a deep breath, letting the words out of him in a rush. "I came over to offer you a job. I was thinking you could work nights at the restaurant and just bring the baby with you. My chef is starting to feel overwhelmed during the day trying to get all the management stuff done for the kitchen and doing the desserts, too, and seeing as you already know what you're doing, I thought you could help me out for a while. At least until your therapist gig works out." He looked at me expectantly.

"Do you really think it would be a good idea for us to work together?" I asked, dubious.

After a moment's pause, he corrected me. "You'd be working *for* me."

I took a deep breath before responding to him, annoyed by his proclamation. "Oh, well. *That* makes the offer much more attractive. *Thanks*." Kyah stirred in my arms and I jiggled her lightly until she settled.

"I meant that I'd barely be around," he explained. "You'd be there after hours, mostly after I'd be gone for the night. The pay won't be tremendous, but I thought it might help." He shrugged, then stood, holding his hands out, palms up. "But if you're not comfortable with the idea —"

I stopped him. "I'm *comfortable* with it. It'd actually be ideal. Are you sure there won't be a problem between us?" I fingered Kyah's blanket nervously until he finally responded.

"Why would there be a problem? You're a baker. I'm a restaurant owner who needs a baker. No problem that I can see." His tone was laced together with even strings of teasing and gravity; I couldn't unwind one from the other.

It struck me then that maybe the job offer was the only reason Garret had come, that even though he had apologized for his reaction to seeing me with Shane and explained about Jackie, he had changed his mind about the two of us. I straightened in my seat, suddenly businesslike. "Well, then. If that's the case, I'd be happy to work at the restaurant. Thank you for thinking of me."

Garret sat back, a sly smile spreading across his lips. "Of course, there'd be certain requirements of the job, things I normally wouldn't ask of an employee."

"Really," I said flatly. "Like what?"

He paused, then stood to take a step toward me, his hazel eyes finally smiling. "Well, there would be a beginning-of-the-shift kiss for the owner. That goes without saying."

Hope coursed through me again and I responded with a tentative smile. "I think I might be amenable to that." My smile grew wide and I laughed out loud. "Yes, sir," I said. "I think I could handle that just fine."

Epilogue

I stood on Nova's front porch, a December storm whipping at my hair, twisting it around my face in a blinding whirlwind. I made sure Kyah's blanket was securely tucked around her cherubic face, then huddled my shoulders over her as I dashed toward Garret's waiting car, grateful when he jumped out to open the door for me. I arranged my peacefully sleeping daughter in her car seat, then trucked around the vehicle to the front passenger seat.

"Whoo!" I said as I fastened my seat belt, shaking out my now-soaking wet head. "It's raining cats and dogs out there!"

"Eww, Nicole!" Gracie exclaimed from behind me. "You got me all *wet*!"

"You were already wet, Peanut," Garret comforted. "I put the heat on high so we'll all be dry soon."

"Before we see Jenny?"

"Yes, before we see Jenny. We have to drive for a while, so there's plenty of time to dry off."

"How *long* do we have to drive?" Gracie whined, kicking the back of my seat as Garret revved the engine and pulled the car out from the curb.

"A little longer than one *Sesame Street*," I said, having learned this handy trick of children's time-telling from the past three months spent under Nova's roof. It depressed me a bit that kids learned to gauge time passing by the length of television shows, but at least it worked. "I have a job for you, though, okay, Gracie? Since you're sitting closer to her than I am, I need you to keep an eye on Kyah and let me know when she wakes up. Can you do that for me?"

"Yes. Can I wake her up now?"

Garret twisted his head around to glance sternly at his daughter. "No, you may not. You may read your books and talk to Nicole and me if you want, but do not under any circumstances start poking at that baby—you hear me, Gracie Mae?"

"Okay, Daddy."

I reached over to squeeze Garret's hand, smiling. He smiled back at me, pulled my hand to his mouth and kissed it. We were taking things slow, he and I, spending lots of time talking, learning all we could about each other in the brief moments we were able to be alone. He sometimes kept Kyah and me company the nights I worked at the restaurant, leaving Gracie at Nova's. Through cloudlike puffs of flour and over the roar of the industrial-sized mixer, we told each other our respective stories, weaving together the thin strands of communication that form a lasting bond. The first time we made love was a revelation; during it, I felt something within me similar to the opening of a rose when the morning sun first touches its petals. Then, of course, Kyah began to wail like a banshee in the other room and Garret and I laughed, stepping down from our personal heavenly cloud to rejoin the reality of life.

It was, however, a reality I had quickly grown to love. With how busy I was caring for an infant, working, and gearing up to start a therapy practice, I often felt crazed, though utterly fulfilled. I had finally fallen into a rhythm of life that made sense to me. And though this was only my third trip to see Jenny, I was excited to bring her back home with us to celebrate Kyah's first Christmas.

My sister had adjusted well to life in Sunshine House, thriving under the homelike routine and detailed care she experienced there. Mom went to visit her every weekend; Kyah and I made the trip once a month. Jenny lit up like a Christmas tree whenever she saw the baby, her eyes glittering with a happiness I recognized as the one singing in my own heart since Kyah came into our lives.

She was an amazing little baby. I found wonder in every minute thing she did: her soft cooing, the surprisingly loud gas she passed from both ends of her tiny body, the crinkle of her indigo eyes when she blessed me with a gummy smile. It was my touch she longed for when she cried, my skin, my voice; no one else would do. It thrilled me to know that the comfort she took from me was something only I could give her, an emotional connection irreplaceable by anyone or anything. It reminded me of what I had always shared with Jenny, this unbendable, unbreakable link.

My few months as a mother had taught me many things about myself, about what was truly important. But perhaps most important of all was the realization that my coming home to Jenny wasn't a matter of needing redemption. Maybe between those who love each other—sisters, friends, mothers, daughters, lovers—trespasses are simply forgiven by feelings that can't be severed. The connection is always there, and no matter what pain or time or distance separates you, the language you've shared is held in your heart, waiting to once again be spoken.

Author's Note

My sister, Angie, was one of the first individuals in the United States to be diagnosed with a recently discovered neurological disorder called Rett Syndrome (RS). While it is important to say that this story is a work of fiction and both the characters and the events in the novel are products of my imagination, I wrote it with two purposes in mind. First, I wanted to testify to the emotional truth of a family's experience of living with a special-needs child. Second, I hoped to publicize the characteristics of a disorder that occurs in as many as 1:10,000 female births yet is often misdiagnosed as autism, cerebral palsy, or nonspecified developmental delay. For more information and support, please contact the International Rett Syndrome Association (IRSA) at www.rettsyndrome.org.

Photo by Wendy Bailey

Amy Yurk earned a bachelor's degree in sociology only to discover that most sociologists are unemployed. She proceeded to work in publicity, pour lattes, and decorate cakes before settling down to write. She lives in Bellingham, Washington, with her husband and two children. *The Language of Sisters* is her second novel. To contact Ms. Yurk and learn more about her work, please visit www.amyyurk.com.

The Language of Sisters

❖

Amy Yurk

This Conversation Guide is intended to enrich the
individual reading experience, as well as encourage us
to explore these topics together—because books,
and life, are meant for sharing.

A CONVERSATION WITH AMY YURK

Q. What inspired you to write this story?

A. Though the plot and characters are fictional, the emotional truth of the story is rooted in the relationship I have with my own sister. The idea for the book grew out of a strong desire to communicate the gifts and struggles that come along with having a severely disabled sibling. I found that families with special-needs children are most often portrayed as idyllic, always full of perfect love and acceptance of their challenging situation, when in reality this isn't usually the case. It was important to me to show a balance of emotion, that however much love Nicole had for Jenny, she also had the dark side of her that experienced the same frustration their father did.

Q. Who in the story are you most like as a person?

A. There's a little of me in all the characters, but those who know me would probably say I'm most like Nova. I meant her character to be sort of an amalgamation of all my cool chick girl-friends who are also mothers, but in the end, she sounds a lot like me: mouthy, generally good-natured, and hopefully, compassionate.

Q. Both of your novels have dealt with themes of motherhood. Was this a conscious choice?

A. I believe you write best what you know best. I've found motherhood to be a consuming state of being: I think, breathe, and eat it. As a writer, story lines tend to develop from what swims in your mind on an everyday basis. The books just followed. I also believe the relationship you have with your mother shapes a great deal of who you are and how you experience the world; it's a vast pool of dramatic potential.

Q. How long did it take you to write the book?

A. I wrote a terrible draft of the emotional side of the story several years ago, but it had no semblance of an acutal plot. I was three months pregnant with my son when the idea of Jenny's rape and subsequent pregnancy came to me, so I put my daughter into day care two mornings a week, and four months later, the first draft was complete. It's amazing what you can accomplish in eight hours a week.

Q. Jenny has terrible things happen to her: violent abuse by her father and then the rape at Wellman. Do you seek out dark subject matter?

A. I wouldn't say I seek it out, but ugly experiences are often what spur growth in life and character transformation is what I love to write about. Jenny's rape is the catalyst to Nicole's journey to find what she truly wants. Writing about the horrible side of things leaves room for me to explore the sheer goodness that balances it. Nicole finding Garret, Nova and her family, as well as Gracie's connection with Jenny are examples of this.

Q. Are you working on another project?

A. Ideas are always brewing somewhere within me, but for now I'm hoping to spend some time with my kids without working on a book. Of course, that's what I said after my first book came out, and here I am, done with a second before my daughter has even turned two. I literally dream of hours in front of the keyboard uninterrupted by diaper changes and temper tantrums; next to kissing my babies' sweet little toes, writing is my favorite thing in the world.

QUESTIONS FOR DISCUSSION

1. Nicole has stayed away from home for ten years. After all she went through growing up, do you think she was justified in not going back to see her sister sooner? If she had gone home before Jenny was raped, do you think she would have resolved things with her mother?

2. Joyce, Nicole and Jenny's mother, is incredibly distant from them when they first move home. Why do you think she is like this? Is she justified in her feelings? Do you think she should have taken care of Jenny after Kyah was born instead of letting Nicole find the group home? Should Nicole have kept Jenny? Would you have cared for Jenny?

3. Shane is portrayed by Nicole as a shallow individual. Do you think she is unfair in this assessment because she's attracted to Garret? If Nicole had been truthful with Shane from the beginning about wanting to adopt Jenny's baby, do you think he might have had a change of heart?

4. Nova and Nicole reconnect as friends almost instantaneously. Do you think this was realistic? Are there friends in your own life you've been separated from, and yet when you meet again, it's almost as though no time has passed?

5. Who do you think influences Nicole most regarding her decision to adopt Jenny's baby? Do you think Nicole would have adopted the baby if she hadn't met Garret and Gracie?

6. Do you think Garret overreacts to Shane's surprise visit? If something did end up being wrong with Kyah, would Garret still want to be with Nicole?

7. Do you think Nicole's decision was the right one or was she simply motivated by guilt? Will she keep Kyah if something turns out to be wrong with her? Would you?